Report to General Shinseki

To Lady,

enjoy

Tom Barnes

ISBN: 978-1-449565-69-5

Printed in the United States of America.

This is a work of fiction. All characters, dates, times, places and events are either fictitious in themselves or completely fictitious representations of the thoughts, actions and behaviors of real people.

This is not meant to be read as history but as a novel. This is a work of fiction that hopefully gives insights into the world view of veterans and specifically disabled veterans in the United States in the first decade of the 21st century.

Report to General Shinseki

A novel

by
Thomas Michael Barnes

Contents

Preface

THIS IS MY fourth self-published book. This book and all of the others can be purchased at Amazon.com . The websites for my previous books are as follows:

The McGurk—TheMcGurk.vpweb.com

Finnegan Tales—FinneganTales.vpweb.com

A *Distant and Clear View*—ADACV.vpweb.com

And the website for this book which explains the back story to this novel can be found at RTGS.vpweb.com

I honestly believe that the back story of any book is just as necessary to understand as the subject matter in order to grasp the ultimate meaning of the book itself. It gives the book a context within which to understand the author's point of view. Nothing exists in a vacuum. A book cannot be written or understood without a background with which to measure its depth and breadth. Everything in the universe has or should have a context within which it can be understood, experienced and explained. The website is an attempt to explain that context. I hope you visit it prior to reading the book. Once you are done reading, I hope you leave your comments on the website. As an author, I truly appreciate your feedback on what I write. It keeps me right sized.

This book was written out of my own personal experiences with fellow veterans. I am a retired Coast Guard warrant officer with over twenty four years active service and I am a totally disabled individually unemployable veteran. This is normally termed an IU disabled veteran in the jargon of veteran's disability adjudication prevalent in the early part of the 21ˢᵗ Century. It means that I am too disabled to find full-time, steady and meaningful work. So I write. It fills the time and gives my life context (there is that word again!).

Above all else, veterans and especially disabled veterans want to be understood. They may or may not be able to fully communicate their service experience to someone else. That all depends on the mind set of the veteran and on whether that experience was mundane or horrific. Service life is often both of these. In any event, no veteran of the armed forces wants to be seen as a whiner, slacker or ward of the State. That is especially true of those who have seen combat or intense hostile action as in Coast Guard units in a drug interdiction at sea that has gone bad. I have personal experience with that last scenario.

At the same time, these men and women do not want to be ignored when they have legitimate needs that are frustrated by a government bureaucracy ferociously attempting to keep costs down and therefore keep pensions and benefits minimal at the expense of the individual veteran's quality of life. Veterans constantly find themselves fighting with their own government to have benefits delivered in a timely fashion with fair adjudication by professional staffers. The fight can be hellish, especially if the veteran is disabled. It is not a pleasant experience to be a disabled veteran. Ask anyone who is dealing with that situation.

This novel is an attempt by one disabled veteran to get the reader inside the mind of the American disabled veteran. His complexion and his mind set might have changed from one time period to the next in our history. But his need to be understood by the government that placed him or her in harm's way remains a constant variable that must always stay in the forefront of the interaction between the two parties, i.e. veteran and government.

I want to thank all American veterans of all time periods for putting on a uniform and taking up arms at the order of their government to ostensibly protect home and hearth, to keep the trade lanes open for American commerce and to defend the American way of life from all encroachment from without or within. Sometimes those fights were righteous, sometimes they weren't. But the American veteran lives knowing that when he or she was asked to shoulder the burden of national defense, he/she did just that.

If historians later decide that his or her efforts were manipulated due to political forces outside of their control, veterans do not share in the responsibility for that deliberate misdirection of national purpose. They followed legal orders. They manned the barricades. They believed that their national leaders knew what they were doing when they asked them to take up arms. They put themselves in harm's way to protect their communities. That is a hero.

For that trust, I salute all veterans and I thank them for their service to our people and our national ideals.

CWO3 Tom Barnes, USCG (Ret)
2 September 2009
Alexandria, Virginia

Acknowledgements

THERE ARE SO many people to acknowledge for helping me write this novel that I am not going to be able to do it. For those persons or groups that I have not mentioned, I ask your indulgence for my error.

First of all I want to thank all members of the warrior classes from the various colonial armies and navies manned by people who would eventually see themselves as Americans up to the present day armed forces of this nation. From our earliest times on this continent until the present day we have had warriors and therefore veterans. All peoples of all nations and tribes living here answered the call to arms at one time or another to defend village, town, encampment, kin, region or community of one type or another. From the Braves of the various indigenous tribes here in North America to the English, Dutch, French, Swedish, Spanish, Russian and other European soldiers and sailors who defended the rights and lives of their citizens who came here, I offer a humble 'thank you'. As you grew older and left the bearing of arms to younger men, you were the first veterans living on the continent. For the many privations and injuries that you suffered for your people, many of you even dying in poverty and neglect as a result of your service to chieftain or king and a far off country, I offer a heartfelt apology. You deserved better than that. I want you to know we learned from your experiences.

For the colonial Americans who would fight for foreign kings in the various continental contingents of foreign armies and navies that vied for control of this continent in the 17th and 18th Centuries I give you thanks. Most especially for those Americans who fought under the British in the Continental Army against the French and their Native American allies prior to the Revolution, I thank you for your bravery in establishing the roots of this nation through the fire of war. When the time came for Americans to win their own freedom from British rule, most of you made the hard decision to fight against former comrades for the sake of your families and your future.

Some of you formed yourselves into Tory Regiments and fought for the king. Whatever you decided, that could not have been an easy decision. At no time did more than 20% of the American population openly support rebellion against Britain. Our first war was highly unpopular with the American people. Thank you for persevering. Those of you who fought under Washington gave birth to a nation. Those of you who fought for the king followed your conscience and lost your birthright to American citizenship. I thank you for your honesty in making that hard choice. A nation was born out of that struggle and veterans returned home from that prolonged and bitter fight to start shaping our nation's initial infrastructure into a purely American community.

I wish to thank all Native Americans for defending their rights to land and culture against European American encroachment. You showed all of us what courage is by your defiance in the face of overwhelming odds. Your spirit is now part of the American soul and many of you have served in our armed forces with distinction. Thank you for giving us your warrior spirit in a particularly North American way.

For all minorities of all groups that ever fought in an American uniform, I thank you for the nobility of spirit that you have shown through the centuries in defending a country and a way of life that did not fully include your needs or wants. You showed incredible strength of spirit and courage in embracing the defense of a nation that did not always honor your ways and a people that did not always treat you as equals. Your patience and grace under pressure has taught us all the true values of the warrior spirit. You fought and died alongside people who did not always fully recognize your sacrifice or adequately honor your deaths. You taught us more about courage than you will ever know.

For all Americans of all colors, religions, ethnic groups, regions and language groups who ever served in the American armed forces,

I thank you for your sense of duty and your willingness to meet your obligations squarely and without flinching, especially those of you who have seen hostile action and combat. For those men and women of the U.S. Coast Guard with whom I served for over twenty four years, I thank you for what you have taught me. Thank you for the security you provided all of us. Your efforts were not in vain.

Next I want to thank all American veterans who work for veterans' rights and benefits in a very difficult atmosphere within the political environment of this country. In the end, it is a fight for resources against heavy competition and you never give up. Thank you. I especially want to thank the various veterans' organizations and the staff and management of the *Veterans Today* web site. The ones I need to thank the most are John Allen, Gordon Duff and Bob Hanafin. These men work very hard for veterans and I want to publicly thank them now. I have the privilege of being a staff writer for the site. I treasure that distinction and my association with the men and women who write for the site. I want to thank the members of the House and Senate Veterans Affairs committees. You are appreciated more than you will ever realize.

I am a lifetime member of the Disabled American Veterans and a member of the American Legion for many years now. I wish to thank these organizations for constantly educating me per veterans' issues and for handling my adjudication over many years on my own disability case. I would only ask these two organizations to go lightly on the politics and get primarily back into the business of representing veterans and obtaining better benefits with timely deliverance in a big way. That is a hint. Please take it.

I want to thank Darlene Bothner, MSW for her help in explaining to me the various psychological ramifications of mental illness for the seriously physically disabled. I want to thank Kantha Raji Stoll M.D. for her help in understanding poly-trauma victims and their predicaments in life. Dr. Stoll has a practice in Alexandria, Virginia and served as an Air Force physician for many years, leaving the Air Force as a major prior to starting her own practice. I would also like to thank Zulma Weeks, a widow of a disabled veteran and a disabled veteran herself. She has helped me to understand the problems that a family endures while strugling with the disabilities faced by the veteran. As a former Air Force nurse, her compassion is deeply rooted in the veteran's experience.

I want to thank Gwynne Spencer for her never ending support as my writing mentor and Karen Gilden for once again formatting my book, constructing the cover and interfacing with the publishing arm for Amazon.com, CreateSpace.com.

I also want to thank my father, Thomas Carroll Barnes Jr. for his combat experience on Guadalcanal with the First Marine Division in Word War II. I learned many lessons concerning what I believe were symptoms of lifetime combat PTSD from his life experience. His postwar life taught me and my siblings and my mother how important treating lifetime combat PTSD can be to an entire community. He went untreated his entire lifetime for combat PTSD. That oversight carries a tremendous cost to the veteran and the family. Untreated combat PTSD in a father and husband can destroy any chance of normal functioning inside a family. It is a cost of war that is rarely taken into account. The effects of this dysfunction span generations for many people. I speak from experience here.

Lastly I want to thank the roughly 22.9 million American veterans that are alive right now in the summer of 2009. You routinely did more than was asked of you and delivered the goods during critical times when any other group may not have been able to accomplish the mission. I thank all of you most of all. Thank you for giving all of our people the opportunity to remain a nation. Your courage, grit and sacrifice were not in vain.

Tom Barnes
IU disabled American veteran

NOTE ON RESEARCH

The following websites were perused, read and/or extensively used in the research aspects and/or writing of this novel.

veteranstoday.com

minnpost.com

csbaonline.org

osdir.com

dailymail.co.uk

afji.com

nytimes.com

mshistory.k12.ms.us

americanfamilytraditions.com

www1.va.gov

arlingtoncemetery.net

1215.org

asianamerican.net

aaets.org

giftfromwithin.org

iamputees.blogspot.com

scientificamerican.com

spiegel.de

en.wikipedia.org

ropercenter.uconn.edu

liu.edu

uswings.com

footnote.com

history.com

archives.gov

cuw.edu

slate.com

pbs.org

If I have not named all the resource websites that I used in research, I apologize to the fine writers and researchers who contribute to those sites and whose insights I have used in the writing of this novel.

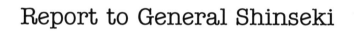

Report to General Shinseki

I.
Living with disabilities

The Pain of It All

CHIEF WARRENT OFFICER Rogier Maarten Magritte was a
56 year old individually unemployable (IU) totally disabled veteran of
the Gulf War. He was a retired U.S. Army helicopter pilot with almost
twenty five years active duty to his credit, having retired from the Army
in September of 1999. He was also a combat veteran who had taken a
direct hit on his Apache helicopter by an Iraqi shoulder borne rocket.
In the summer of 2009 he could still feel the pain of that evening in
1991 throughout his entire body.

This left him a man with crushed testicles that had to be surgically removed along with other severe internal injuries, chronic colitis,
bladder problems and a slightly dislodged brain that sat slightly off its
stem and gave him moderately blurred vision at nighttime or in the
dark. The attack also presented him with an injured and minimally
workable penis and therefore a very bad attitude due to that unfortunate event and its outcomes on his body, mind and sex life. Chief warrant officer Magritte was not often a happy man. But he was basically
good natured and quiet, so his discontent was not usually obvious.

To make matters worse, the fact that he was missing his family
jewels made it necessary that routine testosterone shots be administered to him at the Veterans Hospital in Washington D.C.. Otherwise
he feared that he might start growing breasts, wearing sun dresses and
begin shopping for really fashionable red pumps at Lane Bryant. Roger
did not want to see that happen. He had enough problems already
without having to deal with potential gender issues due to low testosterone levels. Still and all, immediately after the shots were administered, Roger would be unnaturally aggressive for a few days.

It was really a lousy situation all around, especially for his girlfriend. The upside here was that the day that he received his shot his libido was way up. His girlfriend would often say "Get your shot today?" when he would call her at work to ask to see her that night. It was the only time he ever called her at work. The shots made him horny.

To add to the bizarre nature of this entire odd state of affairs, the doctors had replaced Roger's testicles with two small prosthetics that more or less resembled small sponge balls set inside his scrotum. He would always laugh to himself that he must be careful because if he sat down on a chair too hard, he might bounce up to the ceiling. His "balls" might have looked natural to the casual observer who might be in the position to see them, but they felt like sponge balls to the owner. It was just one of those things that disabled veterans learn to live with during the course of a lifetime. There were worse things that could happen to a disabled veteran then having sponge balls for testicles. "At least I can still walk" Roger would often mutter to himself when considering his condition.

The trauma of being blown up in a helicopter had injured his penis to the extent that he had needed to get a penile implant consisting of a canister filled with fluid in his abdomen and a pump cylinder inserted into his scrotum which was then connected to inflatable rods inserted into his penis. When he wanted to have intercourse, he would squeeze his scrotum gently a few times. Then the pump reservoir in his scrotum would fill up with the fluid from his abdomen apparatus. At that point the fluid would be pumped into the inflatable rods in his penis. This was the only way to make his penis hard enough so that intercourse could occur. It was also the only way that he could have anything that even resembled normal sex in his life. As he and his woman would prepare for sex, he would normally say to her "Just give me a minute to prime the pump." She would usually wait patiently for the hydraulic wonder to finally rise to the occasion.

He often thought of the Frankenstein monster every time he put himself and his girlfriend through this drill with his semi-mechanical, hydraulic genital system. Between the sponge ball testicles, the testosterone shots every other week, the pump in his scrotum and the rods in his John Henry that he needed in order to force an erection he felt like a character in a Japanese adult cartoon series. But it was the only way that he could be intimate. One does what one has to do in order to at least approximate a normal life when one is severely disabled. Roger knew that quite well and relearned it every day.

When a disabled veteran has to go through all of this just to get some intimate time with his lover, the miracles of modern medicine do not mean a whole lot on a personal level. It is just one more thing to suffer through. But Roger would often mutter to himself at such times "at least I have a penis. A lot of veterans do not."

But he did have some limited choices in this regard. There was another type of penile implant that he could have had implanted, the semi-rigid inflatable rod type. In this method, one literally had semi-rigid rods placed into their penis and the penis could be bent up for intercourse or down to place it back into one's pants and therefore have it lay out of the way in a semi normal fashion for walking and sitting. The implanted rods bent more or less like pipe cleaners.

But Roger did not want to have to work his penis like a little boy would bend a pose-able toy in order to get his plumbing to work at intimate times. So he decided to have the more complicated pump and reservoir affair surgically implanted into him. It made him feel more normal somehow. Disabled veterans can be hard to figure out sometimes. Even they do not always know what their reasoning truly is.

Known as "Roger" by his Army pals because his Belgian name Rogier was difficult for an American to pronounce, he had a low key manner and was not prone to whining. A Vermonter by birth, he was raised almost directly on the U.S.-Canadian border by strict parents who were Belgian immigrants and war refugees. They settled in the U.S. in 1946 which was right after finding themselves displaced in the aftermath of World War II. Rogier was born in late 1952. He enlisted in the Army National Guard in 1973 and then went active duty as a helicopter mechanic in 1975. He went to helicopter pilot's training at Fort Rucker, Alabama in 1985 and eventually piloted an Apache helicopter in the Gulf War.

The AH-64 Apache helicopter is a four bladed, twin engine helicopter used for the attack with tricycle landing gear, a tandem cockpit that is designed for a crew of two people. The machine is forty eight feet long, twelve feet high and can weigh almost 21,000 pounds maximum at take-off. Top speed is 184 miles per hour. It's range is 300 miles and it's service ceiling is 21,000 feet. It was originally developed by Hughes Helicopters to replace the AH-1 Cobra which was first flown in late 1975 and was deemed no longer suitable for Army operations in modern warfare. The helicopter features a nose mounted set of sensors for targeting and night vision and is armed with a 30 mm M230 Chain Gun mounted between the main landing gear. It also carries a mixture of AGM-114 Hellfire and Hydra 70 rocket pods mounted on stub-wing pylons. It is a mighty war machine.

It is designed with double and triple redundant aircraft systems to maintain adequate survivability in combat and crash survivability for the pilots. It has a unique Kevlar armor bonding framework molded directly onto the airframe and inside the cockpit there is a shielding plate between the two crewmembers to act as a blast shield. This is intended to protect each crewmember if the other is blasted away. The downside to this cockpit configuration is that the shielding often captures the full effect of the blast inside the cockpit for the poor slob that gets hit.

In Roger's case, this shielding layout in the cockpit cost him his testicles and slightly dislocated his brain. His copilot and weapons systems operator was simply knocked unconscious for a few seconds and suffered a mild concussion. From his point of view, the blast shield worked. From Roger's point of view, it just made a bad situation worse. War machines are often like that. They tend to be partial answers to difficult questions which are posed at the most inconvenient times in very strange surroundings.

The Apache was first used in combat in 1989 during the invasion of Panama by American forces in something dubbed Operation Just Cause. Roger did not participate in that event. Both the AH-64A Apache and the AH-64D Apache Longbow have played large roles in several Middle Eastern conflicts. They were used in Operation Desert Storm, Operation Enduring Freedom in Afghanistan and in the invasion phase of Operation Iraqi Freedom in 2003. They are fine tank hunters and have ultimately destroyed hundreds of Iraqi armored vehicles. But their war record is not this one sided. If it was, Roger would still have had his nuts.

There are roughly one thousand Apache helicopter pilots in the entire U.S. Army. The community is small. They all know each other. Roger was well liked and respected as a hot stick prior to his being shot down. In the 100 hours of Gulf War I, two hundred and seventy seven AH-64 helicopters were used and they destroyed over 500 Iraqi tanks and numerous armored personnel carriers. Although Roger's aircraft was not shot down, once he was injured his copilot brought the chopper back to base. An RPG round had slightly penetrated the airframe and exploded half in and half out of the helicopter. It left a hole in the airframe the size of a beach ball. Roger's life would never be the same.

He stayed in the Army another eight years after his mishap but he spent three years in hospitals and on rehabilitation leave trying to heal from his wounds. He was left with a slight limp. He had fairly constant headaches. After his release from medical hold he had low level administrative jobs at various Army airfields. He finally decided to retire in 1999 on almost twenty five years active duty. He had experienced enough fun for one lifetime. When asked by his Army buddies upon his retirement if he had any regrets he simply said, "I regret that I only had two balls to give to my country." No one laughed when he said that.

He was declared IU totally disabled by the Department of Veterans Affairs after three intermediate appeals and one final appeal to the Board of Veterans Appeals in January 2007. It was a frustrating fight that lasted seven and a half years to finally be declared 80% disabled and individually unemployable. He was initially declared 40% disabled upon his retirement and he subsequently got help from the Disabled American Veterans in filing his several appeals. It was early 2009 before he ultimately received all of his back pay. It totaled over $40K in monies owed him by both the Army and the Department of Veterans Affairs. The Department of Veterans Affairs can be as slow as molasses in January when it comes to paying out entitlement money. And the Army isn't much faster. Roger had learned that the hard way.

But finally he received his money. His girlfriend convinced him to refurbish his thirty year old condo with the back pay. The place needed to have the kitchen and the bathrooms remodeled. It needed a new paint job and new interior doors and shades. It would cost about $40K. It was money well spent since he spent a great deal of time in his place. Having to suffer with severe colitis he spent over an hour on the toilet every day, usually divided between five or six trips to the throne in any twenty four hour period.

It was not easy for Roger to travel anywhere. So his condo was pretty much his world for most of the day. Roger made just enough money with his Army pension and his veteran's pension that he did not have to work. He was not wealthy, but he made enough in pension money to live a quiet life without having to worry about his ability to survive. At least he had that much going for him. He would often think that he was relatively lucky. Most working class Americans were not as secure as he was.

He lived at the Sentinel at Landmark Condominiums on Stevenson Avenue in the 'condo canyon' section of Alexandria, Virginia. It was near the mall on the west side of town. It was a mostly uneventful life. He spent most of the day walking his cocker spaniel and reading the paper, visiting the library, working out in the exercise room on the first floor and walking the mall while running small errands. He had two daughters from his one marriage of years prior and he tolerated an ex-wife who was now involved with another woman. Apparently she had been having lesbian affairs throughout their entire marriage.

Roger was to find this out years after their very bitter divorce had become final. His wife had fought the divorce bitterly. She did not want it. Roger was finally made to understand that he was more of a meal ticket than a husband. Sometimes it works out that way in a marriage. "It was just one more fine decision in a life long string of fine decisions!" Roger would often think to himself sarcastically about his nightmare marriage.

Roger, being a professional soldier, was often away from home and his pay check made her life quite comfortable. Her girlfriends made her life quiet exciting. Once Roger decided to leave her because she was so unstable, she fought the divorce realizing full well that now she would have to support herself now that her meal ticket was flying the coop. Sometimes, military wives can be extremely hard to understand. But after all, a soldier's pay buys a soldier's woman.

She worked low paying jobs in Pennsylvania where she now lived and would make Roger's life uncomfortable whenever she could. It was her reason for living now. Roger just accepted the situation to keep peace with his daughters, what else could he do? He had been married to a bitter and unstable nut. It seemed to Roger to be the American way. At least he thought so since many of his army friends were in similar situations relative to their ex wives. This misery was everywhere. Go figure.

Constructing a Life

Roger's girlfriend, Afet Wanly, was a Muslim American of mixed Turkish and Egyptian background. She was three years old when her family moved from Libya to Florida where her father had been a college professor. He received his Ph.D. in Florida after the move. She held a Ph.D. in theoretical mathematics and taught graduate level math to students at Howard University in Washington D.C.

The daughter of an imam, all of her siblings were highly educated. Her father had taught Muslim Studies at Howard University for decades and all of her sisters had attended that school as undergrads. She had attained her Ph.D. at Princeton University and her sisters were a physician and a psychologist. One worked at George Washington University hospital and the other was on the payroll for the Department of Defense in a highly classified job.

Afet had one brother who had been a U.S. Marine in the initial assault on Baghdad and had played a big part in capturing Sadam

Hussein. All of the siblings spoke Arabic in the Egyptian manner and her brother, Gamal, was now an analyst with the Defense Intelligence Agency. Roger had met her in a coffee shop in a strip mall next to an Egyptian restaurant near his condo. Roger did not realize that there actually was such a thing as an Egyptian restaurant in Virginia until he met her.

The sex between them was very passionate, considering the handicap that they were working with due to the condition of Roger's appendage and its affiliated supporting machinery. Afet was unusually understanding of the situation. She would wait patiently for Roger while he went through all the mechanics of getting himself ready to make love to her. While he was squeezing his scrotum getting his penis inflated he would usually say something like "Hang on honey. Let me just get finished with all the bells and whistles here!" She would laugh. They usually spent part of Saturday night together at Roger's condo. It was not easy considering the medieval attitudes of her sons relative to sex. They had to do it on the sly.

Afet had two sons in college so staying at her place was out of the question. Staying over night at Roger's place was equally impossible. The young men were both mosque attending Suni Muslims and very active in the Muslim Student Association at George Mason University. Afet was a believer, but hardly very religious. Since the boys had both attended the Saudi Academy in Springfield, Virginia they were rigorously semi-Wahhabist in their personal belief systems. They could be quite radical and anti-Israeli as well as anti-Zionist.

The Saudi Academy seemed to be very good at producing ultra conservative Muslim Americans less than twelve miles from downtown Washington D.C. It was just an odd piece of Americana that was often overlooked in the hubbub of urban life in northern Virginia. The F.B.I. almost certainly hoped that nothing dangerous would ever develop out of this. That agency had warned the academy three times prior to 2006 to alter the anti-Israeli and anti-Jewish agenda it preached. The results coming out of that series of warnings were never clear. The academy was almost certainly under constant federal surveillance.

Chapter I

All of this meant that Afet and Roger had to hide their sex lives like teenagers from her two very religious Muslim sons. These guys were college age American kids and they had the personal value systems of a tenth century Bedouin living on the Arabian Peninsula. It was really quite incredible. For American born young men, as far as Roger was concerned these two guys were really out-to-lunch relative to modern social norms. But then, Afet was loyal and pretty and sexy so Roger suffered the charade in silence.

He was getting quite an education about Muslim America from being her boyfriend and lover. It was nothing at all like the uninitiated might think. It was like dating a strict Calvinist in the 17ᵗʰ Century. You had to get your fun on the sly. Roger often referred to Afet's older son, Salem, as "the Imam." She hated it and would get angry with Roger when he did that. "His name is Sa-LEM!" she would scold Roger. Roger would laugh at that, and she was just get angrier. It was the only time that the two ever really crossed swords.

Roger had spent Thanksgiving Day the previous November at Afet's townhouse in Springfield with her extended family and Muslim friends. He was the only person at the gathering from a Christian background and her family was quite religious in their conversation. In fact, Roger was surprised to see so many highly educated and scientifically trained American citizens who were Muslims engage in open proselytizing at the dinner table. In fact he was stunned. He had never seen anything like this before.

They were all M.D.'s or Ph.D.'s or highly educated professional people and they discussed the Quran for over an hour with Roger. They all were believers in the literal truth of that sacred book. Roger was silently astonished. He had never experienced anything quite as eerie as this. They pushed hard for him to see their faith as true and unique and worthy of consideration for his full acceptance as his own. Roger had not attended church since the 1970's and did not see himself as much of a Christian, though he was raised Catholic. He was really taken back by their aggressiveness but he said nothing in order to be polite to Afet. "These are highly educated people" he thought to himself. "How could they be this fundamentalist in their life view?"

11

He held this thought throughout the entire evening. The situation was very uncomfortable for him. Still, Afet was his girlfriend and a longsuffering and tender lover and considering his physical situation Roger suffered the preaching silently. It was bizarre.

In attendance at this makeshift and ad hoc madras were her brother, her two brothers in law, two Yemeni friends who worked for the State Department and were married and their two sons were also present along with her five nieces and her three nephews. The meal was turkey with all of the traditional American fixings. Roger was asked to say the opening blessing to the meal but he declined and said that since this was a Muslim family, a Muslim prayer should be offered. Roger offered, "That is the very spirit of Thanksgiving. The family thanks God for the blessings and trials of the previous year. The prayer should be in the family religion." They smiled and said a prayer in Arabic. Roger had no idea what it meant but it was obviously heart felt. The evening was calm, filled with conversation and had a highly religious overtone. Roger frankly was not sure what to make of it all. It was a unique evening to say the least.

It always left Roger mildly irritated to be in the company of such a religiously fervent group of highly educated people. Could they not see how ridiculous they seemed to him? A scientific background mixed with a fundamentalist approach to an ancient belief system always seemed a contradiction in terms to Roger. It did not matter to him whether it was Muslim, Christian or Jew. A believing scientist seemed to be the ultimate oxymoron to Roger. But he really was fond of Afet and so he played along. Her brother Gamal sensed it and agreed with him. He was about as much a Muslim as Roger was a Christian.

They both had learned the hard way through service experience that god talk could be a lot more dangerous and empty than it could be soothing and helpful. It was often a flimsy excuse to simply kill people in the name of a god. They had both suffered war in an American uniform in the Middle East. Neither felt very good about it. They seemed to sense in each other this kindred view. They grew close that evening as a result. It was unspoken and subtle, but their common combat experience drew them close. It was unmistakable in their demeanor toward each other.

Gamal had just been welcomed back into the family fold. His two tours in Iraq with the marines had disenfranchised him from family for years. The men in the family, including the nephews who attended George Mason University would openly and bitterly argue with the war veteran. "Can you not see that you are a Muslim warring against Muslims? This is sacrilege!" they would shout at him. The sisters had eventually arranged a truce.

Before Gamal came to dinner, the men in the room quietly outlined their bitterness toward him so that Roger would understand how deeply offended they were with his soldiering for America. Roger pointed out to them that Gamal had been born here in the U.S. Roger also noted that every one in the room except the Lebanese brother in law either presently worked for the U.S. Government or previously had done so. It seemed to make no difference to them. Roger then quietly said to the men as he looked them all in the eyes, "It might be something you would want to think about. *This* is your country now." They visibly cringed at his statement. They knew it was true. It did not sit well with them, true or not.

Roger then asked them a simple question. "Did the Muslims in Iraq have any problem trying to kill Gamal, an American-born Muslim?" The brothers in law stared at Roger. They were a Lebanese Druze who had converted to Islam in order to marry into a Muslim family and a Pakistani who had been raised in a non-religious home but was now quite fervent. The men were struck silent. They did not know how to answer. Roger found it more than interesting that the Lebanese immigrant owned a liquor store in Maryland. Religious Muslims do not drink. The Pakistani immigrant was a physician who had only recently re-embraced Islam as a believer. He had lived a very long life into his mid-forties as a drinker, carouser and womanizer. He had recently found Allah again and grown a beard to show that to the world. There was more than a little hypocrisy here.

Roger moved off to another subject. But he had made his point. The proselytizing stopped abruptly at that point. No more Quran lessons for the Christian, the American "messihi", that day. "Thank God!" Roger muttered to himself when he realized that they would stop all the Quran talk. He thought he would scream if it continued much longer.

Gamal proved to be a serious student of Muslim America and its history and Roger was intensely interested in what Gamal told him. Gamal spent considerable time that afternoon explaining Muslim American history to Roger.

It seems that the history of Muslims in America stretches back to the 16th Century when Estevanico of Azamor (1500-1539) is mentioned in a few contemporary expeditionary logs kept by the Conquistador Cabeza de Vaca's as a slave servant in the Spanish explorer's party. Roughly translated as Stephen the Moor, Estevanico was sold into slavery in Azamor, a Portuguese town in Morocco. It is unclear whether his parents were blacks from Senegal or that he was brought to Morocco via the trans-Saharan slave trade. In any case, he made several trips into what was to eventually become the Southwestern United States and the Caribbean nations with various explorers. He was probably the first person of African descent to set foot in the Americas.

A former Presbyterian that had grown bored with Christianity and had dabbled with Buddhism became America's first Anglo-American Muslim. Alexander Russell Webb is considered by many American historians to be the earliest prominent Anglo-American convert to Islam in 1888. He traveled to India to study Islam and ultimately converted his American wife and children to that faith. Although there are no reliable records to support any contention that slaves sent to North America starting in 1520 continued to practice Islam, it is certainly true that roughly half of them came from areas in Africa where Islam was the dominant religion.

Small scale migration to America by Muslim Yemenites and Turks began about 1840 and stayed fairly constant until right before World War I. They settled mostly in the areas surrounding and encompassing Dearborn, Michigan, Ross, North Dakota and Quincy, Massachusetts and Ross is the site of the very first mosque and Muslim cemetery in the U.S. It was left to decay and was later torn down in the 1970s but a new mosque was built in its place in 2005.

In 1906 Bosnian Muslims founded the Jamaat al Hajrije, a social services group put in place to help Balkan Muslims in the U.S. The community still existed as of 2009. In 1907 the Tatar communities from Poland, Russia and Lithuania founded the first Muslim organization in New York City. In 1920 the first Islamic Mission in the U.S. was started by an Indian Muslim and in 1934 a mosque was built in Cedar Rapids, Iowa. In 1945 a mosque was built in Dearborn, Michigan. There are more mosques today in California than in any other state.

The Nation of Islam was started among the African American community in 1930 and is still controversial in many ways among the Muslim community in the U.S. It presently has about 70,000 followers in this country. There is no accurate overall count of Muslims in America. The number varies from 1.1 million to 8 million depending on who is doing the counting and what the political agenda of the census taker might be. American Muslims seem to adhere to virtually every political leaning possible.

At the present time it is not possible to draw a clear picture of a basic political agenda shared by all American Muslims, the community seems to be too diverse across economic and societal backgrounds for that kind of homogeneous approach to life in America. Like every other American ethnic or religious group, American Muslims seem to be moving into all corners of the political landscape.

Since Gamal himself was a former U.S. Marine and presently worked as an analyst for the D.I.A., Roger could clearly see that there was no common agenda for American Muslims anymore than there was for any other religious group in America. The two men genuinely liked each other and had a lot in common. Gamal excused himself early from the dinner table and family gathering and left to see his girl-friend, an Irish American who worked with him at the D.I.A. Roger hoped to see him again and told him that as they parted.

Roger helped Afet with the dishes and when the guests left, he snuck a kiss or two from her so that her oldest son would not catch them in the act. He would not have reacted well to this. Roger found him to be very odd for a college kid. Conservative was not a strong enough word for his outlook on life. The kid was downright reactionary and Roger thought that there might be mental health issues involved here. He was correct. There was. Afet would speak about it every now and then and the young man's aggressive behavior toward any man who was around his mother was a dead give away that something was odd. It made Roger think hard about going forward with Afet.

Roger drove home from Springfield to his condo in neighboring Alexandria later that night after all the guests left Afet's home. She was very pretty, very smart and very accomplished. Roger really liked her. But she openly talked about Roger and her marrying and the need for Roger to convert to Islam if and when that happened. And *that* was just not going to happen, not ever. Roger found her very sensual, very loving and very sexy but there was something about the veto power her oldest son held on her behavior which really bothered Roger. It was like something out of the Middle Ages.

And she was terrified that the boy would catch Roger kissing her. Hell, they were having sex often but telling the oldest son they were just friends. Roger did not like this aspect of their relationship one bit. It was just too Middle Eastern for his liking. But for the time being, he decided to let their relationship ride. Hell, no one else was interested in him and Afet was very pretty and very nice. It was just the whole "Muslim thing" that was too much for Roger to deal with over the long run, and he knew that. He was going to have to resolve all this internal conflict at some point.

Open Wounds

When he got home Roger went straight to bed. He was an early riser, which meant he was an early-to-bed kind of guy. It had its advantages and disadvantages like anything else. He woke up and worked out for a half hour with weights and did light calisthenics and then got a shower and started his day. It was a typical day. He ate his breakfast at the computer while reading the morning news online. He then turned to other business.

He often contributed as an unpaid staff writer to a left leaning veterans' website called *Veteran's Now*. He liked its progressive point of view. It had a staff chock full of disabled veterans who were volunteering their time and talents to get out pertinent and pragmatic news to veterans of all ages and all time periods in the Service. This morning he wrote an article and posted it on the website concerning Gulf War veterans and his impression of their understanding of the Muslim American community. He used a lot of the information that Gamal had given him the previous day. He felt oddly satisfied when he had written and posted the article and he got 125 hits on his article that day. That was not bad for this small website.

Most of the staff writers were Viet Nam era and Gulf War era veterans. Many had been high ranking officers who had been placed in key positions. There was a lot of good information on that website that made Roger proud to be a contributor. It did not try and tow the party line. It was a website for independent thinking veterans. They were usually angry at their lot in life and Roger understood that point of view quite well.

Roger ran some errands at the local mall in the Landmark section of town which was only four blocks away from his condo and then ate lunch alone at a local Chinese restaurant. He was partial to Mongolian beef and would frequent any Chinese restaurant that had it on their menu. He went to the library only ten blocks away from the restaurant and returned some books and read a *Newsweek* magazine and then drove over to the other side of town to see a movie at the Potomac Mills Mall cinema. They had sixteen screens and he enjoyed the atmosphere there. Roger's day was proceeding nicely. It was relaxing and there was no pressure to do anything. He liked that.

Roger telephoned Afet at work and left a message on her office phone. She taught three classes a week at Howard University and spent the rest of the week in research. She was always writing another text book. She had already published two and was close to publishing a third. Afet was brilliant and Roger admired her. She had asked him the previous weekend once again to consider marrying her as a Muslim in the mosque that her family infrequently attended. Once again, Roger just stared at her when she posed the question. He never knew what to say to her.

The whole question seemed just too surreal for him to entertain it seriously. Roger had been killing Muslims in the Gulf War, not out of hatred but out of a soldier's sense of duty. Somehow or other, becoming a Muslim in order to marry Afet did not square with his previous experience in the Gulf. It would also be a core value system change that seemed too strange to him.

After he left Afet the message Roger drove over to Walter Reed to visit the seriously disabled Iraq and Afghan War veterans in the wing for the amputees. It was always hard to see these young people like that. As a bona fide seriously disabled veteran himself and one who was a member in good standing in several veterans' organizations, he could get access to the wards. Bur even more importantly he knew one of the senior Army doctors who worked in one of the wards for the seriously injured. Roger had served with him years before in the Gulf War and that fact alone let him get the access he needed.

The injured soldiers were always glad to see Roger. They liked Roger's easy going manner. He was a no nonsense kind of guy and he had helpful information and experience in living with serious wartime injuries but he was also oddly calm and pleasant. The young soldiers picked right up on that. His message was always the same to them; take care of your mental health first and your physical health will follow. Even if it doesn't, a strong and positive frame of mind will help a seriously injured veteran get through any day. He knew that much from personal experience. The injured were always grateful to hear that message, even if they did not always show it.

Because of the oddities of modern warfare in the 21st Century, wounded service members were now dealing with what military medicine terms 'poly-trauma' in unprecedented cases. This is a number of serious injuries that would have killed young Americans in uniform in previous wars. But due to Kevlar armor for both personnel and vehicles and due to the survivability factors of the modern battlefield with forward operating surgical hospitals practically in the battle area, Americans with grave combat injuries that would have killed them only a decade earlier are now surviving.

This poses a dilemma for all concerned in military medicine. What is their quality of life going to be if these severely injured soldiers and marines survive their battlefield injuries? That question has just started being asked in the circles of military medicine. It has not been answered yet.

Roger entered the first ward he would visit that day. He found that one soldier from North Dakota, a Sergeant Hicks, was lying in a bed staring at the ceiling. Roger approached Sergeant Hicks and shook his shoulder to get his attention. The soldier slowly turned his head and stared blankly at Roger who said "Hi! I'm Roger and I'm a disabled Gulf War vet. How are doing?" The soldier smiled a weak smile and continued to stare blankly. "What happened here?" Roger asks. The soldier slowly and with halting language told his tale. It was heard for the soldier to concentrate or to speak clearly. Roger could see that.

It seems that Sergeant Hicks was blown out of his Hummer by an IED planted by the Taliban while he was only three months into his tour in Afghanistan. The blast threw the young twenty nine years old National Guardsman threw the window. His spleen burst, his left lung collapsed and one of his kidneys was torn. The blast was so powerful that it knocked the fillings out of his teeth, shattered his right hip and the force of the blast shattered his shinbones. Roger could see that he is missing three fingers on his right hand and part of his heel has been blown off his right foot. The concussion in his head was so severe that it slightly rocked his brain off its stem. His short term memory is gone. He thinks he got hurt in basic training sometimes. At other times he has no idea what happened. His eleven years in the Army and the National Guard are gone; he cannot remember them. He only remembers basic training.

He has no memory of Afghanistan. He is mobile only when he uses a wheelchair. He has a German wife and two sons from his regular Army days in Germany prior to the war. His wife visited him the first few months he was here at Walter Reed but has since returned to North Dakota with her sons. Hicks has not seen them or heard from them in four months. She does not contact him anymore. The sergeant lies in his bed most days and just stares. His wife is AWOL and moved on with her life he suspects. That is, he suspects this when he can think straight. He can rarely think straight. It is not an unusual case. Sergeant Hicks is more the rule than the exception in these unfortunate circumstances.

The young man told the story in a monotone voice without emotion. This sent a chill down Roger's spine. He worried for the young man and did not know exactly what to say. He patted him on the shoulder and said "Hang in there trooper" and moved off. He noticed a tear streaming down the young man's face as he walked away. Roger's heart was pounding and he wondered if the man would have been better off dying. The doctors on the ward wondered that also. The man didn't wonder. He *knows* he would have been better off dying.

Roger approached another young man, this time it was a sailor according to his rank card above his bed. Roger was surprised to see him at the Army hospital. "Hi! I'm Roger, and you are...?" Roger asked. The young man smiled and said "I am Dave." Roger moved in closer. "How did a swabbie end up here?" he asked. Dave laughed. "Well actually I was simply a courier for Navy Operations in the Middle East and I got blown up by a rocket in the Green Zone in Baghdad while I was sleeping in my rack." Dave laughed a nervous laugh. "I am not much of a hero am I? And that is not much of a hero's tale!"

Dave's two legs were missing below the knee and one eye was gone. He was once a very handsome young man, Roger could see that. Those days are gone. Dave was nineteen years old. "They are trying to fit me with prosthetics for my eye and they are not sure how they want to proceed, so I am still here in the ward" Dave offers. Roger nods. "Anything I can do for you Dave?" Roger asked. Dave laughed. "Can you find me a real eye and two brand new real legs?" Rogers laughed too. "Good luck!" Roger said laughing mildly and moves off.

He waved as he left Dave. Dave waved back. They share a bravado common among seriously disabled veterans and the term black humor does not adequately describe the mentality. When there is nothing left to do, laughter is always an option.

When a human soul is imprisoned in a young but virtually destroyed body it lives a half life between the living and the very gates of hell. Only the seriously disabled can understand the overpowering and ever present despair that comes with this distinction. In order to keep one's loved ones and surrounding souls from being infected with despair the disabled veteran commonly adopts an attitude with the world that can only be described in this fashion. "What can you do to me now? You have taken everything. So go ahead and take whatever else I have. What difference could it possibly make at this point?"

There is a sort of "brotherhood of the damned" mentality that takes over the mind. One sees it all the time with seriously disabled veterans, especially the younger ones. They might continue existing, but a meaningful and productive life is often simply left in the war zone or in the dangerous situation that took away their life's dreams in the first place.

Somehow or other the human spirit rallies when it realizes it is no longer in danger of losing anything. Everything of value has already been taken. In a way that cannot be adequately explained, the seriously disabled young veteran finds solace in this thought. In a manner that only those who have faced death and somehow survived can understand, death now holds more fascination, even serenity, than it holds fear.

When a nineteen year old has been in combat or in some dangerous situation that is life altering and lost both legs and an eye, why should he not laugh at his predicament? There is nothing else left but the constant realization that life is indeed a tragic joke.

The broken man can draw strength from this realization, but this cannot be explained. It just is. Perhaps this is what it means to participate in the godhead, something that ultimately all the world's religions strive to have their adherents attain. This truly is crucifixion in every way. And for the strong ones and the ones that somehow learn to transcend the pain and the horror and the disfiguration, resurrection often follows the crucifixion.

When life has been so tragic that it no longer matters whether or not one lives or dies then a certain calmness can descend upon a broken soul. A very quiet but persistent whisper can he heard in the stillness of the night, like awakening from a dream. It says, "Wait. Just wait. This will end someday. This will not continue forever. The day will come when the horror of life is over and you can rest. Just wait a little longer. Death will come for you. You have that much to hold onto at least."

Roger continued his walk through the wards and his greetings. He fought to keep a smile on his face while greeting the dozens of young men in the wards. The women were in their own ward and were often visited by female veterans. It was pretty much the same situation there. The horror of modern warfare does not discriminate among the genders.

Shattered Minds

It was always hard for Roger to walk through the wards of the seriously injured that were often filled with multiple amputees who were younger than his own kids. He had two daughters aged twenty nine and thirty two and so many of these kids were ten years younger than that. And they had so very little left in their lives to make a living with; their limbs were gone or brains were scrambled, or both. Roger knew that he was spending time with the living dead. He hated it. He loved it. These young people were his people more than any one else on the planet, and he knew that. They were his and he was theirs'. It was really that simple.

He was home when he was with them, no matter how uncomfortable one of them might make him feel at the moment. And the most obviously wounded were not in the largest group of the maimed and wounded. The biggest and most seriously hampered group and the most dangerous group of wounded veterans were those without visible wounds. Modern warfare was so intense and so brutally efficient in its longevity and ability to return the wounded to the battlefield again and again that it was crushing the human personalities of the warriors. It was simply squeezing the humanity out of them.

Modern warriors, unlike their ancient forebears, were dying slowly from psychic violence brought on by intense and lengthy combat tours and extremely violent service experiences. Modern warfare crushes the mind as well as the body. It leaves a human being with terror that will last until he draws his or her last breath, even if that is decades later.

From the attacks on 9/11 until the last week in May 2009, almost 1,900 men and women had committed suicide while on active duty or while serving in Guard or Reserve units, both stateside and overseas. The Center for Disease Control informed the Department of Veterans Affairs in early 2009 that 18 American veterans from all wars combined commit suicide every day in the United States. That is 6,500 veteran suicides a year. Roger realized that the implications are staggering. And the situation is even more tragic than this.

As of February 2009 there were 184,000 American troops of all kinds assigned to Afghanistan and Iraq. About 15% of these troopers, marines, airmen, sailors and even a handful of coast guardsmen suffered from concussions as a result of munitions blasts. In a survey completed in that month by the Army, many of the soldiers were suffering from lasting and chronic headaches. 30% of these soldiers were suffering with headaches 15 days a month. And this number did not include the soldiers who had lost consciousness for more than thirty minutes or that have an injury that can be detected on an MRI or a CT scan.

It is known by military doctors across the world that headaches are a common complaint following a mild brain injury but there are other problems like nausea, light sensitivity, balance problems as well as cognitive and behavioral problems that follow on a brain concussion. Depression and post traumatic stress disorder also might follow trauma to the brain.

There were many more unidentified wounded from the wars in the Middle East raging at the beginning of the 21st Century than there were identifiable casualties. That was now becoming apparent as they came home. Their lives were exploding in a much greater number of cases than random statistical analysis would support. Suicide and homicide inside the families of returning service men and women was off the scale relative to what should be expected from a random sample of the American population. The hidden injuries were literally killing people. The war was never going to end for many of these wartime veterans. That much was now becoming painfully apparent to military medical personnel and veterans organization staffers.

And something else was becoming very apparent to psychologists and psychiatrists working with enormous numbers of unstable wartime veterans of the Iraq and Afghanistan wars. It was now suspected by military medical personnel that the unprecedented number of days exposed to danger and combat or potential combat conditions was literally driving huge sections of the American armed forces into a state of permanent craziness.

Too much combat exposure for too few troopers meant that the very few who were carrying the burden of combat over and over were possibly being subjected to personality disintegration at an unprecedented scale. And many professionals were claiming that the stress and near psychosis that was born out of this unprecedented exposure to combat could not be corrected with traditional psychological interventions.

Roger could see with every visit to Walter Reed Medical Center that the situation was getting worse for the mental states of the soldiers he came across and many of them did not look seriously injured. Many of them were simply dead inside. They no longer had the capacity to engage Roger in even simple, nonthreatening conversation. They were emotional zombies. They were dead men who were moving around, their personalities had disintegrated beyond reach. Roger was beginning to suspect that they were beyond healing. A secret report to the Joint Chiefs of Staff at the Pentagon concurred with Roger's assessment. These men were beyond healing.

Roger could see that new and completely radical approaches to mental health must be found quickly to save the American troopers involved in these wars from a lifetime of depression, suicidal thoughts and broken lives. As far as Roger was concerned thinking completely out of the box was now mandatory to grab hold of a problem that was growing exponentially worse with no end in sight. A crazy army, navy and air force served no one's needs. It was also useless in national defense. It was time to listen to the radicals within the counseling community. These were often the marginalized geniuses in the mental health profession. The traditional approaches to healing trauma were not working with this group of injured young people.

But Roger had read up on this problem and knew more than most people. It was after all, a personal thing for him. He found that as usual in matters of psychological survival, the Israelis were far ahead of everyone else.

The Israeli government pioneered psychological interventions for victims of terrorist attacks and one of the leading experts in that field, a Professor Irwin J. Mansdorf, published a book in Israel in October 2008 outlining various techniques for debriefing victims of this trauma. Some military medical personnel were presently lobbying to get his methods accepted by the American military establishment for combat veterans seeking help with mental trauma following combat. One thing was sure however. No single method was accepted by mental health professionals as appropriate for combat veterans dealing with psychological trauma and there was plenty of evidence from various studies that early debriefing of trauma victims oftentimes hurt more than it helped.

In his readings on the matter Roger found that various psychological surveys and follow up studies have come to the unfortunate conclusion that there is no evidence that individual psychological debriefing is a useful treatment for the prevention of post traumatic stress disorder (PTSD). A screen and treat model is now the preferred method for discovering and treating early symptoms of PTSD. But this would not be helpful in treating war veterans, many of whom would carry psychological scars for the rest of their lives.

Truly *jumping* out of the box was needed here. Simply *thinking* out of the box was not going to be enough. Roger could see that plainly every time he visited the amputee wards. So what were the options for treatment of lifetime combat PTSD? Roger talked to many experts and their findings were sobering.

The medical people in the armed forces and the veterans organizations could continue doing what they were doing and get lousy success rates or a completely radical approach could be attempted. Roger had done some serious research based on his need to find a personal answer to the decaying mental states of the wounded warriors he was advising and he came up with some partial answers.

Roger had found two therapists / researchers who had extensive experience with trauma victims and who had worked out an actual plan for trauma victims to follow in their life patterns after the trauma. Doctor Erwin Parson and Ms. Luerena K. Bannon had spent years working with trauma victims of virtually every type and had found a common set of self-help strategies that their patients could use to make the mental pain bearable while the mind healed itself.

Roger had their plan printed on cards with a few editorial changes that he felt were relevant for combat trauma victims and he handed it out to every seriously wounded soldier he came across at Walter Reed.

The card read as follows:

What Can I Expect After Trauma?

(1) You can expect the "quick-fix" impulse that will completely, overnight, eliminate your current suffering. But remember you will need time and lots of patience for post-trauma healing and recovery to occur.

(2) You can expect to learn first before you are gaining control.

(3) Being realistic, you recognize what you have been through was a very difficult experience for yourself, and that the trauma will challenge and test every capability you have.

(4) Expect sleep problems.

(5) You can expect to find your self becoming very irritable and angry over the slightest provocation and to feel depressed, sad, and alone.

(6) Go easy on yourself, again, exercise patience; you are going through an extraordinarily difficult time, but you can choose to get out of it.

(7) Expect ordinary life events to become more distressing than they were before the trauma.

(8) You may expect to find your heart rate increase and pounding, feeling spacey, with perspiration, sometimes tremulousness, and increase in anxiety and fear.

(9) Allow yourself to mourn the loss that occurs when trauma robs you of your sense of self—your motivation to go forward, ambition, ideals, identity, internal security, dignity, and aspirations for the future.

(10) Keep in mind that even the most ordinarily loving and well-intentioned person may find it difficult hearing your story, and maintaining the level of empathy you need. But don't give up; don't get discouraged. Be patient with your self, be patient with and even understanding of others' limitations to comprehend the enormity of your trauma-based suffering.

What Can I Do and What Should I Resist Doing After My Traumatic Ordeal?

(11) Do reach out to family and friends with whom you can talk, and who will offer you their attention, and empathic commitment to offer you support.

(12) Do writing your experience down on paper is also a helpful way to process your trauma.

(13) Do seek a self-help group if you believe this would help you. In these group you will meet fellow survivors who are suffering but are able to communicate and share feelings with group members, and who are not so distressed they require professional intervention.

(14) Do search for individual and/or available therapy groups with survivors of combat related trauma if your symptoms get worse and interfere with your life. Ensure that the group is led by a person with professional training and experience in combat induced trauma and PTSD.

(15) Do all you can to engage in health-generating, mood-brightening activities:

Do reach out to others.

Do engage in meaningful hobbies, finding fun things to do. Do put forth the effort to engage in regular physical exercise and relaxation procedures.

Do plan to eat well.

Do get sufficient rest.

Do learn how to reduce the "flightiness" (or being out of control) of your breathing.

Do things to normalize your life and its routines by having meals, sleep, work, and exercise at the same time of the day.

Do make a diligent effort to remain free of alcohol or drug use as ways of coping.

(16) Resist eating heavy meals, drinking coffee, and intense physical exercise several hours before going to sleep.

(17) Resist using anger to keep others away, as a "trauma technique" to remain safe from questions, safe from others' piercing scrutiny, and from feeling vulnerable to the return of dissociated trauma thoughts, feelings, and behaviors.

(18) Resist tendency to stay away from people, and from shopping malls, activities, and places you were accustomed to before the trauma.

(19) Resist tendency to make home into a defending fortress.

(20) Resist making sweeping changes in your life at this time; for example, like moving away, changing careers, getting divorced, or dissolving long-term relationships—until, as they say, further notice.

(21) Do remember that intrusive thoughts to the trauma are normal and predictable.

(22) Do remember that your trauma intrusive thoughts are mere constructions of the mind; they are not real. That is, the recurring image or thought of the trauma does not mean the original traumatizing experi-

ence is reoccurring in the present as your mind-out-of-control would have you believe.

(23) Do seek and get new knowledge about trauma and PTSD's effect on your thinking, feelings, behavior, and on your perspective for the future. Knowledge is power, and information is truly how you get it. So, it's also important for you to learn all you can about what happened to you, about your stress responses, and what you can expect whether you decide to deal with our ordeal alone, with friends, or by using professional assistance.

(24) Resist the tendency that is prevalent among PTSD victims to use alcohol and drugs to reduce anxiety and get sleep.

(25) Since trauma responses take you away from the present, telling you that, despite the fact that you know the trauma is behind you, that, "in reality", it's still reoccurring in the present:

(26) Resist the tendency to reduce pleasure in your life.

(27) Resist becoming a workaholic to stave off memories of the trauma.

Do use relaxation skills.

Do use all your senses to ground you in the present. Thus,

Visually, focus on the color of objects in your immediate environment ("it's green," "long and sharp," etc.). Keep your eyes open, and take note of where you are.

Auditorily, do focus on identifying the various sounds you're hearing at the present time.

Tactilely, do touch objects close to you and describe the experience in detail. Touch something cold, warm, or hot and describe the sensory experience.

Olfactorily, do become aware of the various smells in your immediate environment.

Gustatorily, do think back at something you recently tasted, or select something to eat and describe the taste.

Do use self-soothing approaches:

Talk to your self in a reassuring language, reminding your self of who you are, where you are, and where you're going.

Say compassionate things to your self.

Think of the last time someone said something that you found inspiring, and repeat it to yourself, now.

Remember your favorite poem and recite it.

This was not a cure-all for the serious trauma that combat veterans face but it seemed to help them. They often said so after seeing Roger again in the wards months after he gave them the card. It seemed to work for many of them and many said that they were helped greatly by the card. Roger wrote a note to the researchers and thanked them. He never heard back from them. He hoped that they had received the note. One never knows the tremendous good that one can do by simply caring about how other people cope with life. When people act like that, heaven must be a sure thing for them.

The sad truth was that an overwhelming number of veterans were suffering from PTSD. It was reliably estimated in 2005 that over 30% of Viet Nam veterans currently suffered from PTSD. By some estimates taken at the Department of Veterans Affairs in 2008 (D.V.A.) 12% of Iraq war veterans and 6% of Afghanistan war veterans in the U.S. Armed Forces currently suffer with lifetime chronic PTSD symptoms.

As for Gulf War veterans, some statistics indicate that as of 2008 about 15% still suffered from PTSD. To make matters worse, the normal PTSD interventions that are used for trauma victims of sexual assault, physical abuse in childhood and things such as trauma due to murder in the workplace or involvement in a death by fire do not seem to work well with combat PTSD victims. A solution was needed that specifically addressed the trauma of combat veterans. Roger was to find the answer, at least in part, from a very odd place.

Jumping Out of the Box

Roger often asked friends in the therapeutic community what could be done here. The answers that he got were enlightening. They taught him a great deal about the present state of affairs in the treatment methods for trauma victims.

It seems that in therapy and psychotherapy training for a therapist, psychiatrist, psychologist or social worker there is a mentoring process or some sort of classroom training that involves the concepts of transference and counter transference in a counseling environment. Simply put, transference occurs in a counseling environment when the therapist either represents something to the client or says or does something that reminds the client of his or her traumatic past. This then creates a sort of emotional flash back in the client and that in turn dredges up all the emotions of that past time surrounding that event. The emotions transfer the client's psychological state of mind from that moment into the present. It can be very dramatic and often quite emotional in a negative sense for the client.

Counter transference is when the therapist must learn to identify and then consciously redirect his/her own feelings toward a client. Or put another way, the therapist is taught to quickly identify and then immediately redirect his/her emotional entanglement with a client since it will almost always result in a failed professional relationship with no resolution of the client's problem. Training to identify this dynamic immediately is crucial. This not only serves to help the therapist regulate his/her own emotions in the therapist/client relationship but even more importantly it gives the therapist valuable insight into exactly what the client is attempting to draw out of the therapist with his transference behavior.

But Roger had to simplify this if he was going to explain it to the powers that be at the D.V.A. To state this in very simple American English, the therapist and client are doing a psychological dance with each other at all times. The therapist must always be the partner that is leading, never following. He or she must remain in control of the therapeutic dance at all times. Whether the client realizes it or not, he or she is attempting to elicit an emotional response from the therapist. The therapist must be aware of this and act according to the client's psychological needs for a more stable frame of mind. He/she must consistently point out to the client that the client is attempting to get a response from the therapist through unconscious or conscious manipulation of the emotional environment.

To state this even more simply, the client will create a mini-crisis or construct an artificial issue in the client/therapist relationship in order to get a familiar emotional response. This may not always be a positive response, it is simply familiar. And the client is attempting to get a familiar emotional response, one that he or she has confronted previously. It does not matter to the client if that response is negative. The important thing is that it is familiar.

Roger realized that this might be the answer in healing combat PTSD suffering. It is now thought by some therapists looking for a radical new way to arrest lifetime PTSD suffering in combat veterans that this may be at least a partial answer. If all combat veterans suffering from PTSD can be taught the same strategies to deal with their PTSD triggers and their need for crisis in the same fashion that therapists are taught to recognize and control their own counter transference toward a client with whom they experience negative feelings and emotions then PTSD symptoms might be controlled. Then the PTSD event can be seen by the sufferer for what it truly is, a perception, and perhaps be controlled by the sufferer.

Roger found that if the sufferer from combat induced PTSD can be taught to construct and maintain a sort of "inner therapist" to whom he or she can turn when the PTSD triggers are present in their environment, they can literally turn off their own reactions to PTSD triggers. They can short circuit their own tendency to act out by simply objectively seeing how they are setting themselves up for a crisis and then they can refuse to play along with their own desire to act out.

Roger was discovering that many therapists who worked with PTSD sufferers from combat experiences were using their own medical school and social work training to teach these veterans how to literally "see" themselves and their maladaptive behaviors from a mental viewpoint above themselves. They then might be able to stop these maladaptive behaviors before they took hold of their emotions as a result of a trigger in the environment.

Put in infantry terms, the veterans suffering from lifetime PTSD were learning to identify the enemy (their need to act out). Then they could control the terrain (control the environment that allows them to act out). And then they could subdue the enemy (stop the urge to act out before behaving badly). This would be done with the overwhelming firepower of refusing to cooperate in maladaptive behavior that stems from their fears. Many therapists believe that these skills can be taught. Roger hoped that they were right, for the sake of those with shattered minds and dead emotions.

This odd approach might be the key to opening the door to successful treatment. If the veterans with lifetime combat PTSD could be taught to see themselves from a point above themselves and stop the behavior of that person that they are observing from a vantage point outside their own bodies, figuratively speaking, combat PTSD behaviors and symptoms might be controlled.

Roger spoke to many therapists who worked with poly-trauma in service men and women. He even spoke to a few that worked with trauma victims in the civilian community and they generally agreed that so far, this new approach held promise. This was completely out of the box thinking, but a radical approach had to be tried. The traditional approaches were failing. Radical approaches had to be sought out and attempted. Young lives were at stake.

A key factor here, Roger was to find out when talking to the therapists involved in this research, was the therapists' willingness and ability to completely empathize with the combat PTSD sufferer. If the therapist took too clinical an approach with the suffering veteran, the veteran would simply walk away. He/she would shut the therapeutic relationship out.

Unlike other trauma victims, lifetime combat PTSD sufferers demanded complete empathy from the therapist in a way that PTSD sufferers from other types of trauma did not expect to find. The perfect therapist in this regard would be a therapist who had undergone the trauma of combat himself/herself. Very few therapists in the USA have that kind of experience. This was a major problem to this approach and Roger knew that.

A completely radical approach to the personnel administering lifetime combat PTSD therapy had to be found where combat veterans who had seen extreme trauma but had learned to control the behavior associated with PTSD were themselves administering therapy to combat PTSD sufferers. This was an incredibly non-traditional way of conducting therapy in that almost none of these men or women would be properly trained therapists in the traditional sense of that word. But the need was immediate and the long term success rate for arresting maladaptive behavior among combat PTSD veterans was low. It was time to try a new approach to combat PTSD therapy or to accept failure in a huge percentage of cases.

But getting permission from the Armed Forces and the Department of Veterans Affairs to train and then immediately implement this approach was proving impossible. This would be a sort of 'hands on PTSD therapy corps' drawn from well adjusted combat veterans. The approach would be that they would serve alongside the medical corps in a temporary status as a sort of emotional ombudsman for lifetime combat PTSD sufferers to use as a role model for healthy behavior. He/she would be a mentor who would teach the lifetime combat PTSD sufferers the various techniques that he/she personally used to identify and control the maladaptive behaviors in his/her own daily emotional environment.

It would be very much like a sergeant teaching a private exactly how to execute any particular soldier's skill, except this time the skill set would be mental and emotional. It is assumed by many therapists that support this idea that at this point some sort of loosely organized fellowship would evolve from this technique. There would be frequent meetings to talk out the problems of combat PTSD and reinstate and/ or reinforce the mental interventions that were learned to continue to control the outbursts. Theoretically this could work. Pragmatically it was proving impossible to get off the ground. Service politics and government bureaucratic wrangling were killing it before it was born.

Turf battles within the therapeutic communities of both the Armed Forces and the Department of Veterans Affairs were ongoing and fierce. The professionals were doing everything that they could to short circuit this approach. No one wanted to hand responsibility for treating combat PTSD veterans over to non professionals. On many levels that is completely understandable. Roger could see how this could go very wrong if not strictly administered by top notch professionals. He had been told as much by many Army mental health professionals.

However, the problem was that professional counseling was not working for this group of sufferers. The professionals did not have credibility with the clients. The basic roadblock to success was that combat PTSD sufferers did not trust anyone who had not personally come under fire themselves to handle their inner conflicts related to combat. Someone had to show courage at the highest level of government to take a chance on this radical approach to treatment of combat PTSD but so far, that leadership was lacking. Roger felt helpless because in fact he was helpless to do anything more. Maybe someday somebody in power would try this approach. Roger could only hope.

In the meantime, the suicide and homicide rate among wartime PTSD sufferers continued to climb. The professionals were out of answers precisely because they were professionals and not combat veterans. They were looking for answers in text books and psychological theories that applied to non combat related psychological damage. They would not find answers there. The salve for these psychic wounds had to be found in human comradeship between broken and fallen warriors themselves. Of that, Roger was sure. Sometimes the only way to heal a wound is to have the medicine administered by someone as deeply wounded himself as the fallen warrior. It made no logical sense, but the mind is not always logical. Sometimes it needs a miracle to heal itself.

Roger learned in his conversations with therapists that sometimes "like minds" must meet in order to merge their experiences, one to the other, in a way that fellowships have found to work time and again. These therapists told Roger that this healing through structured fellowship works for alcoholics and drug addicts and victims of incest and gamblers and dozens of other sufferers. Could not a fellowship approach to healing also work for combat PTSD sufferers? Roger hoped that someone in authority would see this soon and facilitate an approach that would work. It was long past due. Traditional therapy for lifetime combat PTSD victims was simply failing.

This was just one facet of a point of view that Roger was gradually developing. He held a bachelor's degree in Psychology from his undergraduate days at the University of Massachusetts and he held a master's degree in Organizational Development from Marymount University in Arlington, Virginia. He understood the human psyche and the dynamics of small groups in a structured setting working toward a common goal with measureable and attainable goals. The key seemed to be constant and valid measurement against verifiable group goals that had been agreed upon by all group participants as necessary and integral to the group's ultimate mission and purpose.

To put this perpsective in American business management terms, if everyone in the group had "buy in" the chances for success relative to any group goal increased enormously. That would include an agreed upon approach to healing PTSD wounds among combat veterans themselves. They would in effect construct their own therapy on many levels.

This meant in implementation terms, the old rules and procedures must be discarded. If combat PTSD veterans were assembled into small groups and then made up their own rules has to how they would proceed to control their own maladaptive behavior based on common 12 Step Program rules of conduct in a fellowship composed entirely of other combat PTSD victims, the chances for success were relatively high when measured against current success rates. "Hell, what did they have to lose?" Roger thought frequently but so far he had not gained access to anyone in a high enough position within the Department of Veterans Affairs to use his approach.

Chapter I

It was all very sad and all very routine for Washington D.C. The Old Guard refuses to move off even when surrounded by the corpses of its own failures. It was an old story in this republic. Power never goes away gracefully from its haunts; it has to be driven out. It is just the way it works.

Roger went home exhausted and completely spent. But he knew that his efforts to console fellow wounded warriors was therapeutic for both himself and the newly wounded veterans at Walter Reed Medical Center. Even with all the pain involved, it was a winning situation for Roger and the young wounded vets. They had gotten through another day together.

II.
Managing people with disabilities

The General Takes Over At D.V.A.

"I AM LATE for work!" the general said to his driver as he got out of the car and hurried into the building elevator to get to his office. Usually bright and early for work, the general got caught in traffic on his way to work and arrived unexpectedly late. "I hate being late!" he thought to himself.

General Erik K. Shinseki had just been appointed the new Secretary of the Department of Veterans Affairs (D.V.A.) a few short weeks after the election of President Barak Obama. He was new to the job and trying to snap himself into a new government agency after having served ultimately as the much marginalized Army Chief of Staff under the Bush Administration. He knew what the price of leadership could cost a man. After a fine military career he was professionally locked out by other generals and Defense Department people for telling the truth to Congress. Sometimes we learn the big lessons late in life. "Retirement is not such a bad thing" the general would sometimes mutter to himself after he left the Army.

Shinseki was punished by the Bushites with professional isolation to the point where he had to retire from a distinguished military career as a fine soldier and leader because he spoke out on Capitol Hill in 2003. Prior to the invasion of Iraq he told Congress that huge amounts of soldiers would be needed to properly subdue ethnic violence in Iraq after their armed forces were defeated. He used the term "several hundred thousand" in interviews. This went directly against the philosophy of Secretary of Defense Donald Rumsfeld. Shinseki was to pay for his candor to Congress with being sent to the hinterlands of government accessibility. He quietly retired and was never thanked by Congress for his courage.

The Obama administration reinstated him by placing him in control of the much maligned and morale-broken D.V.A. hoping that he could lead them back into their primary mission, serving veterans. Shinseki was one of the few flag officers that the Obama Administration felt that it could trust with such a tough assignment. "I went from the frying pan into the fire" was something else he now muttered to himself. Anyone who might overhear hear talk like that would certainly agree.

And the general was no stranger to hard decisions or difficulties. An Asian American from the state of Hawaii, Shinseki had a highly distinguished Army career after his graduation from West Point in 1965. He had several critical and high profile command assignments, including Commanding General, U.S. Army Europe and NATO Commander in the Balkans. Early on in his career he was wounded twice in Viet Nam, losing a major portion of one foot in one incident. He had to fight hard to stay in the Army after his wounding. He held a graduate degree in English literature and taught at West Point for a time after his combat experiences. He was known as a respectful and attentive commander by the soldiers that served under him. That is a rave from a foot soldier's point of view.

He came aboard the D.V.A. publicly acknowledging that brain trauma and PTSD were the characteristic and signature wounds of the Iraq and Afghanistan wars. General Shinseki also publicly stated that he wanted to continue the same efforts with the D.V.A. that he started with the Army, that is, to make D.V.A. more agile and more immediately capable to solve problems for its core constituency, the veteran himself/herself. This was a very good start as far as veterans were concerned. It showed that he was in touch with the needs of the common veteran.

When Congress asked General Shinseki what he thought that his focus should be during his confirmation hearing, he said the following. "For the V.A., the single focus for transformational change should be the veteran — providing for generations of veterans, who have done their duty, the support and services they have earned and we have promised."

Roger was impressed with the man and followed his newly appointed D.V.A. career closely. He felt that real and substantive change was coming under this man, at least he hoped so. Only time would tell if his hopes were reasonable. The bureaucracy at the D.V.A. had been known to crush people literally to death. Roger hoped that the general had the strength to stand up to the insolence and intransigence of the government bureaucrats who had a stranglehold on the D.V.A. for generations. In many ways they would be the toughest foes he ever faced. "This guy is in for the fight of his life if those wonks over at D.V.A decide to resist him. They will put up a fight that will make him think his Viet Nam experience was a training exercise" Roger would often tell disabled veterans who were close friends. They usually agreed with that statement.

Roger was very aware of the kind of personal character that Shinseki brought to the Secretary's job. A combat general's toughness was going to be needed and Roger hoped that the general would not take it easy with his subordinates. Roger hoped that he would demand the kind of 'out of the box' thinking that was going to be needed to meet the tremendous demands on the Department that PTSD and brain trauma were now presenting.

The D.V.A. is the second largest department in the government. Only the Department of Defense is larger. The need to take care of veterans who have fought in almost constant wars, police actions, and various types of hostilities and "hot flash" military events throughout the world from 1941 continuing into 2009 was becoming more and more well known to the average American. The needs of veterans were growing with every military or naval intervention around the world. Roger could not help but think to himself, "This is the price of having an Offense Department in place of a Defense Department; constant war and constantly wounded warriors."

American imperialistic tendencies overseas were now producing very real problems at home among the veteran's community and their supporters. "There are just too many broken old warriors and too few resources to take care of them all" Roger would often tell anyone interested in hearing.

The financial and socials costs of a constantly deployed Armed Forces was huge and success was not always apparent in the treatment methods of the wounded, especially the broken in spirit. With Army and Marine reservists and Army and Air National Guard units deploying to western Asia to see hard in-your-face combat over and over again, the 'social contract' that these people had signed with the federal government and their state legislatures had been ripped to shreds. Frankly, a very real case could be made that they were illegally exploited. They never signed on to the Army or Marine reserves or the National Guard to constantly be sent into combat overseas in an undeclared war. What is worse, they knew it. There was always danger in betraying a social contract with a man who held a weapon.

To be quite frank, these people had been betrayed by several layers of American government and American society as a whole. And they knew that too. Their rage at government underhandedness in their lives was palatable and slowly simmering to the boiling point. This was part of the problem with returning veterans from the wars in western Asia. Roger often heard them speak with bitterness when he came in contact with them. "One weekend a month my ass!" is what many wounded and severely disabled reservists and national guardsmen would often mutter to him. Sometimes the depth of their rage actually unnerved him. "They lied to me. I was supposed to do a weekend a month and get money for college. I was supposed to help people in my state during hurricanes, tornadoes or floods. Instead I lost my legs in Afghanistan. Why?"

These young people had been used as stand-ins for conscripts in wars that had no immediate bearing on national defense and it was obvious to anyone involved. The 'stop loss' program was the worst example of this betrayal, but not the only example. Although the draft had ended officially in 1973 the poor, the working class who could not find work and the marginalized among the lower middle class made up the bulk of the volunteer armed forces when it started in 1974. It was conscription by an individual's necessity to survive and the dearth of other economic choices. Wealthy kids almost never wound up

wearing a uniform after 1973. And this unofficial draft was not the
only issue that burned into the hearts of these unwilling heroes.

Quality of life issues were most especially needed in helping the
injured veteran to re-enter society in a fashion that would be acceptable as something resembling a near normal American style and
standard of living. Roger knew the general would tackle these tough
problems if his staff kept him informed. But would they? Roger
doubted it. It had too much experience with government wonks to
trust them very much.

The record for being proactive in solving veterans' problems was
spotty at best at the D.V.A. Veterans as a whole tended to not think
very highly of the department. It had a history of being much more
concerned with good public relations than with solving veterans' many
problems. Roger often heard disabled veterans say "If they spent half
as much time on trying to help me as they do on trying to prove how
invaluable they are, I would have been out of this situation years ago!"

It is not so much that disabled veterans look to the personnel
at the Department of Veterans Affairs for answers to their personal
problems as they look for leadership that is consistent, just and timely
in its application. And that was the problem. Disabled veterans have
a phrase that is used for disability adjudication that spoke to their
desperation. "Deny, deny, deny, until they die." It was hoped by all
disabled veterans that since the general was a disabled veteran himself,
this phrase would justifiably go out of fashion with veterans. It was just
a hope, but it was a big hope.

And there were all sorts of ancillary problems that were going
to affect the general's effectiveness for the veterans he served that he
had little control over. For example, veterans' disability payments were
supposed to be sacrosanct. No one was supposed to be able to garnish
them. However, in reality, that federal law was constantly being put
aside by judges in divorce courts and family courts relative to alimony
and child support payments whether the veteran was solvent or not.
Instead of taking the money outright, which was blatantly illegal, the
courts all around the nation were simply freezing the accounts and

then garnishing all the money from the accounts that the D.V.A. was using to pay the veteran. They were ignoring the law and a lot of these veterans were literally living and dying in poverty as a result of this.

And the problems and the fallout circumstances were even uglier than most people knew. There were the homeless veterans to be considered by the D.V.A. Population estimates suggested that on any given night in the U.S.A. there are 131,000 homeless veterans on the street. Both male and female veterans continued to be over represented in the general homeless population as late as July 2009. Male veterans were 1.4 times more likely to be homeless than non-veteran males in the U.S. by federal estimates in that month. Female veterans, according to the same study were between two and four times as likely to be homeless as their non-veteran female counterparts in the population and many of them had children involved in this tragedy.

To make the situation even more poignant some studies were beginning to show some sort of indirect connection between combat exposure and homelessness.

More research needed to be done on this last issue, but if early indications were true, the impact this would have on veterans' benefits in the near future would be astronomical. Stated simply, if the government sent a man or woman into combat, they were increasing his or her lifetime chance of homelessness by somewhere between two hundred to four hundred percent. "That is a game changer" relative to benefits for combat veterans Roger often said to friends. "This could get very expensive very quickly" he wrote to his Congressman.

Roger wrote to his Congressman a lot, in fact, he often carried a copy of a letter he had written to his Congressman so that others could use it as a matrix for their letter to their congressman or woman. Roger asked people to write Congress at every available opportunity.

The letter read as follows:

> I am asking you to introduce legislation for immediate passage in Congress to increase disabled veterans compensation for totally disabled veterans 25% over present amounts. This would be in order to compensate for quality of life negation by the severity of their service

connected disabilities. This would be for both schedule rated 100% totally disabled and individually unemployable totally disabled veterans and should be enacted immediately so as to take effect in 2010.

The 2008 General Convention of the Disabled American Veterans passed a resolution concerning this problem of quality of life inequity for totally disabled veterans. Page 14 of the resolutions passed at that convention reads as follows:

14

RESOLUTION NO. 058

INCREASE DISABILITY COMPENSATION

WHEREAS, it is the historical policy of the Disabled American Veterans that this Nation's first duty to veterans is to provide for the rehabilitation of its wartime disabled;

and

WHEREAS, the percentage ratings for service-connected disabilities represent, as far as can be practicably determined, the average impairment in earning capacity resulting from such disabilities in civil occupations; and

WHEREAS, compensation increases should be based primarily on the loss of earning capacity; and

WHEREAS, disabled veterans who are unable to work because of service connected disabilities should be entitled to compensation payments commensurate with the after-tax earning of their able-bodied contemporaries; NOW

THEREFORE, BE IT RESOLVED that the Disabled American Veterans in National Convention assembled in Las Vegas, Nevada, August 9-12, 2008, supports the enactment of legislation to provide a realistic increase in Department of Veterans Affairs compensation rates to bring the standard of living of disabled veterans in line with that which they would have enjoyed had they not suffered their service-connected disabilities.

ALTERNATE REQUEST FOR TAX EXEMPTION LEGISLATION

If the request outlined above cannot be met due to excessive cost, I am asking you that in place of this legislation, other legislation be enacted. The alternate course of action is to allow totally disabled veterans both schedule rated 100% and Individually Unemployable Totally Disabled veterans to be exempt from taxes. I am asking as a back up request that legislation be introduced to exempt all totally disabled veterans from taxes up to an amount of $125,000 dollars per year gross income. The overall effect on totally disabled veterans would be the same as a pension increase and they could meet their financial commitments.

All veterans gauge the government's degree of responsibility toward veterans by how the government treats totally disabled veterans. That treatment is the measuring stick of effectiveness for all veterans. The totally disabled vets are in dire need of money now. Their lives are crumbling. This situation is critical and needs to be resolved in this legislative year. Their sacrifice is not being properly compensated and they are very aware of this fact. They often feel betrayed by the very class of American business elites whose interests they were in the Service to protect.

The recent wars in Southwest Asia coupled with the American overseas military adventures of the last fifty years have brought us volunteer armed forces manned almost entirely with the sons and daughters of the working class or the lowest of the middle class. It is now clear that they have been introduced to Service realities and the danger of action for the almost exclusive benefit of America's elites and their business interests. Such things as 'stop loss', abuse of the Reserve and National Guard for war fighting overseas that has no clear mission, multiple amputations due to wounds and severe brain damage due to IED explosions harden their thinking and radicalize the political views of many veterans of all ages. This abuse of the armed forces for the financial gain of the elites in society and the fact that veterans' health and pensions systems are antiquated and do not take into account quality of life issues now have made a veterans abuse issue a very serious national security concern. You need to understand the dangers here.

We no longer have a Defense Department. We have had an Offense Department for several generations now. The working class and lowest levels of the middle class have carried the burden and injuries resulting from overseas escapades for many decades. The price of that folly may very well be massive social unrest. I believe that potential violence is brewing among the abused who have served in uniform. The key to quelling any potential violence from this abuse of soldiers, sailors, airmen, coastguardsmen and marines is to upgrade veterans' benefits to realistic levels of support. Injuring these young people for the financial gain of relatively few wealthy Americans is unethical. But largely ignoring their needs once they have been injured and are unable to care for themselves is flirting with civil war. You must take this warning seriously.

When among themselves and believing that they cannot be overheard, they often talk of organized violence due to this betrayal. We are talking about more than 22 million people with military training. The Republic would fall if this sort of fury was unleashed on a lethargic population that has no idea of the level of rage that has been building among veterans for generations. This is an extremely dangerous situation that must be handled immediately.

Large numbers of disabled veterans and their supporters among the veteran population now believe that this outright manipulation by the elites has existed almost continuously since the Spanish American War in 1898. What was once seen as mere government unwillingness to shoulder full responsibility to appropriately care for veterans, and specifically totally disabled veterans, is now seen as something much more sinister. It is seen as outright government manipulation of working class people to provide fighters to protect the overseas business interests of the elites without caring for them properly once they are disabled.

The disability system is broken. We all know that. Veterans are watching very closely as to how the government will rectify the long-

standing abuse and neglect of disabled veterans. Properly taking care of the totally disabled veterans is the key to defusing this situation. It will be a bellwether measure for action by veterans. Totally disabled veterans are in a situation that approaches a nightmare reality few of us can appreciate. Please take care of them now, in this legislative year, for all of our sakes.

I do not need to be contacted however, if you wish to reply to this message, please contact me at my email address noted above. Please act immediately on legislation that enhances quality of life for totally disabled veterans.

Sincerely,

Name of Veteran

And then there was the social awakening of the individual gay sol- der and sailor, airmen and marine which was now beginning to show itself in the veteran population.

In late May of 2009 an Asian American West Point graduate and recently discharged First Lieutenant in the New York State National Guard, Daniel Choi, took part in a street demonstration in Beverly Hills, California in order to bring the spotlight onto the needs of gay active duty personnel and gay veterans. He defied a police constraint order to salute President Obama on national television outside of the designated free-speech zone. The picture was in the media all over the country. Hopes were high among gay soldiers and sailors as well as gay veterans that finally their needs would be addressed.

If the same demographics from the general population applied to the Service as it did to the population at large, then roughly 10% of the Service and the veterans' community were gay at any one time period. The time to realize that was fast becoming obvious. And the gay community has its own health problems and social expectations. Would the D.V.A. help or hinder this group's aspirations for fair treat- ment? And what about the health problems that gay veterans bring to the D.V.A.; would they be hidden?

And the debate did not end with one cashiered gay lieutenant. On 19 June 2009 the former Army chief of staff from the period 1993 to 1997, General John M. Shalikashvili, wrote a compelling article in the Washington Post calling for a renewed debate on gays in the military. His argument was that emotions were ruling the day in the U.S. and that the data did not support disallowing gays to serve in the military.

He argued that Europeans have already allowed this with no problem to speak of presenting itself. By extension, if gays were allowed to serve in the military then they would have medical and social needs inherent to this group and its life style. AIDS and life partner benefits would need to be taken into account for gay soldiers and sailors and later on, as veterans. If this happened, would the D.V.A. be able to cope and rise to the occasion to support these needs?

And then too, there was the problem of under representation of medical care and procedures needed by female veterans.

A Democrat by the name of Congressman Leonard Boswell had just introduced the Women Veterans Access to Care Act in the Spring of 2009 and the general was quite interested in attempting in any way that he could to help get it passed. The Congressman had found some very disturbing data about women veterans that were behind his legislative efforts on their behalf.

As of the summer of 2009, 43.4% of all eligible female veterans from Iraq and Afghanistan had sought out the D.V.A. for health care, and almost 85% of these women have visited the D.V.A. healthcare facility in their area more than once for outpatient treatment. It is estimated that by the year 2020, 15% of veterans using the D.V.A. for health care will be women. And that could cause a problem since currently D.V.A. healthcare is primarily tailored to the needs of men.

Female veterans are more likely to have lower incomes than men. Proportionally, more female veterans than male veterans suffer from poor health. They are also less likely to have private insurance than male veterans. Their health needs are served at a minimal level at best at D.V.A. and there is a great need for expansion and upgrades in reproductive care, primary care and other areas for women veterans.

The Congressman wanted all this to change and since he was a re-tired Army Lieutenant Colonel and aviator from the Viet Nam era, his opinion was solid and sought after. General Shinseki was interested in this piece of legislation and asked the president to help get it passed in Congress. "I promise to give it all the support I can" the president told the general.

There was also the problem of amputations simply being so incredibly devastating that they effectively ruled the life of a disabled veteran. Roger knew that the D.V.A. was working on some sort of amputation mitigation medical research but it was all hush-hush. Since Roger had a lot of experience with amputees from the Gulf War and the Iraq and Afghanistan Wars he looked into the extant research personally. It was a little more encouraging than people might think.

It seems that a Mexican salamander called an axolotl can com-pletely regenerate a limb from a group of cells that occur naturally called a blastema. It is presently being studied in the hope of regen-erating human limbs at the Center for Regenerative Therapies in Dresden, Germany. A researcher there named Elly Tanaka had been recently interviewed by British journalists and expressed excitement at what they had found there. Another researcher named Malcolm Maden from the University of Florida that had taken part in axolotl regeneration research also said that it might point the way toward hu-man limb regeneration. And at the Wistar Institute in Pennsylvania, a group of lab mice had been genetically altered to allow limb regenera-tion in some cases.

Roger knew that this was a lot more important than most D.V.A. people realized. If limbs could be regenerated for severely disabled soldiers, the life crushing effects of lifetime disabilities could be essen-tially nullified. This would go a very long way in completely changing the landscape for disabled veterans.

The D.V.A. had a lot to answer for; their recent track record with veterans was abominable. Things had happened from destroying re-cords deliberately at D.V.A. offices to clients getting AIDS from dirty medical tools to veterans being deliberately denied the full panoply of benefits that they had earned because it was too costly. The general needed to change this immediately to win veterans' confidence. Only a combat general could do this. And retired generals involved in veterans' affairs had a long history in American politics. They often gave the job a needed shot of candor sent straight to its bloodstream. Roger was hoping that General Shinseki would take the lead of those generals before him and ruffle some feathers.

Actually, the time for ruffling feathers was over. Roger really wanted the general to actually kill some chickens. "We need him to kick some ass!" is actually what Roger normally confided to friends who were interested in the issue.

Roger had been involved in disabled veterans support since he retired from the Army. But the veterans' organizations often lost their vision in the political fog in Washington D.C. It was not just Roger's membership in the Disabled American Veterans (DAV) that oftentimes shamed him. It seems that for all the good that the organization did, it was so well connected among the Washington political elite that it oftentimes left the disabled veteran and his needs behind.

Often it had so political an agenda that it had spent generations turning a blind eye toward absolute malfeasance at the D.V.A. in order to gain access to the White House and to the power blocs in Congress. The rank and file members were painfully aware of this and had to live with the results of such an agenda.

A huge slice of American veterans believed that the DAV oftentimes wanted to play a bigger role in American foreign policy, defense budget construction and domestic politics than it wanted to help veterans in need. It was undeniable that the directors had now become wonks for the hard right in American politics. The needs of the individual members who were disabled had taken such a low priority with the organization that it left Roger breathless. He was a lifetime member and stayed on the membership rolls as a result of that status, but in his mind the DAV had as much to answer for to the disabled membership as did the D.V.A. Neither organization ranked very high in Roger's mind for removing roadblocks for veterans. They often seemed to actually create them.

And Roger was also a member of the American Legion, another powerful veterans' organization. It had a very checkered past and was often aligned with the radical right in American politics. This bothered Roger. "You've got to be kidding me!" is what he said to himself when he did some research on their history. General Smedley Butler, a much loved Marine who had been a state director of the American Legion for years and had won the Congressional Medal of Honor twice, had gone on record concerning the American Legion many times. Roger kept the quotes and would often read them to himself to keep his priorities straight.

The record on this sad state of affairs concerning the American Legion bordered on the unbelievable.

It seems that in 1932 General Butler, then retired, was approached by representatives of the Morgan Bank who offered to fund any effort that he would be willing to establish in order to project a dictatorship onto the American people to replace Franklin Delano Roosevelt's administration. Butler refused to cooperate with this right wing conspiracy and went to the national press. Many of these conspirators seemed to have had deep connections to the American Legion. An author named Jules Archer wrote a book called The Plot to Seize the White House concerning this series of events. It was Roger's favorite book. He would often think nowadays, "I need to send a copy of that book to General Shinseki. He could use the insights."

And Butler was by no means a pushover for the right wingers. One of his most famous quotes to a newspaperman was Roger's most favorite. It read in part : "I spent 33 years (in the Marines) . . . most of my time being a high-class muscle man for Big Business, for Wall Street and the bankers. In short, I was a racketeer for capitalism. . ."

"I helped purify Nicaragua for the international banking house of Brown Brothers in 1909-1912. I helped make Mexico and especially Tampico safe for American oil interests in 1914. I brought light to the Dominican Republic for American sugar interests in 1916. I helped make Haiti and Cuba a decent place for the National City (Bank) boys to collect revenue in. I helped in the rape of half a dozen Central

American republics for the benefit of Wall Street. . . ." Yeah, Butler did not mince words. Roger liked that about him.

But there was more to Butler than this early sound bite. It went even further. He also said: "In China in 1927 I helped see to it that Standard Oil went its way unmolested . . . I had . . . a swell racket. I was rewarded with honors, medals, promotions.... I might have given Al Capone a few hints. The best he could do was to operate a racket in three city districts. The Marines operated on three continents."

This last quote was printed in The World Tomorrow, October, 1931 and mentioned in the New York Times on August 21, 1931.

And perhaps the crowning glory of quotes from General Butler came in his testimony before the House of Representative's Committee, Investigations of Nazi and Other Propaganda in 1935 when he said the following. "You know very well that it (the American Legion) is nothing but a strike-breaking outfit used by capital for that purpose, and that is the reason we have all those big clubhouses and that is the reason I pulled out of it. They have been using the dumb soldiers to break strikes." This was a powerful comment coming from the former State Commander of the Connecticut American Legion!

General Shinseki was in good company. General Butler had blazed a trail for General Shinseki to follow. Take care of the veteran as best you can; screw the politicians. They were all out for money anyway as far as General Butler was concerned. General Butler was perhaps a foreshadowing of powerful veterans speaking their mind to power. Roger was hoping that General Shinseki would take up the torch. And he had other pathfinders in that regard.

General Omar Bradley, one of the very few five star generals this nation has ever had, was named as Director of the Veterans Administration by President Truman on 15 August 1945. He really did not want the job but he accepted it because the Veterans Administration was in complete disarray. As unbelievable as it may sound, the Veterans Administration at the end of World War II was responsible for pensions for five million veterans with a few widows' and dependent disability pensions cases stemming from incidents in the War of 1812!

By the end of the next year, 1946, seventeen million veterans were on the rolls of the Veterans Administration. The expansion was beyond the government's capabilities. But it came anyway.

Bradley completely remodeled the V.A. based on regional needs and he insisted that the staff at the V.A. put the needs of the individual veteran above all other organizational needs at all times. In the past political considerations governing such things as the placement of Veterans Hospitals had held sway. Bradley killed that thinking outright. With the aid of Major General Paul Hawley, General Eisenhower's Theatre Surgeon, Bradley completely overhauled a medical care system that Hawley described as medieval.

General Bradley revised and extended educational benefits for former G.I.'s, put in place vocational training programs for returning war veterans with no work record previous to Service, established a veterans' loan program and administered a program with phenomenal growth in insurance claims and disability pensions. In the two years that he held the job, Bradley transformed the medical services of the V.A. from a national disgrace to a national model.

Even our first commander in chief, General George Washington had something to say that General Shinseki could use relative to establishing a better policy for the handling and treatment of veterans by the government. Washington said, "The willingness with which our young people are likely to serve in any war, no matter how justified, shall be directly proportional to how they perceive veterans of early wars were treated and appreciated by our nation." Roger could not agree more. He had placed that quote above his computer screen and read it every time he logged on. He thought that General Shinseki would probably agree with it.

So General Shinseki met his first days in the job with the same determination with which he forged his Army career. Roger was impressed. He met frequently with President Obama to give him updates on revamping the D.V.A. and so far, veterans at large were willing to give the general the benefit of the doubt. But major out-of-the-box thinking was going to be needed in order to care of the nearly 23 million veterans that were still alive in the U.S. Things were going to be difficult, especially since money was tightening up in an environment that followed the financial crash around the globe in the mid Fall of 2008, months before the Obama administration took office. A tougher situation would be hard to imagine.

Somehow or other, the major veterans organizations had to be thanked by the Obama administration for doing a good job, while at the same time they had to be recognized as being just as much an impediment to the well being of veterans as they were a benefit. They were too involved in politics to really matter to most veterans. They operated more like foreign policy lobbying groups than they did veterans' organizations. They represented perhaps a total of eight million veterans and the actual number of veterans in the country was three times that number. These groups were too encased in generations of bad habits that constantly put their organizations' needs ahead of particular veterans, even their own membership. "This has simply got to change!" Roger told the DAV commander in a personal letter.

The 'wave the flag, my country right or wrong' philosophy of the major veterans' organizations was now seen by most veterans as more of an irritant and a hindrance than a help. It was an antiquated and marginally effective approach to veterans' problems to the former servicemen and women struggling with service connected health problems and social readjustment stemming from the wars in western Asia. It was outright nonsense to the much younger veterans leaving the service with a stop-loss event in his/her short and brutal military career. To state this simply, even members of these organizations suffered them more than celebrated them. That much was obvious at any veterans gathering.

They had been designed in another era to handle a totally different mindset among returning veterans of the Great War of the early part of the 20th century. They very likely may have outlived their usefulness. Roger was quickly gravitating to that point of view. If they were going to survive and serve a useful purpose in the 21st century they must rethink their goals and do serious research on their future constituency and its needs. They were decades behind the times at the very least.

The general walked cautiously when strolling with these organizations through the needs of veterans as they laid them out to him. Having served a lifetime in the Army, he knew full well what group-think and organizational politics was all about. He also knew that vested interests in any federal organization that had a budget as big as the D.V.A. would always have hangers-on in the lobbyist sector. He was no fool. He would tread lightly and listen politely before he spoke. It was his trademark leadership behavior. It served him well in this job. But because he was polite did not mean he was in agreement. Roger could see that in his press releases.

As for the Veterans' Organizations, the American Legion and the Veterans of Foreign Wars were two of the giants in this arena. They had unbelievable influence on policy at the D.V.A. for many decades prior to 2009. They came to be so important that they often times actually set the paradigms in place for how America viewed the veteran and they also claimed to speak for the veterans benefit in an almost exclusive way. Along with the Disabled American Veterans, their power in veterans' policy areas was more or less unchallenged and unchallengeable.

The American Legion and the V.F.W. had originated more as political groups then veterans groups. One was pro labor and one was pro management. They seemed to have lost their way when they were accused of turning a cold shoulder to Viet Nam era veterans returning from the war with the reputation of 'baby killers'.

But perhaps there was an even more pragmatic reason for the leadership of these groups being apprehensive about including massive amounts of Viet Nam era veterans in the decision making process. For decades their leaders were drawn from World War II and Korean War veterans. The Viet Nam veterans threatened to overwhelm the medical system at the D.V.A. and this threatened the delivery of services to the earlier group of veterans in many cases. These two groups also historically took a weak position on any problems discovered within the D.V.A. system.

They were largely silent for a very long time when the Gulf War, Iraq and Afghanistan War veterans began to complain about destroyed documents, deliberate claims backdating by the D.V.A. and other more or less obvious travesties of justice. They were much too involved in the grand picture of attempting to set national policy on non-veteran issues instead of working to help out the individual veteran with a claim or a personal problem. And they were not alone.

The Veteran Service Officers in most veterans' organizations were often ineffective for the latest group of veterans from the western Asian wars. Their problems were just too massive for the old cut and paste approach to patching up a veterans broken life with a ten minute talk between a Veteran Service Officer and a D.V.A. adjudicator. Things were much too medically complicated for that approach to be effective anymore, if in fact that approach ever was effective. That era was now being blown apart by the massive injuries and needs of young, broken married veterans with children.

These new wars in western Asia were not only severely injuring soldiers, sailors, airmen and marines. They were breaking apart the lives of fathers and husbands, mothers and wives in the disabled veteran population on an unprecedented scale. And the spouses were going AWOL at a rate that no one could predict. It was a travesty and military marriages were fast becoming a joke when the military spouse was severely injured. The healthy one would often simply take off. The whole picture was played out every day in the lives of hundreds if not thousands of severely injured veterans. It was heartbreaking. And there seemed to be no way to end the exodus of the spouses from the lives of the shattered. The general had to be made aware of how this affected the overall health of the shattered veteran.

What Roger really wanted to see the general do in the job was to take an approach that reflected a completely different view of the American veteran. The view would be one that grew out of the American civil rights dynamic. This new view would see the veteran as an extreme demographic minority in American culture and politics relative to his or her needs and his or her limited access to resources.

What Roger felt was needed was to somehow find a way to get professional historians and researchers to look at the history, trials and tribulations of American veterans in exactly the same way that civil rights activists had spent decades educating the American public about race hatred and its debilitating effects on society at large. Racism hurt many more people than simply the human being that was being held down. It held society back. Eventually Americans came around to seeing this point of view. Minorities achieved a new status. The same thing needed to be done for veterans.

But that would need massive funding and Roger had no idea how that could come about. Still he dreamed of a time when the non-veteran and the various legislators and agency heads in the nation could see the veteran's life from a framework that would adequately describe how isolated he/she had actually become from the American mainstream. The veteran was becoming a dangerously isolated sub-cultural phenomenon within American society.

"This just ain't funny anymore!" Roger would often complain to friends. "Hardly anybody knows a soldier or sailor anymore. Hardly anyone has them in their immediate families these days. That ain't good! That is a recipe for revolution when only a small minority of people are doing the fighting and dying and the larger group is blissfully unaware of the dangers and the hazards. Too many people are reaping the benefits from the suffering of too few. This is a disaster waiting to happen."

Entire families were now going generations without a single member of that family ever having served in uniform. The wealthy among the American population were beginning to see uniformed service as something that "they" needed to do, not "me" and not "mine." It was certainly not something an Ivy Leaguer should ever need to attempt. This was extremely dangerous and Roger and his veteran friends understood that. The nobles in American society felt no need to actually defend it. When nobles do that, they lose the castle quite quickly. History has shown us that over and over.

A "veterans' class" had now been born among the same working class and disenfranchised and sometimes marginalized segments of the population. It filled the ranks of the volunteer Armed Forces since its inception in 1974. This was not only unfair to the veterans; it was dangerous to the populace at large. But this had happened before, that is to say, one segment of the population had borne an unfair proportion of the burden of military and naval service and combat to the point where violence ensued.

The Irish rioted in New York City in 1863 when they were being drafted into the Union Army in massive numbers due to their inability to protect themselves from this government encroachment on their freedoms. They were poor, uneducated and virtually unrepresented in the country so they were easy targets to conscript. The stop loss program instituted by the Bush Administration to keep the ranks filled with trained soldiers to fight the wars in western Asia had literally broken young minds, spirits and bodies in many cases. It was a backdoor draft, not all that different from the injustices that caused the draft riots of July 11th-13th of 1863.

About 100 people were killed in the New York City riots and President Lincoln had to deploy federal troops to New York City that stayed encamped for several weeks in order to restore order. The situation stayed ugly all throughout the rest of the war. The Irish in America felt that they had been singled out to be the soldiering class that was conscripted en masse in America's Civil War. Irish Americans have never quite forgotten the slight.

Americans on the margins of society had a long history of literally being forced into soldiering and sea faring by poverty and under- representation in government. When they became veterans they had a long history of having their needs ignored due to the same weak status they held in society.

In 1932 a group of World War I veterans reacted violently to being driven out of Washington D.C. at bayonet point because they claimed that they were denied a promised bonus by the federal government. This so-called "Bonus Army" is today seen as a matrix for organized veterans' resistance for those who are planning the same. This thinking was going to be quite dangerous if this continued unabated into the 21st Century.

General Shinseki was taking notice. He was no fool. He could smell a battle coming.

"Honoring" veterans is empty if the real heart of the situation is window dressing to cover up blatant abuse of an under-represented segment of American society that could be bought off with an occasional parade or patriotic words on Veterans Day by any politician and damned little else. The situation was getting quite routinely predictable. Veterans were waking up to their true status in society. And in many cases they did not like what they saw.

In March of 2009 there were about 22.9 millions veterans alive in the U.S. per best government estimates. As an interest group they were gaining momentum. Combat veterans especially were beginning to see that they were stand-ins for rich kids and other connected people that went to Ivy League schools, got the best jobs, had the best connections, lived the best lives, retired with the most money and never served a day in uniform. Those who had given the least to American society were routinely garnering most of its fruits. And that was by having 'connections' not by serving the community at large in uniform. This might even have been acceptable to most, if not for the death toll among the veterans.

The seeds of civil war along class lines were being firmly planted by the beginning of the new century.

Things were now so out of balance in the country's social contract with its citizenry that less than 1% of the population had outright control of 23% of the wealth. Proportionately, very few of the wealthy had served in uniform. And of the few that did, even fewer were subjected to combat. And combat veterans, the very same people who had offered blood, sweat and often their own body parts to keep the trade lanes open and protect American economic interests overseas were dying in poverty more and more in a 'homeland' that cared for them less and less.

This highly unbalanced social phenomenon was not going unnoticed by veterans. The blatant and lopsided injustice of "he who does the most gets the least" was beginning to become apparent to more and more veterans as the economy worsened. Insurrection was certainly not out of the question. In fact, it was now a general topic of discussion when disabled veterans met.

Cable television, news documentaries, community colleges, public libraries, internet web sites and talk radio were educating veterans like never before to the realities at work relative to their own marginalization within the society that they had served so trustingly and naively. They had become a recognized class within society now, and a class that was becoming more and more militant and more vocal about its needs. In 2009 it was estimated that less than one half of one percent of the U.S. population of 307 million people was presently in the armed forces as of April of that year. Fewer and fewer were being asked to do more and more.

Veterans were starting to feel abused before, during and after their uniformed service. And veterans were growing increasingly aware of this imbalance of both economic and social opportunities and they made up about 8% of the total population and therefore 8% of the electorate. The general was learning hard lessons every day. Veterans were angry and their anger was not always properly directed. Recent American history had shown the real terror that could result from ignoring veterans' needs. Homicides often occurred due to imagined injustices on the part of disturbed veterans. And sometimes that was on a massive scale.

Timothy McVeigh and Terry Nichols had both served in the Gulf War and were decorated veterans, yet they killed and injured hundreds of people in the Oklahoma City bombings due to their extreme political beliefs. There is some evidence that either the Army and/or the Department of Veterans Affairs were aware on a low level that these men were mentally unbalanced. The U.S. government was very aware that there were hundreds of people like these two veterans in the U.S. Could the D.V.A. find them and treat them for mental duress before they caused more damage to the American infrastructure, both physical and social? That was in part General Shinseki's job. He knew it. It was not an easy assignment. In fact it might be an impossible job.

Shinseki would need massive amounts of unprecedented cooperation from the American people in order to identify these mentally fractured veterans before they could harm anyone. And how many were there? No one knew. Would the American people cooperate in identifying veterans with broken psyches, especially those in their own families? No one could really tell. But these people could do tremendous harm, using their military training and weapons skills against American society. It had already been shown to be possible in Oklahoma. What would be next?

With this development what was normally considered to be a veterans' health issue was quickly turning into a national security issue. This often happens when the abused and used realize that they have been 'had'. And the realization was growing every day among veterans. These were dangerous times because of the potential violence inherent in any group that is facing prolonged inequity.

It was especially apparent to the veterans who had been severely injured mentally or physically and were then largely ignored by a D.V.A. that seemed too inept to help them reintegrate in a timely and appropriate fashion. Add to this situation several hundred thousand people with an AWOL wife, a dislodged brain, missing limbs and/or an inept disability adjudication process. Throw in a decaying employment picture for wartime veterans of west Asian wars returning to a fractured economy. Couple that with an untimely decision making machine within the D.V.A and throw in physical pain due to service connected disabilities. Now place into the equation an uninvolved population largely unaware of veterans' issues. Add it all up and Americans were now sitting on a potential powder keg of social inequity ready to explode in the country's collective face.

From many disabled veterans point of view, too many powerless and socially unconnected people from the margins of society had been used for too many generations as fodder to keep the sea lanes and trade routes open to American influence. Too many poor Americans in uniform had been made to fight so that American interests for the American social elites were protected. This was while the warriors were largely ignored or their needs minimized once they were hurt or severely disabled.

In many veterans' minds this was now a matter of simple justice. Desperate people will turn to violence when they are ignored or shut down too often. Roger hoped that the general was aware of the dangers here. Roger often told his friends when they asked about the present state of affairs with what he was doing with veterans that "the whole situation is a bomb waiting to go off!"

These really were quite dangerous times for virtually everyone involved in veterans' issues and by extension, for the general population. Many professionals involved in veterans' issues knew this, this was no secret. A wounded giant was awakening and the lunatic fringe within the veterans' community had been talking about taking up arms against the government for years. Now the moderates were starting to join that conversation. The social contract between the wounded and severely disabled veteran and the American government had to be reinforced immediately for safety's sake, if for nothing else. McVeigh had taught the country that lesson quite savagely.

With the routine shredding of documents at D.V.A. offices around the country and incredibly long periods of times passing before veterans were awarded earned benefits it was well past time for a special prosecutor to be appointed by the president to investigate crimes within the D.V.A. leveled at veterans and intent on destroying their case for benefits or disability support money. This was outright thievery disguised as benign neglect or incompetence.

Veterans were beginning to suspect that they were being deliberately kept at arm's length from the real reasons that the D.V.A. was so inept. Many credible investigative sources were now openly saying that the neglect was all about money. And it was all about keeping large sums of money out of the hands of veterans so it could be used by the wealthy for this or that pet economic "boost" which was usually someplace where they had their money invested.

People involved in this travesty that had been seriously hurt and had benefits denied for decades were beginning to seriously talk about insurrection. Lives had been ruined and entire families had been disenfranchised due to this neglect. Roger hoped that the congress, the president and General Shinseki were listening. Time was quickly running out. The very real threat of violence was looming and everyone who worked in the veterans' rehabilitation community knew it.

Roger really wanted the veterans' story told from the point of view of the minority in American society that the veteran actually is. He did not know how to do that. But life has a funny way of coming around full circle and affording opportunities in the strangest ways. Roger's day had finally come.

III.
Dreams can come true

The Virginia Lottery

ROGER AND AFET would often talk in a joking manner about his winning the lottery. It was a constant fantasy of his. "I am going to win Afet! Just you wait and see!" he would tell her every time he bought a ticket, which was at least three times a week. Roger had been buying lottery tickets since he was nineteen years old and he was now fifty six. It was time to win and the Fates agreed.

On a Saturday afternoon in late May Rogier Maarten Magritte, late of the U.S. Army, bought the winning ticket to the Mega Millions prize in the Virginia Lottery. He bought the ticket at the corner Sunoco Station just up the street on Stevenson Avenue from his condo. He won thirty five million dollars in the Virginia Lottery. Life could be so strange! And it could be so wonderful.

Roger checked his numbers on Sunday morning via the internet. He started screaming out loud when he realized he had won. "I won! I freakin' won!" he screamed over and over. He did not get any sleep that night and drove the twenty miles down to Woodbridge, Virginia on Monday morning to the official lottery office and registered his win. The staff greeted him pleasantly and filed his claim. He opted to be paid over twenty six years and was to receive about one million, twenty three thousand dollars every year for twenty six years.

It took six weeks for Roger to receive his first payment which was delivered by direct deposit into his Savings Account at Sun Trust Bank about two miles from his condominium at Seminary Plaza. Roger was now a bona fide millionaire, and among other things, a favorite customer at his bank. Just as he approached every thing else in his life, Roger decided to use his new found wealth slowly and with great deliberation. He was a very careful and deliberate man in many ways. That approach to life had served him well.

Roger took Afet to Turkey and Egypt as soon as summer break at Howard University commenced. Her classes were over until September so they spent two months out of the country visiting her family. He had severe colitis so travel was a bit difficult at times, but Roger always stayed as close as possible to a men's room, carried toilet paper with him at all times in a back pack and he very closely watched what he ate. It seemed to work most of the time.

When they would spend most of the day in a vehicle travelling, Roger had to wear an adult diaper to keep the embarrassment factor down, but travelling made Afet happy so Roger travelled. He really did not like it, but Afet lived to travel so he did it. While travelling they discussed Roger's responsibilities now that he had plenty of money to spend. Roger never tired of thinking about how to responsibly spend his fortune. That is the way he was built. There was not an irresponsible bone in his body.

He had always promised a childhood friend who was a Catholic priest, a Father Viktor Zobias of the Glenmary Fathers and Brothers, that he would take care of the 95 or so professed members of that Catholic home mission society. They had all lived a life of poverty to spread the Christian message and labored in the deep south of the United States in order to provide for the few Catholics there. They did social work and parish work in counties that might have no more than sixty Catholics in total. Viktor loved what he did. He was a good priest. And he was poor, in weak health and closing in on fifty seven years old. Roger was going to change that situation as best he could.

Rogier Magritte and Viktor Zobias had grown up together in Vermont and attended Catholic schools together from first grade through high school. Viktor's parents were war refugees from Lithuania who had settled in Vermont right after World War II so Rogier and Viktor had a lot in common. They bonded immediately the first day that they met in the fifth grade. They were lifelong friends.

When Roger entered the Army Viktor entered seminary that same year to study for priesthood. Viktor became a home missioner and had spent a lifetime of hard work with the poor and disenfranchised in the South. It is what Glenmary did. It is what Viktor wanted to do. Roger had actually visited the headquarters of the order in Dayton, Ohio once when Viktor took ill years before and had to receive quadruple bi-pass surgery. The order was poor and there was nothing put aside for the retirement of the priests and brothers.

Roger had stopped practicing Catholicism in the Army, he was not very religious. But Viktor was his oldest friend. Roger would always joke that if he ever won the lottery he would start a retirement fund for Glenmary as long as Viktor remembered Roger's 'special intention' at daily Mass. Apparently Viktor had kept up his end of the bargain. As far as Glenmary was concerned, the lottery winning truly was god sent!

Since Roger now had the money to make good on his promise he contacted Viktor at the Glenmary formation home in Kentucky. Viktor was now the Director of Prospective Postulants for the order and ran the house where the prospective applicants spent a year in initial formation and screening. Since the order had no retirement system to speak of, so Roger opened a trust fund for each to get $3,000 dollars a year for twenty years to be placed in their name in a personal retirement fund for these impoverished missionaries. Since that was roughly $300,000 dollars a year expended, Roger next moved onto his family obligations.

He had two adult daughters who were more or less estranged from him most of the time. They blamed him for the divorce from their mother. They did not know about their mother's track record with women in the marriage. Roger never told them and they were too young at that time to suspect anything odd. The young women had a strained relationship at best with their father. He might get a phone call from one of them once a month. The older daughter would contact Roger perhaps once a year, and that was in a good year. They lived in the Boston area. The younger daughter had two kids that Roger adored. He paid off their bills and sent them both a check for $50,000 dollars. That brought his first year outlay to about $500,000 dollars. He was going through the lottery money quickly.

Roger gave Afet $75,000 dollars to pay off most of her bills and to buy a new car. Roger bought a new $23,000 dollar Hyundai. That brought his total outlay to about $600,000 dollars and Roger invested the rest of the money he had received for that year in a couple of old mutual funds he had maintained over the years. He was five months away from another deposit from the lottery commission at that point. It would again be a deposit of over a million dollars. It was going to start raining money for Roger. Oddly enough, he was a tad uncomfortable with the situation. He wasn't yet fully prepared for the freedom that money gives a person. Roger was learning that it could be overpowering at times.

His native New England common sense took hold of him immediately however and he watched every dime that he spent. He realized that the money could go quite far if he spent it wisely. Roger started to think about how he could use the money to help veterans. This is something he always wanted to do. Afet began to question him about it a lot more now that they had returned home from overseas. She could see how passionately he felt about veterans in the U.S. being odd-man-out for any political decision-making relative to expenditure of national resources. She knew how he felt about veterans not being understood and being widely abused by an antiquated system of benefits and pension support. As an American Muslim she often felt like a fish out of water herself. She knew what it was like to feel marginalized in American society.

So Afet hatched a plan and told Roger about it. What if he paid a university history department to write a newly researched view into the lives of American veterans? What if that university represented a marginalized community within American society? Would not that give a new slant to the story of the American veteran for the D.V.A and the politicians to ponder she argued? Would not that give bold and valid insights into veterans' needs and their mindset from the beginning of the republic until the present time? She continued her argument over coffee at Roger's place.

An overview of American veterans from colonial days until the present would give a rich texture from which new and bold decisions might proceed from the federal government, and specifically from General Shinseki. To see the veteran in his and her full panoply of roles throughout the nation's history could provide new insights for a national leadership that was knee deep in lobbyists. These lobbyists had continually claimed to speak for veterans but in fact had secret agendas that used veterans' rights to get their foot in the door in the halls of power. If the veterans' story needed to be told, better it be told by people who understand what it meant to be overlooked and not by groups that had a long history of using veterans for purposes that ran directly counter to their immediate needs.

Roger liked the idea and asked Afet exactly which university she had in mind? She offered that the history departments at two universities in the area would fit the bill. Howard University in D.C., a traditionally Black college, and Gallaudet University, a college for the deaf in D.C. could collaborate on a newly researched history of American veterans for a small endowment to each school. This effort would definitely capture a minority view of how things really were and still are for this under represented portion of the population, the veteran. The researchers from these schools would have insights that another university would not. The scholars at these schools knew what it was like to be isolated and pushed to the periphery in American society. They had personal experience with being marginalized. Would Roger like their view of things, she asked?

Roger liked the idea. It guaranteed a sort of odd-man-out view of the American veteran from segments of American academia that could genuinely align themselves with such a view. These people would certainly have a feel for being on the outside looking in. That is the viewpoint the veterans needed to make the powers-that-be understand their plight.

Afet received a bouquet of roses, a night out on the town and a trip to New York City that month from Roger in thanks for her help. Roger got a night of loving from Afet in return. It was more than a fair trade considering that sex for Roger was a major undertaking due to the state of his personal plumbing. They were both very happy with the arrangement.

Afet contacted the chairmen of the history departments of both universities by phone the next month. She knew them both personally due to her work with the Muslim Students' Association in the city. The fact that she was a professor in the Mathematics Department at Howard University made the connection with the schools professional and that solidified the deal.

After sending a proposal to both schools, a proposal that Roger had a lawyer friend draw up, it was agreed that the history departments of both Howard University and Gallaudet University would cooperate in writing a report to General Shinseki outlining a minority view of the American veteran throughout American history. In return Roger would donate $100,000 dollars to the history departments of both schools in three increments upon completion and acceptance of the report at each phase. The schools could do what they liked with the money.

All parties were happy. It was a good day for all. Roger told Afet, "Don't you just love it when a plan comes together?" Afet agreed that she did. They made love again the evening that the deal was signed. It only seemed right to seal the deal with a kiss, and a bit more!

The Operation and its Aftermath

Roger was having burning sensations in the muscles in his groin. He went to the urologist who checked for a hernia. Roger had one. It seems that the explosion years before in the helicopter, the same one that took away his testicles, weakened the muscle walls in his groin. He had to strain to have a bowel movement due to his colitis problem and coupled with his age, he simply wore out the muscle tone in his groin and he suffered an inguinal hernia. His bladder was pushing through his muscle wall. He needed an operation to get things right. He was told by the doctor that the muscles in his groin were very weak and he would have to heal for a little while after surgery. That would mean no sex for a month to six weeks.

Afet was not happy. She liked sex, even sex with Roger who more or less had bionic plumbing. The relationship started to break down at this point. They remained friends, they liked each other a lot, but they parted ways as lovers just prior to Roger's hernia operation. Afet was willing to live with a bionic sex partner, but life without sex was too much, even for a month. Her Arab blood was too hot for that sort of monastic response to life is the way that Roger saw the situation.

Roger was secretly relieved. At least now all the "you have got to become a Muslim to marry me" talk would be over. He was glad. He did not have to confront Afet now with the fact that he was not open to becoming a Muslim or to getting married. Roger wanted to be married like he wanted a ten-penny nail driven through his eye.

Having this hernia operation was a blessing in disguise. He got to keep a friend and he did not have to make a decision to hurt her over his unwillingness to accept Allah in a mosque so that he could marry her. Roger did not want to marry anybody if the truth were known. And he sure as hell did not want to become a Muslim. He had been raised Catholic and he did not want to practice his own religion let alone someone else's. He was lucky that they parted good friends and he knew that. That is rare and always a good thing.

Within three weeks Afet was dating a younger professor from Howard University. And his plumbing was normal. Roger thought to himself that this had to make Afet happy and he was pleased for her. Everybody was moving on with their lives. Afet was getting sex again and Roger was completely out of the bind of having to walk away from a marriage proposal he never wanted to make in the first place. It was another plan coming together and Roger was at ease with it all. "I just love it when a plan comes together!" he muttered to himself on occasion now.

Roger entered Alexandria Hospital, had his hernia surgery without incident and took two weeks to recover from constant pain. It took another month for him to walk normally and have a normal bowel movement. Roger was a physical mess. But then, he was a disabled veteran with more pieces missing from him than a five year old Lego sculpture in a kindergarten classroom. He was just grateful to be alive. And he was rich now. He had that to keep him busy!

While he was at home in his condo recovering he had a lot of time to think about how he was going to spend his next annual lottery payment. It was going to be placed into his account in a few months and he was starting to draw up plans for that money. He had decided that he would keep his condo, but in the present down market for real estate he would be a fool if he passed up a chance to buy a nice house at a marked down price. He called the same real estate agent that had found him his condo and she got right on it. She would meet his needs.

He wanted a little but very nice home somewhere near the Delray section of Alexandria off Mount Vernon Avenue. There was a coffee shop there called Saint Elmo's Coffee Pub that Roger really liked to frequent. It was on the other side of the city but the atmosphere was great. It would be nice to be able to walk there.

The real estate agent, Sappho Phyllida Maragos Papadopoulos-Anciani, was an elderly Greek woman who emigrated from Rhodes to the Washington D.C. area in the late 1950's when her much older husband, Rastus Odysseus Papadopoulos died in a car accident. Well it was sort of a car accident.

Rastus had been a wealthy "businessman" in Greece. Actually, he was a high profile crime figure. Sappho was a very beautiful woman when she was young and caught the eye of the middle aged Rastus when he saw her at a party he gave at his villa. He married the beautiful twenty two year old woman within a month of meeting her and died within a year after their marriage.

He died of an overdose of lead when two bullets were found in the back of his skull, leaving him slumped over the wheel of his sports car on a back road in Rhodes. He left her considerable wealth. Sappho always told people that her first husband died in a car accident. It was just simpler to explain it all that way.

She took her wealth and came to America and eventually met a Corsican named Aldo Ghjuvan Anciani who married her very shortly after discovering that she did not mind being with short men. She was six inches taller than Aldo. Aldo had emigrated from France a few years earlier and had served in the Vichy French Air Force early in World War II. He had been a co-pilot in an Axis bomber when a British flyer in a Hawker Hurricane shot him down over the English Channel. The Royal Navy fished him and two crewmates out of the water and turned them over to the Royal Air Force who interned them as POWs.

Aldo spent most of the war as a POW in a camp for Axis airmen in Scotland. He learned English as a POW and spoke the language with an odd combined Corsican-Scottish accent. His accent almost sounded like a bad imitation of Bela Lugosi portraying Count Dracula in an early talking movie. After the war he went home to France for a very short time but quickly emigrated to the U.S. He was a very interesting man and wore a toupee. He looked ridiculous with that rug on his head but Roger liked him too much to say anything. Besides, Sappho seemed to like it. That was good enough for Aldo.

Aldo liked taller women, and that was a good thing because most women were taller than him. Aldo stood 5 feet, 4 inches tall with his shoes on. Sappho stood about 5 feet, 10 inches tall with her shoes off. They opened up a real estate business in northern Virginia in the mid 1960's and were still selling homes together almost forty five years later. Even in their eighties they were lively, healthy and completely committed to their clients. They loved selling homes. They were very rich, very connected and actually they were very warm and interesting people. Roger really liked them. They liked him. They would sometimes meet for dinner. At those times Roger would suffer Aldo's toupee and nutty hybrid accent in silence.

Sappho went immediately to work looking for a house for Roger on the other side of Alexandria. She found one within a month and two weeks later she made an offer on the house for Roger. And within a month after that Roger laid down $200,000 dollars on the purchase of the home and mortgaged another $400,000 dollars from his bank. He did not move in right away. The home needed work and so he contracted with a home builder to refurbish the house. He bought almost $50,000 dollars worth of new furniture to furnish the place and had it moved in the day after the contractor was done painting and fixing up what needed to be fixed. New carpet had been laid down and the home was ready to have a tenant.

Roger decided to keep the condo near the mall on the other side of town. What could it hurt? And besides he would have a place to sleep guests, if he ever got any guests. Roger could go months without someone else ever entering his place now that Afet was out of his life. But who knows? One can never tell about these things. It was possible that at some point Roger would have guests. Hope springs eternal.

Shortly before the purchase of the new home Roger's second annual installment of his lottery money was deposited in his account and he took a vacation for two weeks to California while the new home was being outfitted. "Better to stay in the country this time" he thought to himself. It was just easier that way when he travelled. He disliked constantly asking about the location of the nearest men's room in foreign countries. He felt odd about it.

He rented a car and spent two weeks driving all around the state alone. He liked vacationing alone. There were no rules. And he did not have to bother anyone else with his constant need to find a rest-room. He was getting older now. He constantly wore an adult diaper when he was driving. He was close to being incontinent. His disabili-ties were no joke and had to be minutely managed during travel. It could work on his self confidence if he allowed it. He did not allow it.

The last thing he wanted to do but was to be travelling with a lover and a friend in a crowd and to mess his pants. It was a very real possibility if he did not watch every single thing that he ate. He was so highly lactose intolerant that anything with milk in it could ruin his whole day. It would ruin the day of everyone sitting near him too! He had to be keenly aware of things that other people did not even notice in their lives.

He returned to Alexandria, Virginia after two weeks of travelling in California. He still had not moved into his new place and was living in the condo on Stevenson Avenue. He was not particularly close to anyone in the building but it had been his home and community since he left the army and it was familiar. He was finding it surprisingly hard to leave his condo. This was his home. And when you get right down to it, many times a home is all a disabled veteran has to call his own. In the life of a seriously injured veteran family has evaporated more times than not. It was just the sad reality of the situation.

He was not very close to his daughters. He usually only heard from them infrequently and in fact the older daughter really did not want to have much to do with him. She was too raw over the divorce with her mother some nineteen years previous. She never got over it. She blamed Roger for his infidelities. He never said anything to her about her mother's sexual proclivities inside the marriage. It did not seem right to him. So he mostly lived without family contact. On most days, he preferred it that way. There was too much instability in his daughters' lives. He had enough problems; he did not need to be inviting more into his life. Still it would have been nice to have had a family that supported him. "Hell", he often thought, "it would be nice to have a family that just contacted me now and then!"

Roger was living his life alone. He had done that more or less while he was in the army and he would have to do it after he retired and was learning to live with his disabilities. It really wasn't the loneliness that bothered him as much as it was the disconnectedness with the community at large that got under his skin. He seemed to be nothing more than an open wallet to his daughters and a forgotten phone number to his army friends. So be it. Life is what it is. He had learned that it is sometimes easier to accept than to constantly resist life, no matter what it had to offer in the way of pain.

He would often walk through a mall or go to the beach and walk the boardwalk alone. He would see the people and he would think "I got hurt for these people. They could not possibly care less. They don't know me and they do not want to know me. Why did I get hurt for them? It does not matter to them one way or the other whether I live another year or drop dead right here in front of them. They would walk right over my body on the way to the beach. Why did I do it? Why did I put myself in harm's way for them?"

He could never answer that question. His body seemed to ache more when he asked this question of himself. He hurt a lot more as he got older.

Roger had grandchildren that he barely saw. They had his picture, knew his name, he saw them perhaps three times a year if he flew into Boston but that was all the family connection he had. Now that Afet was moving on with her life with another guy he had no real connection to anyone anymore. In a strange way he preferred it this way. It just made a whole lot of things that much easier to handle.

He did not even have a cell phone. He did not want that kind of a connection with the world. It was too easily abused by people looking for money or wanting to use him one way or another. Roger tried hard not to be cynical but it was difficult in his life circumstances. In fact just about everything was difficult in his situation. When a man has a mostly bionic penis, nothing in life is simple and certainly not his social life.

One day he was down in the condominium gym working out when he met another veteran. He was a Fairfax County detective named Whit Fowler. They hit it off right away. Whit had been a junior officer and a military policeman at Fort Belvoir in Virginia prior to getting a job as a cop with Fairfax County. He was conversant at least on a basic level with veterans' issues. Roger appreciated that.

It was obvious to Whit, a trained observer, that Roger was injured. Roger did not 'work out' smoothly; there were obviously some physical issues at play here. They talked about Roger's physical situation and Whit lent a sympathetic ear. After that day they often met each other inadvertently in the condo gym and the conversation would ultimately turn to veterans' issues. It was good for Roger's soul to be able to talk to another veteran about these things.

That was one of the reasons that Roger had not yet moved out of the condo and into the home in the Delray section near Mount Vernon Avenue on the other side of town. He had a small sense of community in the condo and that was very important to him. Once he moved into that nice home that he had just had refurbished, this sense of community would be gone. It was a small thing but it was something important. Roger was afraid to lose it.

Whit was working a cold case that had him stumped. Things did not add up. He did not give much information out to Roger since it was a case that was still under investigation but Roger understood that Whit was troubled by the facts surrounding the case. Roger was glad during these discussions that he was not a cop. The burden of finding guilty people could be overpowering and Roger could see that in Whit's face when he talked about his work. Roger had enough problems and he was grateful that investigating criminals was not one of them.

Whit was very interested in Roger's work for disabled veterans. Whit had not seen combat in his army career but he could see the results of it in the behavior of soldiers returning from overseas who had served in combat areas. They were somehow different, more edgy, and more fragile. In Whit's army days these guys caused a lot of trouble on base for Whit's M.P.'s once they got drunk. There were always a lot of domestic disturbances involving the combat vets and their wives. Once one got through the macho stories of combat an observer could see scared and often broken men reliving stories of a time of terror in their lives. These were times that they did not want to see again.

Combat stories might be good for a round of drinks bought by the listener but they could be traumatic for the story teller later in the evening. Some memories were best left undisturbed. Whit had seen plenty of this sort of thing as an M.P. watch commander at an army base. As a cop he saw a lot of dysfunction in society and many times combat veterans were involved in violent activities once they came home and entered civilian life. It just came with the territory for both the cops and the veterans. It was a sad fact of life. Neither man had an easy answer to stop the violence, to stop the madness that tears at the sole of the PTSD sufferer. But they saw the charred remains of human psyches that PTSD from combat caused almost every day in the veterans that had seen it.

The First Section of the Report

The researchers at Gallaudet University and at Howard University had by this time delivered their first installment of the combined and remarkably interwoven report to Roger. He had paid one third of the negotiated fee to the history departments of both universities for the delivered work. The report would come in three parts. The first three would be the history of American veterans divided into three historical periods detailing their interactions with society at large. The executive summary would come with the last section. Roger was fascinated by the well documented, highly detailed section of the report that he was now reading. It pertained to American veterans from the pre-colonial period up to the end of World War I. There were footnotes, bibliographies and reading lists attached to the report that would take years for any serious researcher to wade through. It was quite scholarly. Roger was very happy with the work so far.

The report was very thick and opened up with a preface. The initial direction in the preface dealt with a general discussion concerning American veterans in 2007, the last year that reliable numbers were available from the 2008 Census. In that year there were 23.6 million veterans in the USA (that number was known to be about 22.9 million in the summer of 2009). Their annual income in 2007 was $36,053 dollars and 5.7% of them were living below the poverty line for income. In 2007, 1.8 million veterans were women. Of all veterans age twenty five or older in 2007, 25% of them held at least a bachelor's degree. Ninety percent of them held a high school diploma.

The report pointed out that in 2007 there were six million veterans with a disability. 17.4 million veterans voted in the 2004 presidential election and that was seventy four percent of all veterans. 14 million veterans voted in the 2006 congressional elections and that was sixty one percent of veterans overall. In 2006, the last year that figures were available at the time of the census, 2.7 million veterans were receiving disability compensation totaling $28.2 billion dollars.

In 2006, the total amount of funding for the various veterans benefits programs was $72.8 billion dollars of which $34.6 billion dollars went toward compensation and pensions. A total of $33.7 billion dollars went toward medical programs and the remainder of that money went to other various veterans programs such as educational benefits and vocational rehabilitation programs.

It was obvious that there was a lot of the nation's treasure being expended on America's veterans at the beginning of the 21st Century. Roger wondered if all the expenditure was truly achieving all of its goals. He thought not. But he had to admit, enormous amounts of money was being sent toward the veteran to meet his or her needs.

But this was not always the case. Oddly enough, veterans benefits was an idea that grew slowly in the fiercely independent mindset of the typical American citizen. It was mostly a matter of veteran's preference up until the War Between the States. Roger was surprised at what he was reading the report was very specific and showed a marked and definite low regard for the system.

Prior to the Revolutionary War when most "Americans" were really North American born colonials of European powers, veterans of the various continental contingents of the European armies and navies were usually awarded land in North America for service to the king or queen. If they wished to travel to the mother country after being seriously wounded in a North American skirmish with soldiers from an enemy European power they might be awarded a small pension in that country but this seemed to be a rare occurrence.

Wounds and serious injuries were expected to be dealt with by the extended family of the wounded colonist or by the North American colony of the European power in some way. This was certainly true of the American Indian tribes and nations that fought with and against the European colonials. The Indian Nations had no sense of the nation itself owing "benefits" to a fallen or wounded brave. He was on his own if he got hurt in battle. The same spirit seemed to be prevalent among the various colonists from different parts of Europe in North America.

When the American Revolution was fought the situation changed a little bit, but not much. There were proportionately high numbers of American wounded that served in the Continental Army and Continental Navy (includes the Continental Marines), by some estimates, up to 6,188 wounded, 4,435 killed out of a total of about 217,000 colonials who served in uniform and who were now considering themselves Americans for the first time. That is roughly a five percent casualty rate.

The idea of veterans' benefits took hold slowly, probably due to lack of funding and a pioneer spirit of self sufficiency. It goes without saying that African Americans who served in the army and navy were usually slaves placed into combat by masters and so they had no rights whatsoever, including the right to any veterans' benefits in this early period. It is not clear exactly how or if Black freedmen were awarded benefits of any type for Revolutionary War service or injuries.

In fact the entire period in American history prior to the Civil War had a small regard for what we would consider to be adequate benefits for almost all veterans. The mainstay of veterans' benefits was veterans' preference in federal appointments. As hard as this may be to believe, the report showed that there was no legal basis that existed in American government for the treatment of war veterans. Although certain narrowly defined classes of soldiers and sailors were rewarded for their service.

This preference in federal appointments actually extended back to awarding government positions to wounded veterans as early as the Revolutionary War. Other benefits for American war veterans at that time were based on the earlier established European models and had limited use of pensions, bonuses for war service, a small disability allowance and some ability to provide hospitalization of injuries that occurred while in uniform. These were all seen as rewards for wartime service.

It was not until roughly the period of the administration of Andrew Jackson when the "spoils system" of government largesse and the awarding of benefits to the election winner's political backers became more common. This would be the start of veterans' benefits as we would eventually know them in American politics. And even then veterans' benefits were really nothing more than an appointment to a federal position as a reward for military service.

It must not be understood though as all encompassing. These appointments were reserved for ex-officers who had served and were usually tendered to fairly high ranking officers. There was no provision whatsoever to find a job for an injured rank and file soldier with the government. He was on his own. This thinking about veterans continued into the Civil War period.

It should be noted that the British government promised all slaves in America freedom if they supported the British cause in the War of 1812. Tens of thousands of slaves went over to the British side and helped in building fortifications or escaped to British ships which often took them out of the area. Native Americans allied themselves with both sides. Neither of these communities was seen as deserving of veterans benefits by the government. The War of 1812 saw 286,730 Americans serving in the army and navy and 4,505 were wounded with 2,260 killed. That would be about a 2% casualty rate.

Veterans' benefits continued to be mostly federal appointments for high ranking officers. This continued through the War with Mexico in 1848. In that war 78,718 men served in the army and navy (includes marines) with 4,152 wounded and 1,733 killed.

In an odd turn of events, mostly Irish and Irish Americans who were Catholics serving in the U.S. Army under anti-Catholic Protestant officers deserted en masse. They joined the Mexican Army against the Americans, forming the San Patricio Battalion (Saint Patrick's Battalion) under a Captain John Riley of County Galway, a former American officer. They are revered in Mexico to this day. In the U.S. their story is virtually unknown since they were deserters who joined the enemy.

After Mexico lost the war many San Patricio's saw a court martial and were executed for desertion and treason by the U.S. Army. Their reasoning was that they could not support fighting against a Catholic country and serving under antagonistic Protestant officers. Most of these men were Irish but there were some Scots and some Germans among them. Roger was completely unaware of this facet of American military history. Roger was impressed that the report mentioned it. "This truly is going to be a minority report" he thought.

Veterans' benefits more or less stayed minimal until the Civil War when President Lincoln interjected a broader view of benefits for the federal soldiers and sailors who fought. The Civil War casualty figures were horrific. On both sides, 3,213,363 soldiers, sailors and marines served in uniform. 354,805 were wounded and 191,963 died directly as a result of combat. That casualty rate is about 17%. President Lincoln realized that the high price in combat casualties was going to affect American psyches for decades to come, not to mention the economic impact this would have on the post war workforce. President Lincoln started what was probably the very beginning of the modern veterans' benefit system and its paradigms.

He lobbied Congress for substantial benefits for Union veterans of the war. Confederate veterans were not included. However, the former Confederate States had pension provisions for their former fighting men to more or less match or even exceed the benefits afforded to Union veterans. After Reconstruction failed and white Southerners gained total control of their state legislatures again, pensions were introduced for Confederate veterans.

Initially limited to disabled white veterans, oddly enough, some blacks who had served in the Confederacy could apply for and received a Confederate pension. Initially the pensions awarded by North Carolina, Florida and finally all others were to include the poor and indigent by 1898. Widows could also be awarded a pension by these states as long as they did not marry again.

African Americans who had served the Confederacy were initially awarded pensions by only one state, Mississippi. They had served as body servants, combat engineers, cooks or in other non-combat roles and were first awarded pensions by Mississippi in 1888. It was not until 1921 that any other Southern state offered a black Confederate war veteran a pension. By this time these men were quite old and it was hard to document their service in the Confederate Armies so their numbers on the rolls were quite small.

Mississippi, which was the only state to include black Confederate war veterans from the pension program's inception in 1888, had 1,739 African American pensioners; North Carolina, which first offered pensions in 1927 had 121 African Americans on its pension rolls; South Carolina, which first offered pensions in 1923, had 328 African Americans collecting a Confederate Veteran pension; Tennessee, which first offered pensions in 1921, had 195 African Americans on its pension rolls for service in the Confederacy; and Virginia, which first offered pensions in 1924, had 424 Black pensioners as a result of service to the Confederacy.

A review of the applications for Confederate pensions in Mississippi showed about 36,000 recipients of which 1,739 were African Americans so the number was small. It should be noted that Union Army veterans who were disabled as a result of their service during the Civil War were receiving pensions as early as 1868. It should also be noted that in a sort of foreshadowing of things to come on the federal level, Mississippi's pension program for Confederate veterans was initially limited to soldiers and sailors and their former servants/slaves who had a disability sustained during the War Between the States.

The disabilities were such things as a loss of limb that prevented them from engaging in manual labor and to widows who had been widowed during the war by the death of their husband, a Confederate veteran, and who had not remarried. The federal government was eventually going to accept that widows and unemployable veterans should be pensioned. The researchers found it interesting to note that a former Confederate state was the first to understand the need to subsidize veterans and their widows who could not support themselves and not just the disabled which the federal pensions initially covered solely.

Lincoln finally got Congress to pass such a law in 1865 that was the first significant veterans' preference legislation. It read in part:

"Persons honorably discharged from the military or naval service by reason of disability resulting from wounds or sickness incurred in the line of duty shall be preferred for appointments to civil offices, provided they are found to possess the business capacity necessary for the proper discharge of the duties of such offices."

This law concerning preference in appointments was limited to those disabled veterans who were otherwise qualified for the work to be performed. This piece of legislation which was passed by Congress for Union veterans in 1865 stood as the basic veterans' preference basis in law until after Word War I.

Along the way, however, several modifications were made to the 1865 legislation. An amendment in 1871 contained the first instance of "suitability" requirements for job seeking veterans. The language read as follows:

"The President is authorized to prescribe such regulations for the admission of persons into the civil service of the United States as may best promote the efficiency thereof, and ascertain the fitness of each candidate in respect to age, health, character, knowledge, and ability for the branch of service into which he seeks to enter, and for this purpose he may employ suitable persons to conduct such inquiries, and may prescribe their duties, and establish regulations for the conduct of persons who may receive appointment in the civil service."

In 1876 the law was amended again to give reduction in force (RIF) preference to veterans, their widows and orphans. It should be mentioned here that "equal qualifications" of a person entitled to preference for federal employment was left to the appointing officers. For all intents and purposes this ensured that all federal veterans' appointments went to white males. Non-whites were effectively blocked from using these provisions for seeking employment in any significant numbers. In 1888 a Civil Service Commission regulation was incorporated to give absolute preference to all disabled veterans over all other eligible applicants.

In 1889 President Harrison issued an executive order allowing honorably discharged veterans who were former federal employees to be reinstated without time limit. This was the first appearance of reinstatement eligibility as applied to veterans.

In 1892, reinstatement rights were extended to the widows and orphans of veterans. The reinstatement provision was the last significant addition to preference legislation until 1919.

And now injured veterans continued to join the ranks of their brothers in arms before them. In the Spanish American War of 1898, there were 306,760 men in uniform, 1,662 were wounded and 385 were killed. That is a casualty rate of less than 1%. However the figures for World War I are 4,734, 991 men in uniform, 204,002 were wounded and 191,963 were killed. That is a casualty rate of about 8.3%. The numbers of veterans needing care and special consideration were growing much larger in the 20th century.

This was mostly because the force in American economics that would eventually be termed "the military industrial complex" (MIC) in the mid 20th century was beginning to show its will in implementing foreign policy decisions as early as the 1870s with America's march westward. As the researchers showed, the more the MIC grew in importance to the basic stability of the economy, the more skirmishes, international incidents and wars would be fought by Americans, thereby producing veterans with many disabled veterans among them.

Disabled veterans were actually a necessary by-product of an economy based on war industries and their related partners in other sectors of the economy. By the Spanish American War in 1898, this fact was indisputable. We simply went to war to gain access to markets to which we had been denied. This would be a common factor in all wars to come in the century or more following that war.

At this point, the first part of the report that had been negotiated with the universities ended.

Roger was impressed with the scholarship and detail in this first installment of the report. He was especially taken by the fact that the researchers at Howard and at Gallaudet realized that veterans' preference was heavily a white male prerogative and veterans' benefits more or less followed in that same racial vein for most of America's history. Any non-white veteran would have found it difficult and perhaps even impossible to obtain veterans preference for a federal job or even a pension due to war injuries in many or perhaps most cases in the time periods covered by the first section of the report. Racism was rampant in America and that meant denied benefits for many veterans. It was really that simple.

IV.
Time to take command of the situation

The General and the President

GENERAL SINSEKI AND President Obama were meeting in the Oval Office early in the morning on a Tuesday. It was time to "talk turkey." There were more and more veterans and less and less money. How were we, as a nation, going to provide the funds for veterans in such an atmosphere? That was the number one question that they hoped to answer together this Tuesday morning. The two men were to hash out some ideas together. They wanted the highest priority to be placed on this issue of funding veterans' benefits in tough economic times.

"The president will see you now general" the secretary said. The general followed her into the Oval Office.

General Shinseki walked into the room and the president invited him to sit down. Since they both had lived in Hawaii they had a lot in common. They talked for a minute or two about Hawaii and then moved on to the matter at hand. It was just the two of them in the room for a very brief, thirty minute meeting where the general could lay out for the president what he had garnered were the prime issues to be implemented by the congress and the president in the next year. There were so many veterans issues that he did not know exactly where to start.

"General, start at the beginning" the president instructed. "Mr. President, I will do my best. But you must understand, the beginning is a very broad and deep place. To be frank, we must spend years simply playing catch up ball. Here is what I have learned in the few months I have been in charge at D.V.A.." And the general began to brief President Obama on what he had learned and where he thought the priorities lay. He kept his sentences clipped in order to get the most information into the least amount of time.

"Well sir, here is what I have learned." He spoke of meeting with the major veterans organizations. The Disabled American Veterans (DAV) saw an immediate 25% increase in disability funding as needed to satisfy the demands of the Veterans Benefits Commission Report delivered to Congress in October 2007. The commission wanted an immediate quality of life pay raise for disabled veterans and the DAV concurred. Disabled veterans were falling behind in being able to fully support themselves and their families. Both the commission and the DAV saw this payment as a primary and immediate need. But where would the money come from? Neither man knew.

General Shinseki offered to the president that the rank and file disabled veterans that had been polled by the various major veterans organizations had asked for a solution to be put forward in a radical way. The money was needed now and spending years in legislative fights with a half dozen congressional committees was not going to meet their immediate needs. So the rank and file among the disabled veterans polled wanted to know if the president would support and send forward for legislative action a revision to the tax code. This revision would support tax free income for all totally disabled veterans up to $150,000 dollars a year in income.

The president asked "The veterans have come up with this request themselves? This does not come from lobbyists?" The general nodded in the affirmative and said, "As far as we can tell at the D.V.A. this is a big issue with the rank and file of the various major veterans' organizations. They say they need it immediately." The president agreed to consider it. The general continued with his explanation of the request.

There would actually be very few disabled veterans earning that much money, perhaps less than one percent of them. But that income barrier from taxes would see that the overwhelming majority of disabled veterans earned tax free income while at the same time making the wealthy among them pay a fair share of government expenses through taxes. In that way thousands of extra dollars would be freed up in the households of disabled veterans every year to meet expenses and it could be done by the president almost immediately. It would be done by simply asking for a revision to the tax code that was favorable to totally disabled veterans, both schedules rated and individually unemployable groups. The president again agreed to consider sponsoring such legislation.

The general moved on.

His next priority for the president's consideration was D.V.A. healthcare provisions. The evidence that over 10,000 clients at D.V.A. hospitals might have been exposed to the AIDS virus due to the use of unclean colonoscopy instruments deeply disturbed both men. "We are aggressively investigating this mess" the general told the president. However, efforts to enforce better standards for healthcare related issues were hard to enforce. Old ways of thinking were very difficult to overcome inside the D.V.A. bureaucracy. That issue was infecting virtually all other issues.

That is, the people that worked at D.V.A. were so set in their ways of doing things that documents supporting disability cases were being shredded en masse at many locations. Hospital procedures were often dangerous and substandard. In many cases related to medical procedures, the D.V.A. healthcare technicians and doctors were not even following the published guidelines that the department supposedly enforced.

Veterans were beginning to see the depth of the mess at D.V.A. as not only unjust and illegal but actually life threatening in many cases. The general was more than aware of the problem but not sure about the solutions here. Who would be? The president simply asked the general to continue his efforts to uncover the dangers and obstacles to good veteran care and he promised to support him in any way that he could do so. "Be as aggressive as you need to be general. This mess has simply got to stop!"

The president mentioned to the general that he had read an article in the New York Times on 21 June 2009 that concerned a Doctor Kao at the VA Hospital in Philadelphia who had allegedly improperly implanted radioactive seeds meant for prostate cancer clients. That VA Hospital, upon investigation, had been found to have improperly implanted 92 clients with radioactive seeds to treat prostate cancer. This was out of a total of 116 cases investigated. Doctor Kao was responsible for most of these incidents.

To make the matter even worse, a urologist was supposed to be on hand to clear and protect the bladder during such operations and it did not appear that this was the case in these surgeries. Proper surgical procedures were apparently not followed at even a basic level in these 116 cases. This was still being investigated but there seemed to be plenty of blame to go around. Dr. Kao would have normally been trained in internal medicine in his position. The seeds are supposed to be implanted by an urologist. Something was very wrong here with the very basic structure of how these surgeries were done. This was very much like having a baker change the oil in a car. Maybe he knows what he is doing, maybe he does not. Either way, it is not his profession.

To state the matter simply, the clients very quickly became victims of radiation poisoning or related issues. The problem seemed to be lack of any oversight at all by the proper hospital authorities. The President asked the general to take this matter under personal consideration. The general agreed to do so. Within a month the doctor left his position as a contract doctor to the D.V.A. in Philadelphia.

The general then explained to the president the situation concerning the backlog of claims that the D.V.A. found to be prevalent. In FY08 there were about 2.95 million veterans that were receiving D.V.A. disability compensation benefits. As of 6 June 2009, according to D.V.A.'s own records 722,901 disability claims were pending and that included 409,362 cases that were waiting to be rated. The statistics indicated that 22.1% of those cases had been pending at or above 180 days. And that was only the initial rating cases.

Cases on appeal sometimes waited seven or eight years or longer to be finalized through the appeals process. By early July 2009 some veterans' organizations were claiming that about 1.3 million cases were now either waiting to be initially adjudicated or were on appeal! The D.V.A. disputed that number.

In 2008 over 55% of D.V.A. appeal cases that reached the Board of Veterans' Appeals were either reversed or remanded. The problem was going to be difficult to fix because it went right to the heart of the core problem at D.V.A. which was basically a bureaucracy following the old ways simply because that is the way things have always been done. The fear of change was heavy enough to cut with an axe among the staff at D.V.A. Veterans were simply not being served in an organized, efficient and trustworthy fashion. Virtually anyone involved in veterans' advocacy could see this. But the solution was oftentimes elusive.

It was obvious to even a casual observer that the standards for assigning disability percentages were not common and standardized across the country. Some regions of the country were rating very specific disabilities quite high while others were rating the same disabilities quite low. The injustices here were apparent. Disabled veterans with the exact same disabilities were being rated very differently depending on what part of the country they live within. This was a constant topic of conversation among disabled veterans.

There was a rumor floating among veterans that adjudicators who kept down disability pension costs through low-balling the rating decision were awarded bonuses. If this was true, it was an obvious conflict of interest. The general could never really get a straight answer from the career types at D.V.A. when he looked into this area of concern. Something was fishy. "Can't I just get a yes or no answer?" he would often ask his staff. He was learning that a yes or no answer was not always possible in this line of work. It was frustrating. "The jungles of Viet Nam were easier to navigate than this system!" he would often exclaim to his staff.

And then there was the security aspect of D.V.A. work that the general had to consider. There was always the possibility of social unrest if injustices like this became so widespread that the entire system was being called into question. The situation was approaching meltdown. The general realized that the nation was fast approaching a precipice concerning the basic trust of veterans toward the D.V.A. Veterans were watching him quite closely. Vigorous action from the general was needed and was expected by the veterans' community at large.

But what kind of action was needed? "I never dreamed that this job would have such a sharp national security aspect" he once reportedly told his wife. "If this is not handled right, we could have blood in the streets" he thought. And he was right. A lifetime in the army had taught him how to smell a coming fight. He smelled one every day in his job.

The general now briefed the president on priority eight enrollments into the D.V.A. healthcare system of non-service connected disabled military retirees. By October 2010 approximately 270,000 military retirees were expected to be enrolled. This category includes veterans with no service connected disability and income of more than $29,000 dollars a year. The D.V.A. was expecting to send out 500,000 applications to veterans asking them to apply. This would be an initial entrance into the president's national health care plans for this group of citizens.

The social environment surrounding this effort was hazy. Republicans were calling it socialized medicine. Democrats were screaming that it was not enough of an effort for standardized national healthcare. Nobody was happy. The general could see that and to some degree he realized that he was caught in the middle of this heated debate with nowhere to run. It was just one more obstacle in the political terrain of his every day experience at D.V.A.

Finally the briefing was over.

The general congratulated the president for recently winning the Nobel Peace prize and the president smiled and thanked him. The two men shook hands and the general left the president. "You are doing a fine job general" President Obama offered. The president had a very busy schedule and the general quickly exited the Oval Office and walked down the hallway in the White House to his waiting limousine. He walked alone and said nothing to anyone. He was deeply in thought about the things he did not tell the president. And there were many things that the general held back from the president for various reasons, most of which had to do with the hope that these problems could be quickly corrected and never need to be reported.

"I've got to get a handle on this nightmare quickly!" the general reportedly told his wife. "This entire organization acts like some sort of clandestine agency at times. It defies belief. The army was not this Machiavellian. And that is saying something!" Family friends claimed that his wife Patricia often heard him talk like that. The sound of incredulity in his voice was always apparent to her now that he took this job as Secretary at the D.V.A. Some times he simply could not believe what he was hearing from his subordinates. He thought it was crazy enough to be a cartoon series on Saturday morning television.

There was for example the issue in California that had veterans' websites buzzing for months. It seems that the police and security service of the D.V.A. was routinely spying on veterans. On June 28th 2009 an incident occurred between the D.V.A. security services and old World War II and Korean War veterans who had come in front of D.V.A. property in West Los Angeles to protest the alleged illegal usurpation of that property by wealthy Californians. The incident had hit the papers and had given D.V.A. a very black eye. The president did not ask the general about the incident so the general said nothing. He was grateful for small favors. But he knew all about it and the story was not pleasant.

Then there was the related ongoing situation where the D.V.A security services hacked D.V.A. medical files to garner information on PTSD veterans being investigated without congressional or judicial oversight for allegedly faking their symptoms in order to get benefits. Some sources within the D.V.A were claiming that as many as 2,000 disabled veterans were being prosecuted by the D.V.A for filing allegedly illegal PTSD claims based on the hacked files in 2007 through 2009. This was blatantly illegal. All sorts of laws forbid police agencies from looking at medical files without undergoing intense oversight by a judge or a congressional committee.

Apparently neither set of permissions had been sought or received. Furthermore, these D.V.A. employees who were cooperating with media investigators were claiming that the security service at the D.V.A. was openly making medical determinations. This was as to whether or not a particular veteran receiving PTSD benefits was faking symptoms or not. Only a doctor can make that determination. That is not a police matter. This situation was about to get real ugly real fast without the general's immediate attention.

Insiders at the D.V.A. were claiming to media researcher that although the HIPAA Act of 1996 made medical records secure from blatant police searches, D.V.A. doctors were being intimidated by the D.V.A. security and police arms to release confidential medical information to these investigators. These doctors potentially faced license suspension and even civil lawsuits for criminal and ethics violations for submitting these files as a result of inquiries from "unsworn" and improperly trained security arms within the D.V.A. itself.

These D.V.A. sources largely believed they were holdovers from the Bush administration that were infuriated at the cost of veterans' benefits. And it got worse. Some of these veterans who were adjudicated at 100% and who had well documented case histories of chronic trauma-centric behavior over many years faced prison. Assisting these D.V.A. "investigators" was a neo-con think tank, The American Enterprise Institute, all of whose "experts" on this issue subscribe to Dr. Sally Satel's medical theory that PTSD sufferers are largely fakers and liars. Some veterans have already been imprisoned as a result of this mess.

A disabled veteran named Keith Roberts was imprisoned in Wisconsin as late as the summer of 2009 as a result of a conviction based on these questionable D.V.A. police practices and another disabled veteran named Robert Athlon, also of Wisconsin, was facing a similar fate in July of 2009. The larger veterans' community was becoming increasingly aware of this ugliness. This was not good. And it was apparently blatantly illegal. And a lot more of this kind of illegal interference into human lives was taking place at the D.V.A. under the radar.

Federal crimes and their investigations fall under the exclusive purview of the Federal Bureau of Investigation (FBI). Insiders at D.V.A. had told newspaper people in the winter of 2008 that the

FBI had been approached by the D.V.A. to investigate these so called "PTSD fakers" among disabled veterans who were awarded PTSD benefits but the FBI refused to do so. The FBI refused to investigate largely based on issues involving patient confidentiality and strict violations of state medical ethics and various federal laws.

Now this tale gets nasty and the waters here get very, very muddy. When the general was briefed on this it was reported that he just shook his head and said quietly "You cannot be serious!? We have done this? How do we undo it?"

The general was furious. Even a professional soldier with no legal training could see that the D.V.A. was functioning completely outside of all legal guidelines by combining highly confidential medical files with other D.V.A. files. These medical files are legally protected and this violates legal restrictions on the use of medical files. This gets hairy for PTSD sufferers in that every word transcribed on their medical file that was said in front of a psychiatrist or D.V.A. doctor is potential self incrimination and a violation of the Fifth Amendment. The legal rights of disabled veterans as they apply to protections from illegal search and seizure were being routinely sent through a legal meat grinder by D.V.A. employees.

General Shinseki knew from personal experience that veterans are often whacky as a result of service connected injuries and they often say goofy things. They are often very unstable personalities. If veterans are not given the same protections of their medical records as are other citizens then there is potential violation of both the Americans with Disabilities Act and the Civil Rights Act of 1965. The D.V.A. could be sued for millions of dollars.

The general ordered an immediate halt to this practice but huge damage had apparently been done to both thousands of veterans who had been investigated for allegedly faking PTSD symptoms and those who were now facing criminal charges as a result. If immediate steps were not taken to get Roberts out of prison in Wisconsin and the D.V.A. from off of PTSD sufferer's backs, the very real threat of armed insurgency from highly unstable veterans was real. This was very serious stuff.

"I have got to get moving and build a fire under my people" the general thought to himself. Things were turning ominous among veterans and the disabled veterans of the 21st Century were nothing like the much more complacent and compliant disabled veterans of the previous century. They were too educated, too well informed, too ready to take matters into their own hands. They must not be ignored. Ignoring veterans in the new century would come at a very bitter price for all Americans. Timothy McVeigh and Terry Nichols showed the country that much.

The Veterans' Now website had recently posted a proposal by an allied veterans' group, Iraq/Afghanistan Veterans for Change that had outlined very specific proposals that their hard experience with the D.V.A. told them was necessary. The general's staff reportedly read that website daily. He knew that he needed an "out of the loop" source for valid opinions on veterans' issues. The traditional and more mainstream veterans' groups were too hooked into the Washington power circles to be completely trustworthy. The general's staff took note. They were instructed to get back to him in five working days on the value of the proposals and how the proposals could be implemented. The proposals read clearly and involved the following changes.

The newly formed veterans' group web site posted often that it wanted extensive Veterans Service Officer (VSO) training to be implemented immediately at the D.V.A. The present system had VSOs trained by their parent organization and the training was not consistent or uniformly valid for all veterans' organizations. "The government should be training all of them" was their plea.

They also wanted the huge number of claims and appeals that were being remanded to be decided sooner by putting in place a computerized claims system that can process both medical and military records, establishing clear and uniform decision making standards for disability cases, and more attention from the supervisors to claims being paid.

The group pointed out the President Obama had made the following statement: "We have a sacred trust with those who wear the uniform of the United States of America, a commitment that begins with enlistment and must never end." They wanted to make sure everyone understood that he meant what he said and expected that this spirit of this statement be carried forward at all times by D.V.A. The general concurred. These veterans were correct in their assessments.

Back at Walter Reed

Roger arrived early at the Ward 57. This is the official name where the recently injured amputees were housed at Walter Reed Medical Center. It was a hot day and Roger was wearing a very loud Hawaiian shirt and loud lime green shorts with beach sandals. The injured soldiers always poked fun at him when he dressed loudly so he tried to dress as awfully as possible. It seemed to improve their morale. He liked that. He would do almost anything to get a smile from one of them. It meant everything to him.

In modern warfare in the 21st Century, removing troops with poly-trauma injuries from the battlefield within the "golden hour" ensures a much greater chance of survivability. This is possible only because military medicine and battlefield evacuation techniques have been vastly improved since Viet Nam. Battlefield medics also know that if the very seriously injured soldier on the point of death can be treated and removed within the "platinum ten minutes" then even soldiers with horrendous wounds might survive.

A lot of these guys were on Ward 57 at Walter Reed. Many had serious head injuries. Many had much worse. Many simply could not even communicate they were so badly injured. Roger always spent time standing next to them and speaking to them, even if they could not speak back. He considered it to be his most solemn duty. "I owe them at least that much" he often offered to his veteran friends that asked him about them.

Roger approached one badly injured soldier of about 22 years old. He walked up to the bed and saw that the young man was heavily medicated but semi conscious. His legs were missing above the knee and his lower jaw was partially gone. His hair had been burned off up to the crown of his head, he had burn scars over the left side of his face. He was softly moaning in pain. Roger put his hand on the injured soldier's shoulder.

"Hey man, hang in there. I talked to the nurses and they tell me that they are going to give you a new jaw and try and get some new skin over those burns. They say that your prognosis is good. They tell me that you have a lot to live for; a wife and two kids. She called yesterday hoping that you were awake and she is pulling for you man. Hang in there." Roger moved off. His eyes were wet. He went on to the next man in the next bed.

That young soldier was awake. He shook Roger's hand when he approached his bed. He was alert and in stable emotional condition at the moment. "Hi! I'm Eddie DeFalco. I am from Philly. What brings you here?" the young soldier asked Roger, laughing at his loud Hawaiian shirt as Roger approached him. Roger was smiling at the soldier who was laughing at him. "I am Rogier Magritte. My friends call me Roger. I am retired Army. I flew helicopters in the Gulf War. I just came over to visit you guys today. How are you doing?"

Eddie laughed aloud. "That is some shirt Roger! And those shorts are unbelievable! You look like a slice of lime that is on vacation dude!" They both laughed. Two soldiers in the beds across from Eddie started to hoot and laugh. Roger protested in a mock fashion, "What?! I look great, don't you think?" They were belly laughing at his appearance. Roger said, "Just wait, you two are gonna' get old some day too!" They all laughed. They also liked the idea of growing older. Roger could see that in their faces.

Roger walked across the room to the men in the beds who were laughing. "Who are you guys? What are your names?" Roger asked. "I'm Joe Mason. I am from Indianapolis and this guy here is Juan Vega and he is from Puerto Rico, someplace up in the mountains" said the younger man. "Have you guys been here long?" Roger asked. Joe said "Yeah. I have been here about three months and Juan here has been lying in that bed a little longer. Ain't that right Juan?" and the older and darker man nodded yes.

Then Juan said in heavily accented English "You look like a clown man!" and all of them laughed together again. "Yeah, I have been told that before!" said Roger. He moved on. His job was done today with these two. Neither man had both arms, both of them missing an arm each. And Juan was missing part of his left leg. But they were laughing right now. That was a good sign. The goofy clothes worked, again, and that made Roger smile.

The next man down the line was comatose. He was in a drug induced coma that the doctors had placed upon him in order to prepare him for brain surgery. He had been the victim of an IED explosion that had killed every one in his squad but him. It looked like he might be joining his comrades real soon. Roger walked over to him and placed his hand on his shoulder and talked to him quietly for three minutes. The young man did not hear him of course, but Roger felt that maybe a part of the young man's brain would register with his words of encouragement. He walked away slowly and approached the young man in the next bed who was watching him suspiciously.

"What do you want in here dude? You are here a lot. Who the fuck are you?" the young amputee angrily demanded of Roger. "I am Roger and I am a disabled vet from the Gulf War. What's your name?" Roger asked. Roger did not respond in any way to his anger.

"What the fuck do you care? Disabled vet my ass! You look fine to me and you dress like a fuckin' clown. Screw you man! I don't need any do-gooders around me. Go fuck off!." With that last statement, he turned his back to Roger, rolled over in his bed and stared at the opposing wall. The young man was obviously raging at his plight. Of course he was missing both arms below the elbows and also one foot. Roger understood. He understood a lot more about this type of anger than this man could ever know. Roger moved in closer to his bed.

"Are you always in a good mood like this?" Roger asked the young man. The young man turned around quickly in his bed and screamed at Roger "FUCK OFF!" Roger did not move. He just stood there and waited. The young man started to cry. He sobbed uncontrollably for a few minutes and Roger still waited. Finally Roger said to him in a low voice so that the others could not hear, "I know it hurts. Trust me, I know. But you gotta' find a way to deal with all this because its not going away."

The young man just continued to sob and shake in his bed. Roger put his hand on his shoulder. The young man shook it off. Roger said softly. "I am going to leave my card on your bed-stand here next to the bed. If you want to call to talk, call me anytime. I am here to listen." Roger took out a card from his pocket and laid it on the bed stand. He then moved off to the next man. Everyone else in the ward just ignored the outburst and pretended that they did not hear it. It was a common enough occurrence that the men realized that they should not react to it. It was very private grief that was coming out in a very public way. They all knew what the man was feeling.

Roger finished up his rounds and got a bite to eat on the way home. When he got home he saw a message on his home phone, the red light was blinking. He listened to the message as soon as he got into his condo. It was from his Army doctor friend at Walter Reed asking Roger to call back right away. Roger did just that. The news was not good.

The young man who had snapped at Roger had tried to throw himself out of the third floor window and was caught at the last minute by two medics who worked in Ward 57. The doctor wanted to know what made the young man so angry. "I am not sure" Roger offered. "I think it may just have been the light heartedness of my visit. I am not sure that he appreciated it."

The doctor agreed with Roger's assessment and asked Roger to stay away from the hospital for a while. He did not want any other patients upset. Roger was shocked at the request but agreed to it. What else could he do? "I am sorry this happened" Roger said to the doctor. The man simply said, "I am too. But it is best that you stay away now." It seemed final. And that is exactly how the doctor wanted it to seem. There would be no reprieve for Roger. He was not to revisit the amputees on Ward 57. His unofficial permission to do so had been officially revoked.

The Army wanted no more trouble at Walter Reed Medical Center. It had already received enough bad press in the past few years. Roger was reminded of an old Army saying that he had many times. "No good deed shall ever go unpunished." He was going to need to find another way to reach out to disabled veterans. This avenue of approach had been cut off. And it would not be coming back his way again.

The following week the young man who snapped at Roger succeeded in committing suicide. He threw himself down a flight of stairs and broke his own neck. The story was in the newspapers all over the D.C. region. It seems that his young wife had visited him only once when he had been admitted to the hospital. She took one look at the seriousness of his injuries and just turned and walked away. She never said a word. She never returned. That was just a few weeks before Roger had met him. This was not all that uncommon. The wounds received by these young men in this sort of 'combat engagement' might never heal. This was one of those cases.

All of the young men were just as concerned about their loss of sex appeal, their loss of masculinity, as they were about their wounds and disabilities. They perceived themselves in most cases to be shattered men with shattered bodies and diminished manhood. It took a very strong individual to be in this situation and see it otherwise. No matter how much therapy these young men would receive, many could just not overcome the fact that they were amputees and were probably not desirable to their mates anymore. That was true in at least some cases and it was always heartbreaking. Life can be cruel to heroes. And even heroes can lose heart.

Everyone wants to know a hero, but how many women want to be married to one who has lost limbs? How many women want to make love to a man with missing arms, or a chopped up set of genitals? How many men want to have a wife who lost her legs or breasts in combat and is half loony as a result? Roger knew the answer to that question; "not many." It is just the way that life works.

Heroes look great in Hollywood war movies. But attempting to live life as an amputee following a vicious combat experience inside a war that holds no interest or meaning for the majority of Americans is a lifelong sentence to crushing mental defeat and constant self-questioning. Nothing can be worse than losing limbs "for the American way of life" when the common American could not care less about the war, the injured or the problems of living with the aftermath of amputations, brain damage, inability to work and broken marriages. In the end, the broken warrior has no one else to cover his back in life but another broken warrior. No one else could possibly understand. Frankly for the most part, Roger had learned that no one else even wants to understand. In America when something is broken, it is simply discarded.

Heroes generally know all about the depth of cruelty regarding what life can dish out as a result of a soldier, marine, airman or sailor taking a stand. Heroes are usually dead, broken or relegated to the back room for the rest of their lives if they are unlucky enough to live through action that gave them severe wounds. It is just the way it works. To be any other way makes too many people uncomfortable.

The electorate in the U.S. always wants to worship a war hero in his entire broken-bodied valor, as long as it is from afar. No one wants one of these people in their family. They make people ask too many deep questions about the nature of war and the nature of our society. And in a capitalist country with an economy based on a constantly grinding war machine, who wants that? No, Roger understood completely from personal experience that Americans liked their wars in the movies but had no capacity whatsoever to deal with the aftermath of war in reality. We are just too superficial a culture for that sort of meaningfulness in our dealings with each other.

Roger no longer had access to Ward 57 since the young soldier had decided to take his own life the week after he screamed at Roger. It was not Roger's fault. The Army knew that. But with all the bad press that Walter Reed Medical Center had taken in the past few years, they were not going to afford Roger the opportunity to visit any more amputees. It is just the way that the politics of the situation worked. Roger understood but it made him sad. This chapter of his life was closed now.

So, Roger settled in and spent more time writing article for Veterans Now. He was an associate editor and had carte blanche to write whatever he wanted on the web site. He usually spent time on issues regarding how veterans could practically improve their lives every day. It was not an easy tack to take for a disabled veteran, but it was necessary for so many to read. He worked on trying to project a positive attitude toward disabled veterans. He rarely actually felt that way.

The second phase of the report was due and Roger eagerly awaited it. He sent in his payments to the universities that were preparing it and was sent a copy registered mail. It was an eye opener to say the least.

The Second Section of the Report

Roger was pleased with the report and read it voraciously when he received it from the combined Gallaudet University / Howard University team of historians. It opened as it always did with the basic facts in veterans' legislation. Then it moved on to the team's unique view of veterans in America. It was enlightening.

Roger called the heads of the history departments at both schools and thanked them for the report. "This is great stuff and well worth the money. I intend to send the report to General Shinseki at the Department of Veterans Affairs when this is done. I am not sure if I told you this or not. I hope the report makes a difference in the outlook of the management there. It needs to change."

The historians agreed with Roger, the D.V.A. needed a major paradigm shift if it was to meet modern veterans' needs. The Gallaudet group was not all that sure that the report would change much for veterans however. They had spent their lives as hearing impaired people and understood what it meant to be often ignored or misunderstood. "You know, facts do not always change things for a group of people who have been ignored or relegated to the backroom" the department head told Roger via email. "Make sure you do not get your expectations up too high, Roger. The report may do nothing at all to fundamentally change things." Roger answered back in an email to the professor that he understood his point and would keep his expectations in check.

Roger jumped right into reading the report the evening he received it. It started in the time period right after World War I.

The Census Act of 1919 was the first significant change in veterans' preference laws and it was amended almost immediately by the Deficiency Act of 1919. It granted preference to all honorably discharged veterans, their widows and the wives of wounded veterans. It is significant because it no longer emphasized service connected disability for veterans' preference and it introduced the concept of spousal preference in government work. It also redefined eligible veterans to mean both wartime and peacetime veterans. This remained basic veterans' preference law until amended again in 1944.

There were two important changes to the Act of 1919. An executive order was established in 1923 adding ten points to the score of disabled veterans and adding five points to the score of non disabled veterans on Civil Service tests. This was the first time that points were added to tests for veterans. However veterans were no longer placed at the top of the appointment list. In 1929 another executive order needed to be issued to place veterans back at the top of the certification list for federal appointment.

Then in 1938 a rule put in place by the Civil Service Commission required that the decision by the appointing official to pass over a veteran and select a non veteran for a job be subject to review by a commission. This rule was the first time the commission could overturn the pass over decision by the appointing authority if it felt the decision did not have adequate reason to stand on its own merit.

Veterans' preference as it exists in the 21st Century derives basically from the Veterans Preference Act of 1944 which elevated the existing executive order and regulatory policies to national policy. President Roosevelt did everything he could reasonably do to strengthen the veteran's chance at obtaining a federal job. FDR made sure that all future changes to these laws must go through congress as legislation and could not be arbitrarily changed by the whim of the president of someone in the executive branch.

This provided for competitive examinations, reinstatement to federal positions and retention during reduction in force. All positions in government were now covered by the law except for a few high level positions in the Post Office. There were a few downgrades however. Non disabled veterans whose only service was performed during peacetime and the wives of non service connected disabled veterans over 55 years old were no longer eligible for veterans' preference in federal hiring.

In 1948 the law was amended to include the mothers of veterans in many cases. In 1952 the law was amended to include veterans who served in uniform from 28 April 1952 until 1 July 1955. This was a period when Americans were being drafted. The conflict in Viet Nam changed the laws further.

In 1966 laws were passed which provided peace time preference for Viet Nam era veterans who served for more than 180 consecutive days between 31 January 1955 and 10 October 1976. National Guard and Reserve officers were excluded. In 1967 legislation was again expanded to include preference benefits to all veterans who served on active duty for more than 180 days between 31 January 1955 and 10 October 1976. Again, Guard and Reserve officers were excluded.

The end of the Viet Nam war brought with it another law passed in 1976. This law put added restriction on veterans whose service began after 14 October 1976. For post Viet Nam veterans' preference was granted only if these veterans became disabled or served in a declared war, a campaign or an expedition. The various major veterans' organizations, the Department of Defense and other actors in government did not think that preference was appropriate for peacetime service members in the era of an all volunteer armed forces.

The Civil Service Reform Act of 1978 created new benefits for veterans with 30 percent of more disability. It gave extra protection in hiring and retention and under this act, preference was no longer granted to nondisabled veterans who retired at the rank of major (lieutenant commander) and above. In 1988 legislation was enacted that required the Department of Labor to report agencies that violated veterans' preference laws and/or failing to list vacancies with state agencies to the Office of Personnel Management for enforcement. The Defense Appropriation Act of 1997 afforded veterans' preference to anyone who served on active duty in Gulf War (2 August 1990 through 2 January 1992).

The law also granted preference to certain service members who earned campaign medals for service in Bosnia and Herzegovina in support of Joint Endeavor (20 November 1995 through 20 December 1996) and Operation Joint Guard (20 December 1996 through a date yet to be determined). In 2008 a new G.I. Bill was passed to pay for college for veterans involved in the wars in Iraq and Afghanistan. This was a fine bill and pleased mostly everyone involved with it. Veterans' preference also came with service in these wars. In 2009 a bill concerning women veterans was winding its way through the congress at the time that the report was written. It would provide many more protections and health care upgrades for women veterans.

The report then went on to talk about various other issues relative to American veterans since World War I. It basically showed that the end of the draft and the beginning of the all volunteer armed forces in 1974 was a sea change in American defense thinking. The report pointed out that the armed forces grew to be a much greater power in the toolbox of American economic resourcefulness after the Spanish American War ended in 1898. At this time minorities such as the Native American and the African American were allowed to become more and more involved in serving in uniform.

Just prior to World War II the United States had a standing army about the size of that of Sweden. By the end of the war over 16 million men and women were serving or had served in uniform in the USA. What was later to be known as the national defense establishment had now come fully into its own as a result of the power it necessarily wielded in the Second World War. In a speech in 1961 President Eisenhower, a decorated and celebrated five star general, warned all Americans about the dangers of a permanent defense establishment being established in the U.S. It appears that the speech fell upon deaf ears.

The writers of the report showed case after case of the national defense establishment essentially ensuring at all times that war was a necessary and vital part of American economic outreach and power. This newfound status for the Defense Department had enormous impact on veterans. This newly born defense establishment which quickly morphed into an even greater military industrial complex (MIC) had its tentacles into every aspect of American society. And it would soon demand that the country be placed on a constant or near constant war footing. That war footing was known for years as the Cold War. The military industrial complex demanded a near constant state of alert ostensibly to ensure that the Soviets and their empire's minions could not take the West by surprise in a military attack.

But that was simply a front. It was window dressing for much more immediate needs of economic expansion and political connectedness demanded by the captains of this newfound war industry in America. A vibrant war industry cannot long survive without the constant threat of potential war. So that threat had to be constantly exaggerated, exacerbated or simply imagined. This was in order to keep the MIC moving forward with new weapons and related systems. The amount of money that was being made by relatively few individuals as a result of this new war industry was huge.

The report continued in uncharacteristically blunt fashion.

That group of war industries was now in the business of making war whenever and where ever it could, using munitions manufacturing and related industries as a new wedge into the world market place. America's new power as a munitions and war industry giant would propel it into unquestioned economic leadership on the globe for decades. Billions could be made quickly by ensuring that the Western war machine both at home and abroad was constantly stacked with new and better American weapons and related materials and national defense related services provided by American companies. And it was all done in the name of "freedom." It was a great game for many decades. It made a lot of highly connected people very wealthy. And it fit perfectly well within what was to become known as "trickle down economics" in the Reagan era of government and far beyond.

The report then reflected on the psychological impact of the new war based economy.

War is never a problem as long as somebody else's sons and daughters are doing the fighting and the dying. And that was the case for the poor and the working class and lower middle class American families for generations after World War II ended. Their job in this war driven economic scenario was to provide the soldiers, airmen, marines and sailors to do the fighting and dying in this war based economy run by faceless and obscenely wealthy capitalists in the defense industries. It was a quiet and creeping nightmare for the families of the shattered, wounded and dead who were not important enough to matter in any real way to the average American. At this point Americans seemed to adopt and then adapt the old British adage once applied to children in the 19th Century. "Veterans should be seen, but not heard."

The researchers then provided a social backdrop to what would happen in Viet Nam.

As with so many other things, seemingly unrelated and innocuous events had an impact that no one could foresee. The advent of a television set in every American living room allowed all Americans to see up close and almost immediately the death and destruction in Viet Nam on a daily basis. Most American families in the East and Midwest would watch the news around supper time. The West Coast saw the news in the afternoon. By 1967 it was a daily electronic orgy of dying and bleeding North Americans and Asians killing each other with massive weapons systems.

The great spokesperson for the media in America, Walter Cronkite, openly turned against American involvement in this slaughter in a news commentary during the Tet Offensive in 1968 saying that the Viet Nam war was unwinnable. President Johnson later remarked that if he had lost Walter Cronkite, he had lost America. That was probably a true statement the report writers opined. The report then took a very insightful turn relative to veterans' insights after Viet Nam.

In a footnote that caught Roger's attention immediately, the researchers noted that on 1 September 2009 the conservative commentator and social philosopher George Will turned against American involvement in Afghanistan in an article he wrote for the Washington Post. It was inferred that this was the end of solid backing for the wars in western Asia by any thinking conservative in the U.S. References to Viet Nam and Walter Cronkite were inevitable. Will made no mention of American veterans.

Since Viet Nam had been initially fought largely by unwilling conscripts and it had no immediate national defense rationale for the average American the common army draftee became a symbol of the frustration and hopelessness of the American veteran. He was soon to be seen as a hopeless and often homeless pawn of forces within American society that saw him as mostly purposeless and completely disposable.

At this point the American veteran had an awakening that had not been seen since the Bonus Army days of the 1930's. Viet Nam veterans such as Harvard educated naval officer John Kerry who was later to become a U.S. senator and presidential candidate turned the page on how American veterans behaved. He was a major force in civil disobedience by American veterans in protesting the American war machine and its involvement in fabricated wars. He would later run for president against a man who did not serve in Viet Nam, did not successfully attend his required Air National Guard drills but started two wars in Western Asia on a flag waving and pseudo-patriotic political platform. Things are not always logical.

The moral and social landscape had changed. Veteran social activism was born in a new way. And this time the veterans leading the movements were usually college graduates. They were now too smart and too well connected to be misled any longer by fat cat elites of the defense industries. It was now blatantly obvious that the working class who were unconnected were dying in large numbers to make the wealthy and protected even richer.

To make matters even worse for the war industries, by 1985 it had been found beyond a shadow of a doubt that the Gulf of Tonkin Incident, the very rationale for the initiation of the American involvement in the Viet Nam war, had been a fabrication of the Johnson Administration. The war had been based on a massive lie perpetuated by the White House and the Defense Department of the United States in order to get American involvement in that war accepted by the American people. American troops and sailors were sent to their deaths and received massive injuries based on a fraud.

The story was completely fabricated that a North Vietnamese communist gunboat had fired upon the USS Maddox (DD-731), an American destroyer on 2 August 1964 and also two days later. No such aggressive fire was encountered. But the Gulf of Tonkin Resolution was passed by congress on 7 August 1964 which brought U.S. forces into that far-off Asian war. A new generation of broken and abused American veterans was about to be born. They were born of a deliberate lie told by an American administration deciding that American interests would be best served by a war in Indochina.

The story here was like the phony story of the U.S.S. Maine being blown up in Havana Harbor, Cuba at 9:30 PM on 15 February 1898. The U.S. government blamed Spanish mines for the incident. The U.S. went to war with Spain over it. In actuality these legislators almost certainly knew that sea water had seeped into the battleship's boilers and blew the ship up. It was a common problem with early boiler driven ships at the turn of the 20th century. The American government was very aware of it but needed access to South American markets and Spain was blocking that access. The more the world turns, the more it is the same.

So now again in the 1960's the American family had been duped into sending sons and even some daughters into combat in a needless and phony war. This had been done before in the U.S. but never in the age of television. The playing field was now leveled and all Americans had access to basic facts like never before. The American veteran was for the first time in American history seen as a dupe of forces that did not care one way or another whether he lived or died. He would never fully trust his government again. This all played out on television every night around supper time on the east coast and late afternoon on the west coast in every American household with a television set.

The tone of the report was damning. It showed that it was now obvious that the American "government" was simply an arm of the military industrial complex and American veterans were just one more commodity to be taken off the shelf and used. Veterans would be used in any wartime scenario that the defense establishment could create in order to generate capital, protect overseas investments already in place or aggressively assert American influence in foreign markets.

For the first time in American history the "hero" of the American battlefield now clearly saw himself as the victim of American greed. He now recognized that he was a pawn in the hands of greater powers in the American economy than himself. He was essentially a dupe working as a heavy for multinational corporations. There was too much evidence to see this in any other way.

The authors pointed out that flag waving patriotism was no longer rational in this environment. When working class kids are killed for the bottom line in a ledger book held by a munitions company or a related industry, the social contract between the government and the veteran is severed. Going to war to protect "freedom" was now exposed for the fraud that it is.

The Viet Nam veteran had paid in his blood to open our minds and our eyes to the reality of modern warfare. There is no glory in dying to make a rich man even richer. Such is now the legacy of the American veteran. He is largely a dupe.

The report did not hold back. It was incredibly and startlingly clear in all its implications. Roger actually lost his breath several times while reading it. It held uncommon common sense. It was devastating in its blunt assessment of the cold realities inherent in a war-based economy.

This phase of the report ended with the listing of several civil disturbance incidents involving Viet Nam veterans. The third phase of the report would take into account veterans' issues from 1975 to the present day. Roger was fascinated. He did not know what to think. "Nothing was as it seems" he thought.

The overall casualties of various American wars had been horrendous. The ranks of American veterans had swollen to a demographic larger than the total populations of several small countries. The data was overpowering.

In World War II 16,112,566 American men and women served in uniform of which 671,846 were wounded and 291,557 died in battle.

In the Korean Conflict of just a few years later 5,720,000 American men and women served in uniform of which 103,284 were wounded and 33,741 were killed in combat.

In the Viet Nam War 8,744,000 Americans served in uniform of which 153,303 were wounded and 47,424 were killed directly on the battlefield or immediately thereafter.

The number of dead and wounded American veterans was horrific. The expense of taking adequate care of these people with shattered bodies, broken minds and crippled emotions was almost beyond calculation. The military industrial complex was shredding human lives at a rate unprecedented for any industry in the history of the nation. But veterans had long ago awakened to the horror. Recruiting goals were sometimes met and sometimes not met, but recruits saw themselves more and more as short term employees seeking educational benefits more than they saw themselves as careerists. This would later prove to be a problem for all concerned.

Roger finished reading the second part of the report and turned on the television. He watched the late night news and then went to sleep. He was in need of intimacy. He would need to find a girlfriend soon. Explaining his physical situation was always difficult to a prospective lover, but it had to be done if he was to ever have sex and physical closeness again. And he was determined to have at least that much companionship in his life. But it was never easy. His plumbing situation was always a difficult thing to explain. It was the price he was paying for his Army career.

V.
Life often changes

A New House, A New Girlfriend, A Great Cup of Coffee!

IT WAS TIME for Roger to leave his condo on the west side of Alexandria and move into his newly refurbished house in the Del Ray section of that city. His house was near his favorite coffee shop, the St. Elmo's Coffee Pub on Mount Vernon Avenue and it was run by a politically active woman named Nora who was a decent human being. He liked being in there. The atmosphere was just right. It was left wing Democrat country. That was always a good fit for Roger.

He kept his condo completely intact. He had his new home appointed throughout with new furniture and appurtenances from Ethan Allen furniture store. The whole place reeked of New England wealth in a low key way once one entered the home. Roger laughed at that because that was definitely not his background. But it was comfortable and showed that Roger had taste. Well actually, the young woman from Ethan Allen who Roger paid to furnish his home had taste. But who would know that but Roger?

His home smelled of fresh paint, new carpet and newly refinished wood. It had stained glass windows on the front door and a Bay window on the front of the house. It had a small yard that Roger paid a landscaper to keep meticulously neat and ordered. There was a statue of St. Francis of Assisi on top of a bird bath and near a bird feeder. Roger may not have been a practicing Catholic but hey! He needed a bird feeder on the front lawn to attract song birds and one could not go wrong with Saint Francis, right? At least that was his thinking anyway.

Roger's cocker spaniel needed more space and Roger placed an ad in the paper for anyone who was willing to make a home for the dog. An older woman from Prince William County who owned a couple of acres of ground asked for the dog and Roger agreed. The back yard in Del Ray was really not enough room. It was a good decision so Roger moved to Del Ray without the dog.

His next door neighbor was a kooky widow named Adriana Calavetti who was 45 and had the body of a 25 year old woman. Her husband had been an Alexandria Deputy Sherriff and he had died of throat cancer the year before. He left her his pension insurance and they had no children in their marriage and so they had a hefty savings account. They had invested heavily in land prior to his death and when the stock market crashed in the Fall of 2008 their holdings were largely intact. They did not lose any money and in fact even gained a little. This all allowed her to work for herself in an art studio that she now owned within walking distance of her home. She did not sell many pieces of art, but then she did not need to do so.

Adriana was a wealthy woman by the Del Ray standards of Alexandria. And she was pretty. Roger was always a sucker for dark women and Adriana Calavetti, the former Adriana Maria Vallochi, was a dark eyed, brunette Italian American beauty with a killer body, lots of money and her own business. She was a catch and that was for sure. She turned heads routinely on men who were twenty years younger than her. She had that kind of raw sexuality.

She was completely kooky though. Roger saw that immediately. She would tend to her garden for hours, especially after dinner when the sun was going down. She would wear sunglasses and a broad brimmed gardener's hat. She would dress up her dog with a kerchief around his neck and he had his own sunglasses. He was a Chihuahua named Cruz and she would walk him on a leash every night after gardening or before supper and he would bark, and shake at people in that way that Chihuahua's are known to shake. Roger could never figure that out about those Mexican dogs. Roger saw her often in the front yard and decided to call over one night about two weeks after he moved into the neighborhood.

"Hi! I am your new neighbor! I'm Roger Magritte. That is a beautiful garden you have!" he offered. "Hi! I am Adriana Calavetti.

I live here." Roger laughed to himself but said nothing. "Ahhh...yes...
I know. How long have you lived here in the neighborhood?" Roger
asked. "Oh, a very long time" Adriana countered.

That was a pleasant answer but did not really tell Roger anything.
"I mean how many years have you lived here?" Roger asked. Adriana
put down her gardening trowel and took off her sunglasses to show
big and brown and beautiful eyes. She walked over to the fence that
separated their properties and stood near it to talk.

She thought deeply about Roger's question and finally said
"Well, my late husband and I moved into this house after the former
tenant moved out. His name was Mr. Jenson. He was an old man. He
lived here from 1948 until we moved into the house in 2000. So we
have lived here since July of 2000, so I guess that is over seven years."
Roger laughed to himself again. It was July of 2009. That would make
it nine years. But he said nothing to Adriana. Her beauty was captivat-
ing him and the point did not seem to be so important to him right
now. "So she is a little weak at arithmetic, was that really so important?" he thought to himself.

"Well, I just wanted to say hello. I see you out here often and I
want to be a good neighbor" Roger offered. "Oh yes, I need a good
neighbor. Where do you work?" Adriana asked Roger. "Oh I don't
work I am a disabled veteran and a retired Army helicopter pilot so
I have a couple of pensions. I spend my day as best I can by doing
constructive things for veterans and generally trying to keep out of
trouble." Adriana laughed.

"Yes, I always seem to be in some sort of trouble. It seems to
follow me you know!" Now Roger laughed, "Oh I doubt that! You
are too pretty to be in trouble much!" Now Adriana laughed again
and walked back to her gardening tools and shot Roger a look over
her shoulder. It was a "come hither" look. Roger gulped. This could
be dangerous. But he liked that. Afet and he had parted ways months
before. He was getting a bit itchy. This was a good start on a new direction in life. "A very good start!" he thought to himself.

The next day Roger spent the morning at St. Elmo's Coffee Pub
just four blocks away from his home. He read the paper, had two cups

of coffee, sat outside to watch the people walk up Mount Vernon Avenue and just before he got up to go home, Adriana walked into the coffee shop. She saw him and waved. Roger waved back and before you know it, she was sitting at his table on the sidewalk in front of the coffee shop. Roger was completely taken-in by her beauty. She really was an attractive woman and she looked much younger than the mid-forties which was her age.

"Is this what you do every morning Roger?" she asked.

"No. Most times I write an article for a disabled veterans website and then I exercise and then I sometimes visit Walter Reed hospital but lately I have not been doing that. I just needed a morning off, so I walked over here. I like this place."

She nodded, "I like it too!" she gushed.

"Roger lets go on a date. I have not had a date in almost a year."

Roger chuckled. She certainly was not a wallflower. "Okay. Let's go on a date then! When and where should we go on our date?" he asked.

"I don't know" Adriana countered, "I will let you know."

With that she got up, left his table and just walked away. No goodbye, no "I will see you later", not anything. She just walked away. Roger smiled. She really was different. But it was in a kooky harmless way. He liked it.

"I guess I have to wait until Adriana tells me where and when we are going on our date" he lightheartedly muttered to himself. Yes, she was very different.

Roger went home after another hour of reading the paper at St. Elmo's Coffee Pub and then he decided to lay down for a nap. After only a few minutes he heard a rap on his front door. He got up and opened the door to find Adriana. She simply walked into the house before Roger could even say "hello."

"My, what a nice job you have done on this home!" she gushed. Before Roger could say anything to her she offered "Roger I have decided that we should go to dinner at the Evening Star restaurant just down the street from here for our first date." Roger laughed, "Okay. That would be fine. What time should I pick you up?" he asked.

"I will pick you up at seven o'clock tonight" Adriana said. "I will be wearing shorts and a t shirt. It's hot. So shorts and a t-shirt will be fine for you also" Adriana told him.

Roger said "shorts and a t-shirt it is!" And with that Adriana turned and without another word she walked back home across Roger's yard. "I guess hello and goodbye are just not the sort of thing she does!" Roger whispered quietly to himself.

That night they had a nice dinner at the Evening Star. The meals were always prepared with care at the restaurant. Roger appreciated this since he lived alone and prepared most of his meals in his microwave oven. Fine dining was not usually something Roger did often. The conversation was pleasant and Adriana beguiled Roger with her dark beauty and quirky ways. Finally she said, "I think we should spend the night together."

Roger choked on his coffee and said "Excuse me?" and Adriana repeated her thought to him "I think we should sleep together tonight. It has been a long term since I slept with someone and I would like to sleep with you tonight." Roger's jaw literally dropped.

"Ahhm....ummmm...oh...okay, sure!" Roger finally uttered. "What time should I expect you?" Roger asked.

Adriana said, "Well, walk me home. I will give Cruz his evening walk, make a few phone calls to friends, take a shower and then come over to spend the night. Are you sure it's okay Roger?" Adriana asked wide-eyed.

"That would be just fine Adriana. I will be waiting." They finished diner and walked home. Roger took a shower, put on a fresh pair of gym shorts and a t-shirt and turned on the television. Within a half hour of sitting down, Adriana was at the front door. Roger opened it and she just walked in, unceremoniously without saying anything, as was her way.

"Well, are you ready to go to sleep Roger?" Roger chuckled.

"Ahh...ummmm...Adriana it is only 8:45 and I usually stay up watching the news until 10:00. Is that okay with you?" Adriana said, "Well actually, I am kind of tired, so I am going to bed now. Where is your bedroom?"

Roger was now completely overwhelmed with the extreme zaniness of his neighbor and potential lover, so he simply pointed to the bedroom and watched Adriana walk quickly into it. Roger walked back over to the television and watched the news for another half hour. He turned off the lights in the house and went to bed.

Adriana was naked, her incredibly fit and athletic body lying on top of the bed, and she was asleep. She had simply taken her clothes off, laid down on the bed and went to sleep.

Roger stared at her beautiful feminine form for a full three minutes in the moonlit dark of his bedroom. He closed the shades and the room went dark. He then took his clothes off and went to pull down the bed clothes and realized that he could not do that without waking Adriana, so he did that.

He touched her shoulder and rocked her gently and said, "Adriana, you have to wake up so that we can get under the covers." She moaned and then simply stood up next to the bed while Roger pulled down the cover and the sheet. She got back into bed, turned on her side and was asleep again in less than ten seconds.

"This is one different babe!" Roger thought to himself.

They slept naked together, with Roger holding Adriana all night, until morning when she awoke about 5:00 a.m. She woke Roger up with a kiss on his lips. "Good morning good looking!" she said. "Shall we make love?"

Roger awoke with a start at the kiss and the offer of sex. He was now wide awake. The moment of truth had arrived.

"Ahh...ummm...Adriana we have to talk about that. You see, I am a little different sexually" Roger offered.

"You are gay?" she asked.

"No!" said Roger.

"You are bisexual and you do not find me attractive?" she asked again.

"NO!" Roger said, his voice rising.

"You are.." Roger cut her off in mid-sentence.

"Adriana, I have some physical issues that we need to talk about before we can get sexual."

"I am listening" she said. She had an odd look of curious panic on her face.

"Who is this guy?" she thought to herself.

"Well, you know that I am a totally disabled veteran, right?" Roger asked.

"Yes" she whispered slowly with a look of concern on her face.

"Well" Roger continued, "you see, I have several injuries and one of them is that my testicles were crushed in an explosion when a rocket propelled grenade exploded inside my helicopter. So I had to have my testicles removed. I have foam testicles, see?" and with that he took her hand and placed it on his scrotum.

She felt the foam testicles.

"You look fine!" she said with an odd look on her face.

"I know, that is the point of the foam balls in my sac. But I have to do certain things to get ready for sex. I have an implant, a mechanical device in my abdomen and in my penis so that I can get erect. I will show you how it works."

And with that, Roger reached down to his scrotum and started squeezing with Adriana watching. Within a few seconds his penis started to grow as the hydraulics started to work on giving him an erection. Adriana's eyes grew as big as half dollars. Roger could see that clearly in the early morning light.

"Wow!" she said with astonishment. "You have a bionic penis? Cool! I have never been screwed by Robocop before!" she said with excitement.

Roger laughed. "Well, it is a little tricky at first and it will probably feel different to you. I cannot have a wet orgasm but I can have a dry orgasm, of sorts, that more or less feels natural to me. I am not sure whether you can achieve orgasm or not with my John Henry working on full hydraulic, but we can try!" Roger said hopefully.

"The things one learns unexpectedly!" Adriana said to Roger with astonishment in her voice. Then she smiled and kissed him hard on the lips.

Within a minute they were having intercourse. Adriana obviously enjoyed it and achieved climax within a couple of minutes. "That was great!" she said.

Roger smiled. "Yeah, my government reconstructed penis might actually be better than the original model. Who would have guessed?" They both laughed at his comment and then lay in each other's arms another ten minutes before getting up to shower and eat something for breakfast. Roger made scrambled eggs and sausage in his t shirt and boxer shorts. Adriana liked that he was taking care of her. A major obstacle had just been overcome and Roger was at ease now. Adriana watched him closely.

"So you get involved in veterans' issues to fill your time Roger?" she asked over her post breakfast cup of tea, sitting at Roger's dining room table with his robe over her beautiful body.

"Yes, it is how I fill my time constructively" he offered.

"Like what issues?" she asked. "Tell me about what you are involved with now."

Roger smiled and said "This can get awful boring honey. Other than veterans' themselves, not many people are interested in veterans' issues."

"Try me" she said.

So Roger started to tell her what he had been recently doing with veterans. He told her about his visits to Walter Reed and about the recent tragedy. He told her about the fact that he could no longer visit there so he was filling his time with writing for the Veterans Now website and then she asked him to be specific about those issues. So Roger told her more as he sipped his coffee.

"Well, every disabled veteran is going to approach his or her view of the Department of Veterans Affairs in a slightly different way. We all see the agency differently."

She looked at him and then asked, "Well how do you see them?"

"Well" Roger offered. "They are the second biggest agency in government, right next to the Department of Defense. They try to handle the various medical and the life-needs problems of the 23 million veterans that are alive today. It cannot be an easy job. To simply say that they are all jackasses is not fair and does not really get near the solution to any problems. It just causes rancor and there is already too much of that."

"So are they all jackasses?" Adriana asked.

"No, of course not, I am sure that all of them try as hard as they can to help as many veterans as they can on a daily basis. But 22.9 million people is roughly 8% of the general population. And a large number of these people are old, confused, in great need on many levels and without real support from family or friends"

He took another gulp of coffee and continued. "At least twelve hundred veterans die a week in this country and the number is rapidly growing. Most of the dying are from the World War Two and Korean War era. But some younger veterans die from drug abuse, suicide, complications from combat, mental illness, alcoholism and drug addiction and many other related problems that come with combat or just Service experience. It is not a pretty picture."

"So then where is the problem if the bureaucracy is that big and they are willing to help?" Adriana asked.

Roger looked away for a few seconds and then said "It is the shear size of the problems and the number of people who have them that makes this thing so hard to handle. Initially these are truly the most injured, the most psychically broken, the most emotionally destroyed people on the planet. The agency has to find a way to give them back their lives. Sometimes they can. Sometimes they cannot."

" And there are some problems that are systemic, some that may or may not be deliberate and some that just never seem to go away, no matter what their root cause may be."

"Like what would those problems be?" she asked Roger.

"Well, for instance, the D.V.A. is supposed to exist to help the veteran navigate a difficult life after the service or to reconstruct his or her life after a combat experience or a combat injury. But in fact what has happened over the generations is that an adversarial relationship has evolved between the individual veteran and the D.V.A. probably because disabled veterans are so expensive and are seen as an entitled group, mostly by Republicans and Blue Dog Democrats. Like all seemingly entitled groups, the scope of the entitlement is seen as too large, too broad and too generous by the more conservative groups in American politics. It is odd that this is exactly the group of American politicians that claims to speak for veterans. Frankly, it is a set up. The fox is guarding the henhouse here."

Adriana's eyes widened at that last statement. "Go on!" she said.

"Well to put this briefly, I guess I should tell you what many of us who work with veterans every day see as the main issues of contention and that need immediate attention by General Shinseki. He was just appointed by President Obama this year to be the new Secretary of the D.V.A. We all have high hopes for him."

"I hear good things about him" Adriana offered.

Roger countered. "Yes, we all look to him because we need to turn a corner in this country relative to veterans' issues. And he is a strong enough man to make that happen. But there are so many issues that need to be handled that he may not be able to get it done. The job is enormous and the resistance that he will encounter as he moves forward for change will be huge. The old guard within the D.V.A will fight him every step of the way. They seem to see their primary mission as stopping the growth of entitlements, not as helping veterans."

"So what has to change, in your opinion?" Adriana asked.

Roger took his time with this explanation since it was central to what he was telling Adriana about veterans' problems.

"Well, a lot of things need to change and change quickly. A lot of relatively minor things are indicators of problems with much larger implications. For instance, a large percentage of D.V.A. correspondence is signed by people who are very junior relative to the decision maker on that issue. This is important because responsibility cannot be delegated. However, if the decision maker does not sign the correspondence he can always claim that he did not know what the letter said. He can claim ignorance and I believe that too often these high level supervisors do this on purpose to evade ultimate responsibility when things go wrong. Theoretically this cannot be done. But it happens every day."

Roger continued with a sound of tiredness in his voice. "This procedure goes directly against the D.V.A. Operations Manual, M-1. Some issues like status reports to congress and negative decisions on various disability cases cannot be legally delegated to someone lower in the chain of command, yet it happens often. This speaks either to administrative sloppiness, incompetence, inability to take responsibility for the decision being made or all of these. This is not a small matter."

Adriana asked "How often is this done?"

Roger thought about it and said, "No one really knows exactly. How could we? But it has to be investigated because of the obvious implications for greater abuse that is seems to indicate. It happens enough that it has been noticed."

"I see what you are saying. Other problems that worry you?" she asked.

Roger continued, "Every time the D.V.A. investigates itself it comes back with a response that seems to assume that there is an endless timeline with which it should be allowed to fix any problem. It's as if they think veterans will live for two hundred years and five or ten years to fix a problem is a reasonable timeline. It is not a reasonable timeline. These people are dying at about twelve hundred a week and that number grows substantially every six months or so. When the D.V.A. takes ten years to fix a problem well over six hundred thousand veterans will die before that solution is initially brought online. And this is the norm for the D.V.A, not the exception."

"Wow!" Adriana said, "So nobody watches? Nobody has oversight of these people?"

"It's a little more complicated than that." Roger sighed.

He continued on with his explanation of the veteran's disability situation. "There are several House and Senate committees and subcommittees that will get involved when both veteran and active duty service issues intersect. So already you are talking about at least one legislative year wasted while options are reviewed. And that assumes that a study has been done on the problem and the report accepted. If no study has been done and one needs to be initiated, approved, completed and delivered, we can be talking about a five or six year gap between identifying the problem and everyone involved agreeing on a solution. At the very least, a half million more veterans will be dead by then."

"I am beginning to see what you are saying here. The resources are not enough to handle the load." Adriana was paying close attention. Roger liked that.

"Well, yes and no. If they really wanted to see radical change, they could do it in two years if they had everybody within the agency onboard. But they do not." Roger said that last comment with great emphasis.

"D.V.A. is seen by veterans largely as an agency that enshrines process over results, procedures over assistance and rules and regulations over true service in the best of senses. There is an ongoing problem with the Inspector General's office at the D.V.A. and the various security arms of the agency 'investigating' totally disabled veterans who are receiving a pension for PTSD. They believe that many if not most of them are faking. I frankly have no problem with the D.V.A. investigating the medical claims of any veteran receiving a pension but that has to be done by medical people, not policemen or security types. Security people, policeman of any type and inspector general's staff are not medical people and are not qualified to look at a medical file and make a medical determination. Simple common sense would tell someone that."

Roger gulped and continued. He was getting emotional. "Yet there is a 100% disabled veteran imprisoned in Wisconsin right now because the regional D.V.A. Inspector General has decided that he faked his PTSD disability symptoms. His name is Robert Anthon and he has been raped in prison and has received death threats there. Many of us believe that this is not an isolated case. According to some credible reports, the D.V.A. has brought charges against roughly two thousand disabled veterans whom they claim are faking PTSD symptoms."

Roger stopped talking, looked down and caught his breath and then looked up and continued. "But it gets worse, much worse. And to add insult to injury federal law requires that all disability pensions for a disabled veteran must be stopped if he is imprisoned for more than thirty days! That more or less denies any veteran receiving a pension the right to exercise civil disobedience without losing his livelihood since those jail terms for protesting are usually ninety days if the cops can get trumped up charges accepted as real by a judge. His dissenting voice is then effectively silenced. Many of us think that this is not an oversight; that it is done specifically to effectively silence us from speaking out. We believe that this is deliberate coercion for us to keep silent. It is simply wrong!" Roger was now red in the face.

Adriana could see how shaken he was at the thought of this perceived travesty. He was visibly angry.

Roger stopped talking for a full minute. Then he spoke quietly to her. "Are you sure you want me to continue?" Roger asked. "I can get a little carried away emotionally with this stuff!" he said.

"Please go on" Adriana asked.

Roger spoke slowly and deliberately now. "Well, then there is the issue of inadequate compensation. A totally disabled veteran who receives full disability makes less money in a year than the average city bus driver. The money received for "full disability" is a joke. He or she cannot buy a home, he or she can barely support a family if he or she has one and his or her quality of life is minimal at best. The archconservative forces in America's business community and political spheres have kept total disability pensions so low that they are not adequate to fully support a veteran. They always claim that the expense is too high."

"Expense? Did anyone ask about the expense that the totally disabled veteran is paying with mental health issues, lost limbs, internal injuries, broken marriages, chronic medical issues and generally low quality of life? The answer here is 'no'. Even the congressionally mandated Veterans' Benefit Commission report delivered to Congress in October of 2007 talked about an immediate need to increase veterans' pensions by 25%. Nothing has been done. And trust me, veterans have taken notice. I would not rule out violence here."

At that statement Adriana shot him a look. "You cannot be serious! Violence?"

Roger looked at her for a long time and then said. "Adriana, you have to understand how betrayed these veterans, especially the combat veterans and the most seriously injured feel. They have been deceived by the major veterans' organizations and the D.V.A. for generations. They are not stupid."

"Their present level of support is estimated by some experts to be at least 40% below where it needs to be to achieve parity with their working peers. They understand that they are seen as an expense that the nation would rather do without. The potential for violence here is very, very real. A man who has nothing to lose by getting violent is prone to take that action."

Adriana watched Roger's face register real pain as he spoke.

He continued. "The pensions are meager, the quality of life is just above the bare existence level and these men and women are many times mentally unstable due to combat or traumatic service experiences and have severely broken lives. Oftentimes all that they had prior to service life or their traumatic injuries is gone. Their family, friends, sanity, the ability to work, the chance to be part of the larger community are all gone."

Adriana saw the deep pain register on his face. He was having trouble breathing.

Roger caught himself and turned away from her. He then continued. "Unless you are part of this hopeless situation, it is impossible to understand the depths that it will drive a human being into desperation. Many see violence as their only way to make a statement, to be heard, to stop the personal pain of being betrayed by a nation that simply wants them to go away. To state this simply, these people do not matter to the larger community that they live within anymore. And they know it."

Adriana's jaw dropped slightly, then she said, "I had no idea!"

Roger said, "No one does. Disabled veterans are often the sick uncle in the upstairs' back bedroom, the drunken and armless or legless son in the basement apartment, the crazy aunt who has a drug problem and who lives in an apartment above the liquor store and the loony guy next door who stays to himself and only comes out at night to sit with his dogs in the backyard."

"They were driven into a broken life by the rigors of the service and it was made worse if they saw intense combat or some other traumatic service experience that put their life in danger. They were broken by the experience and then often largely ignored by the system of "caretakers" that were supposed to help them heal from their barbaric experiences with incredible violence and unspeakable actions that they were forced to perform in order to stay alive. The bottom line here is this: no one heals from combat or action in a life threatening situation. The best that they can hope for is to develop coping skills that will allow them a life path that resembles something normal."

Roger then lowered his voice and looked Adriana in the eyes. He spoke softly now.

"They were driven insane by national indifference to their plight and then despised for their neediness by a country that worships self-starters and high energy self-reliant mythological figures. A man with a broken mind, a shattered body and little hope has no illusions. "Put it behind you and move on" means nothing to a man in that position."

"The American dream will escape him without enormous help from the community at large. And more often than not that help is given grudgingly by a federal agency that is more concerned with catching potential cheaters than shouldering its responsibilities to help the shattered minds and broken hearts that have seen unspeakable violence."

"It is a situation that every veteran knows about and every disabled veteran knows intimately. When the D.V.A. is at its worst, when it is a mere bureaucracy attempting to exert the least amount of effort in order to move on to the next shattered mind and body with the minimum amount of resources expended, the ideals and dreams of this republic are a cruel joke to those who have paid the highest price for its continued existence. "

Roger then looked off and out his sliding door window into the backyard. He then spoke to Adriana a telling remark. "Once a veteran, especially a disabled and unstable veteran, realizes that he has been left behind by his "unit" to die in the cold and mud of a different kind of "battlefield terrain" filled with an uncaring population something inside of him twists and cannot be put back in place."

"Once he or she realizes that the rules and regulations governing veterans' affairs have been put there to protect the tax payer from the full force of his needs he starts to understand the cruel joke that life has played upon him. He is not a hero at that point, he is a buffoon. And the sad part is that he totally understands the process now. He can never be the same after that. He knows too much now."

Roger swallowed hard and his eyes welled up with tears.

Roger voice was filled with sadness. "He went to war, he sacrificed himself in action or combat, he got hurt or his mind was broken. And now the system laughs at him for his sacrifice by its indifference and its cold refusal to give him his just reward for offering a life for the safety of the republic. He would rather be dead than to live with what he now knows."

"He was used by people who would never see combat in order to make them richer and fatter and even more removed from their responsibilities to the republic. He is no better than a serf. He was thrown into the fray by a laughing and completely uncaring, manor-born, landed-gentry class of elites who used him to increase the size of their portfolios. He was totally expendable. And now that he is broken, he simply does not matter. He is an expense that they can do without."

"Oh Roger, I am so sorry!" Adriana said. There was a tear in her eye.

"So am I" said Roger.

VI.
Old friends are the best sounding boards

Viktor and Roger Talk
All Weekend

ROGER DROVE DOWN to Hartford, Kentucky from Northern Virginia to see his childhood friend, Father Viktor Zobias who was now the primary man in his order for screening and testing new applicants. Viktor's job was to visit any American or foreign born applicant for the Glenmary Fathers and Brothers in his home town and interview family and friends to see if the man was a good match for the society.

Roger and Viktor visited with each other about every three years and the two of them would talk for a day or two. They checked in with each other every now and then by phone to see how life was treating their old friend. It was now something of a ritual event. Roger looked forward to it.

Since Viktor's parents were European like Roger's and since Viktor had known Roger since childhood, he usually referred to him by his given Belgian name Rogier. Roger simply called Viktor "Vic." After a nine hour drive, Roger arrived at the House of Formation for Glenmary and Viktor was at the door to meet him. He had suffered some terrible health problems in the past twenty years and he walked with a cane, was more than a bit overweight and had already had a quadruple bi-pass as a young man in his forties.

But Father Viktor was still hanging on to life. "I have too much to do yet" he would often tell his friends when the subject of poor health or death might come up in conversation. He had an incredibly strong will to serve his God. He had been like that since childhood. It was the strongest sense of Godliness Rogier Magritte had ever encountered in his lifetime. This was one very unique man. Roger was blessed to have him as a friend, and he knew that. He knew from his childhood and never changed his opinion.

Roger pulled into the parking lot of the Glenmary House of Formation and Viktor was there waiting. The two men laughed at the balding heads, graying hair and extra weight each had now manifested since their last meeting and embraced. Since both men had spent most of their childhoods in the homes of the other they were casually acquainted with the family languages of their friend's family. Roger greeted Viktor in Lithuanian and asked how he was doing.

"Viktoras! Kaip tu gyveni? Tai taip malonu matyti tave!" Viktor responded in Belgian a similar greeting to Rogier.

"Rogier! Bondjoû! Cmint daloz ?" and the two men laughed. Their accents were horrible but they always attempted the other's ancestral language when they met. It was a tradition. They walked with their arm around each other into the house, Viktor limping and walking with a cane. Life had been very tough for Father Viktor Zobias of the Glenmary Fathers. It was a price he gladly paid to be a priest.

Viktor had seen academic trouble in seminary, severe health problems in priesthood and he had seen two churches deliberately burned to the ground in the Deep South where Glenmary ministered to scattered Catholics in the rural areas. He had spent his early priesthood mostly in his car, driving from county to county throughout rural Georgia and Arkansas and Kentucky visiting a Catholic population that might number 60 people in three counties. He had been accused of witchcraft by fundamentalist preachers who feared his influence with the thousands of Latin American migrant workers with whom he came in contact on a yearly basis.

He had been accused of debauchery by Protestant ministers who feared his humble demeanor and obvious Christian beliefs. He had been accused by unstable parishioners of meddling in family affairs, in one case, by a deranged son of a murderer who would routinely threaten his life at the communion rail upon receiving communion.

He had been called upon by his order several times to help decide the fate of several priests and brothers who had molested children. He had lost his father at twelve years old and his mother to whom he was very close in his late forties. He had worked very hard his entire life to be a good priest.

And he was a good priest.

And like all good priests he now had very few worldly possessions to show for his service to his God. He was the finest man that Roger ever knew and he was completely ordinary in all his ways, except for his spirit. That was quite special. Roger cherished their friendship. It was good to see Viktor again.

They entered the house and Roger saw several postulants, some American, some Africans and two Asians. Glenmary had just started accepting overseas vocations a few years before. Not many Americans seemed interested in a life of poverty and service to the rural Catholic disenfranchised relative to past generations of Catholics. Viktor said that things were looking up however. More men were entering Glenmary that upcoming year than had entered in a generation. Viktor seemed very happy as a priest, although he found this assignment quite taxing and longed for parish work. He talked about his present assignment as they sat down to eat supper.

Roger listened attentively and realized that there were literally hundreds of people that depended upon Viktor every week for spiritual guidance. It must have been quite humbling to be in that position Roger thought. But when he asked Viktor about that, Vic said that he loved his role as pastor and priest. He said that it defined who he was. Roger did not know what defined him. But who would know that on a deep level but a priest?

As the evening wore on Viktor and Roger sat on the porch of the old house and talked about their lives. Viktor was happy and content with his life. He had done what he had wanted to do since early childhood, he had become a priest. Roger was nowhere near as happy as Viktor and he had become a soldier by default. He simply just sort of "found himself" in the army. He never intended to stay and make a career of it. It just worked out that way.

And like Viktor, Roger now had chronic and severe health problems but for very different reasons. Viktor had health problems because of a hard life in poverty and difficult work while trying to help marginalized people who had no voice in society. He had lost his health in the service of his God. Roger had health problems because he had spent a career in military hardship. He had spent his life training to kill people and sometimes actually killing them. The irony was not lost on Roger.

Eventually they got around to discussing the specific details of their lives. Viktor was spending his days making sure that the newly arrived applicants for the order understood the difficult life that they were about to enter. He spent his days introducing them to the realities of service to the migrant workers, the poor farmers, the Catholics and non-Catholics alike that lived in the rural South where they served. They would serve them all and oftentimes be roundly hated for it. He had to make sure that they understood their calling and were prepared to be tested at every turn.

This was not an easy thing to teach and an even harder thing to learn. Learning to be a priest, accepting one's role as "alter Christus" was a life-changing thing. The terrible clarity of mortality and the crushing realities of the poverty often evident in the rural South and the limited time and resources available to deal with all of it made a Glenmary's life a sharply focused attempt at temporary sanity in a permanently damaged world. The very best people in life always seemed to be treated the worst by life. It is just the way it is on a spiritual journey and Viktor was proof of this axiom.

As for Roger, he told Viktor about his sporadic love life, his physical ailments and his constant boxing matches with the Department of Veterans Affairs to get things straightened out not only for himself but for other veterans. Viktor was impressed with Roger's desire to serve. It had to be a good thing Viktor told him, and it was very rare. And Viktor would know. And he told Roger that. Roger thanked him for that kindness.

"So, exactly what are you involved with these days relative to these young veterans?" Viktor asked. Roger laughed, "That would take a very long time to explain Vic!" Now Viktor laughed. "I have the time. Start at the beginning." So Roger told him.

"Well, they are young and many of them have multiple amputations. I merely lost my nuts and have internal injuries and it is not so evident, so they rarely see me as a peer in misery. I do what I can to give them hope, but it is usually not enough."

" Sometimes they commit suicide to escape the horrible pain of realizing that they will live the rest of their long lives horribly maimed. Very often the wives take off. Sometimes the children go with the wives, sometimes not. As bad as their physical pain may be, their mental pain, their anger, their desperation is often worse. It is all wrapped up in their image of themselves I think."

"It is hard for them to see themselves as sexually attractive young men when their limbs are missing, half their face has been blown off or their mental capacity is diminished due to brain injuries from an explosion. They might be seriously injured but they are not seriously stupid. They see what is going on around them and are powerless to change it in many cases."

"How do you deal with it, the sexual image and all?" Viktor asked. Roger chuckled, "Why Father, I never thought you would ask me such a question!" the two friends laughed at that.

"Well, if you must know, I deal with it as best I can. It is a day by day thing. I usually have a girlfriend and she is open to learning how to make love to a man with a half-bionic penis and two foam balls for nuts, and it usually works out, at least for awhile." Viktor laughed, "Well, I suppose we are all struggling to get through the day! Day after day after day is the struggle. But it must be very hard for someone with such disabilities."

Roger thought about that. Then he said "Well, yes and no. Who does not struggle with something? If you can remember that, your problems can be put into a context of the larger human struggle to make sense out of a human life. Some of the wealthiest, most privileged people on the Earth are some of the most miserable. Just look at the papers every day. They are filled with stories of rock stars and multi millionaire sports stars and media people going from marriage to marriage, entering one drug rehab after another, killing themselves, going to prison for sociopathic behavior. No. Privilege is not what makes someone happy" Roger said.

Viktor laughed again. "Oh! And what does make a human being happy?" he asked Roger.

Roger thought for a half minute and then said, "I think it is a life with a purpose. The purpose does not have to be a particularly high purpose but it has to involve getting out of one's self and serving the interests of other people. It has to be selfless to some degree, even if it is only to a small degree. I happen to be a totally disabled veteran myself, so when I serve their interests' I serve my own at the same time. It is not as selfless as it looks!" The two friends sat quietly for a few minutes. Roger then spoke again.

"Sometimes the situation with these young people is so severe that you wonder whether or not they would have been better off dead. It is a hard question to ponder and even a harder one to answer. But they are not dead, they are alive, and they must be serving some purpose. The trick here is to get them to see that. It is not always possible. I try . I always try. It is my duty. It is my life now. I try to get them to see that their lives mean something, even in their brokenness, their half witted and confused, medicated, poverty stricken, hopelessness that often pervades their thinking."

"They are still young men and women. They still matter to me, to their families and to those others who have a sense of what they have seen, what they have suffered. That is not true for all Americans, that is probably not even true for most Americans. But some Americans know what they have been through and they are grateful for their sacrifice. That has to mean something to them." Roger and Viktor were quiet for a long time.

"You know Vic, a totally disabled veteran in the summer of 2009 rates a monthly payment of $2,673 dollars a month at the basic rate. That equals a tax free payment of $32,076 dollars a year. It would be $2,932 a month if he has a wife and a child. If you add in what he would pay in taxes for that amount of money it is about $39,000 dollars a year more or less. It is an insult. Americans should be ashamed of themselves."

"A typical New York City bus driver makes a median income in the summer of 2009 of about $3,900 dollars a month. That is about $47,000 dollars a year, give or take a couple of thousand dollars or so. This kid that is seriously disabled because his government sent him into harm's way or put him in danger somehow or broke his health does not make that much money. He does not make even near that much. It isn't quite fair is it?"

Roger looked at his friend. His friend could see the anger in the veteran's face and he said nothing.

"Let me draw a picture for you. A young nineteen year old kid enlists in the army. He goes to basic training, comes home on leave for two weeks, goes to advanced infantry training and then heads off to Iraq or Afghanistan. Five months later he gets his arms blown off just above the elbow while on a night patrol. The explosion comes from a bomb planted by the roadside by an Iraqi or Afghani or a Muslim foreign fighter who sees himself as a freedom fighter against the "American crusaders" who he believes are attacking Islam."

"The kid is lucky, his unit gets him out to a field hospital and he gets surgery before he bleeds to death. He spends two months in a hospital in Germany getting stabilized and medicated and then gets flown home to the U.S. and gets sent to Walter Reed Medical Center in Washington D.C. to recuperate and gets fitted with prosthetic arms and learns how to use them."

"More often than not, if he has a girlfriend, she is now long gone. He knows why. He is no fool. So now he is twenty years old. He is a high school graduate, he has no arms from the elbows down, he needs prosthetic devices to eat, scratch his head, go to the bathroom and just about everything else and he will live another sixty or seventy years like this."

"For his sacrifice he is going to be paid for the rest of his life a monthly salary much less than the median income of a New York City bus driver. Now, I have nothing against New York City bus drivers, I am sure that they are fine people. But something is way out of whack here. Something is terribly unjust. The scales are not balanced at all here. And trust me, the kid knows this. And so do all of his friends in the amputee wards and the various veterans' hospitals around the country."

Roger continued. "And it's not only the combat veterans. Plenty of men and women just simply get worn down from years of hard service life. In the service there is always too much too do and too little time to do it with too few people to safely complete the mission. That is true even in the peacetime armed forces. It is just the nature of the beast. And that constant pressure breaks people's health."

"When people are put under that kind of stress for years and years, the human personality degrades, judgment weakens, a person's health breaks and chronic medical problems appear. It is just inevitable. I have seen it in fellow soldiers over and over again during my service career."

He added "and then there is the compensation for all of this. It is too small, delivered too late and the responsible agencies initiate the delivery of the money too slowly in order to have any impact. The bottom line here is that the veteran is not compensated properly or in a timely manner." He then grunted a sort of sarcastic sigh that Viktor understood immediately was the sound of incredulity.

Roger looked off and then returned with his line of thought. "And it really is not that hard to fix. All of these bills governing veterans issues that are needed to fix the source, 38 Code of Federal Regulations, can take years to get to a vote before they go through several committees and finally reach the floor for a vote. Hundreds of thousands of veterans die in those years prior to the vote. All kinds of things could be done to help veterans right now."

Roger was highly animated now. "A tax exemption could be almost immediately voted upon by Congress to exclude totally disabled veterans of both schedule rated and individually unemployable types, from federal taxes. The president could introduce that change to the tax code in less than a month. That would free up thousands of dollars a year almost immediately for totally disabled veterans to use for quality of life issues. That could be done and finalized in the next sixty days. But it won't be. Why? Because there is no political will to be fair to these young people. "

Roger then looked directly at Viktor. "And other things could be done. Totally disabled veterans could be excluded from college and university and training school tuition charges by offering the schools a federal tax credit or federal monies or credits of some other type for every totally disabled veteran that matriculated there. Individually unemployable disabled veterans should be allowed to work and earn more than poverty level wages. As it is now, if they work and earn more in one year than the level of earnings for poverty level for one person, their pension stops! It is insane!"

"These IU disabled veterans are doomed to live their lives in either abject poverty in order to receive a small pension or else they sit at home watching television all day in order to preserve their small pension and the health benefits that go with a totally disabled rating. They often hate their lives. They are damned if they do work and damned if they do not work. What kind of system is that?"

Roger looked at Viktor like a man who hardly believed what he himself was saying.

Viktor just looked away and said nothing. He felt that Roger needed to continue. He could see the tears in his eyes. Roger continued.

"You see, in the end, its all about money. Somebody somewhere so many years ago figured out the cost of a twenty year old losing both of his arms and figured out to the penny what the nation owed that kid in pension money. I am here to tell you, this is a blatant and obscene cruel joke. The kid cannot buy a home, raise a family or even live like a middle class American on his basic pension at the current rates. If he had lost his arms in a traffic accident and he sued the responsible party he would be awarded millions. What does the U.S. government give him? It gives him less than a yearly wage for a Big Apple bus driver."

"And then it wants him to be grateful and thankful for the benefit he receives from the nation that sent him into harm's way in the first place for foggy reasons, with no clear mission in order to protect the interests of the wealthy class. He was sent into combat to ensure that overseas markets were open to American business giants. It is really that simple and that ugly. It is a downright crime and it's immoral. In fact it is an insult." Roger choked up.

Viktor finally uttered after a minute of silence. "So what is the answer?"

Roger said, "the answer? There is no answer. No amount of money in the world can make up for what he has lost. The government knows that and it takes full advantage of the fact. The government is calling all the shots here. If this was a lawsuit in court for damages due to injury, the government would be bankrupt. However, the current amount of total disability payment is a cruel joke. Something needs to be done to make the scales more balanced."

"Totally disabled veterans are being raped by the very government that disabled them in the first place. And the really dangerous part of all of this is that as every day goes by, more and more disabled veterans realize what is happening. Things are actually starting to get quite dangerous. Veterans are openly talking about violence."

Viktor looked far away and said in a quiet voice. "Life really isn't fair is it?"

"No, it most certainly isn't" Roger said quietly.

The Drive Back Home

Roger and Viktor visited for two days and shared pleasant memories, middle aged dreams and hopes and even some fears. When it was time to leave, Viktor shook Roger's hand and Roger said, "Vic, you have been the best friend I have ever had. I want to thank you for that." The two men gave each other a brotherly hug, Roger got into his car and drove away. Viktor waved as Roger drove out toward the highway and back toward Virginia. It was a good visit.

Chapter VI

Roger had a long drive ahead of him but he liked long drives. It allowed his head to clear and his emotions would run to ground. He could get emotionally balanced. He rarely played the radio for more than fifteen minutes at a time. He would turn it on every couple of hours or so. His brain injury made noise in close quarters uncomfortable. Normally referred to as TBI, his type of brain injury had various symptoms.

Roger had a problem with noise in close quarters and his personality changed to some extent after the explosion injured his brain. He got angrier much quicker. He was aware of that and tried to control his anger at all times. Because of this Roger preferred to listen to the slight hum of the engine as he travelled over the interstate highway back to Northern Virginia. It made for a pleasant ride.

He would let his thoughts go where ever they wished. He often thought of his childhood growing up with immigrant parents in Vermont. He would think of his strange and stressful marriage and the insanity of that relationship. He would think of his children and his grandchildren. He would think of his army career, the good times and the bad, the boring times and the terrifying times. They all seemed so far away now, almost as if they were images from someone else's life and not his own. Sometimes they did not seem to be related in any way to the life he was presently living.

He would think of his injuries and his life in recent years. It all seemed so relatively calm compared to the chaos of his early life in youth and early middle age. He was downright staid. What happened? He did not know other than he was tired now and wiser and just a little more skeptical about what life had to offer. He had seen how easy it can be to derail a human life. He had seen how much pain life could generate. He was working with young men who were often just placed on the sidelines of life by either physical circumstances beyond their control or just the general necessity of Americans to move on with their own lives and leave the disabled veteran to figure it all out for himself.

How does a young man or a young woman fight to regain their place in society when there may not really be a place for them to fill?

Americans pay very little attention to former players sitting on the bench. This is a gridiron culture with all of the attention going to the active players. It is just the way Americans are. Disabled veterans have to fight every day just to stay in the game. They struggle just to matter anymore.

And things were always difficult at the level of the small details. Roger was wearing an adult diaper. He had to do that on long drives because his weak bladder and his IBS/colitis condition would often be uncontrollable in places where there was no men's room. Depending on the state of his health for that day, he might be able to control the urge to vacate his bowels and bladder, or he might not. He never knew. So he had to take precautions. It always served as a reminder to him just how delicate the balance of his health truly was at all times. Being a disabled veteran with multiple injuries and medical issues is no fun. And for Roger, travelling anywhere was a major undertaking.

He thought back as he drove past rolling hills and green glens of his days as a child growing up in Vermont, that beautiful green state. He had an almost idyllic child hood; there were no major problems or bad memories that he could remember. His parents had been loving and good people and he never heard them raise their voices. They were gentle and hard working and devout. His mother's health had always been weak and his father's mental state had been damaged during World War II, but they were good people and Roger missed them now that they were long gone.

His army career happened accidentally as a result of lack of anything else to do or anywhere else to go. He did not miss his childhood or romanticize it but he often drew strength from it. It was a good childhood and he never missed his army days. Not much happened in the army until he got injured in combat in the Gulf War. Prior to that, his army days were all a boring and foggy blur. He never intended to be a soldier it just worked out that way. Other than his short combat career he spent his army career as a helicopter mechanic, then onto being a helicopter pilot and then a paper pusher after his combat injuries and preceding his retirement from the service.

Chapter VI

He thought about the young men and women who were so badly injured at Walter Reed and at the various veterans' hospitals and clinics throughout the country. He wondered how they coped with the massive injuries that they received. Roger felt lucky compared to many of them because their injuries were so debilitating. And then Roger wondered why any of them had been injured. "Who gained from this?" he would often think. It was certainly not the soldiers, marines, airmen and sailors who had all been hurt in these recent wars in western Asia. "Why were the wars being fought?" he would think to himself. He could never answer the question.

The missions, the aims and goals and the strategies of these west Asian wars never seemed clear to him. He just did not know why Americans were dying in these places. It did not really seem to matter much to anyone but the families of the wounded, the maimed and the dead. The American people were certainly not involved very much in the totality of the situation. They did not seem to care.

Americans carried on with their lives as if nothing was going on, because for the most part, nothing *was* going on in their lives relative to these wars. The overwhelming majority of them did not personally know anyone involved in the wars. "Why were we hurt?" he would often mutter in these quiet times when he thought of himself and the others and their sacrifice. "Who really cares about us?" he would think. He could never quite answer that question.

His kids had little to do with him anymore. They were adults and had their own lives now. They lived in the Boston area and had their own priorities and needs. He was an afterthought at best as far as they were concerned. He had no family to speak of really, not in any real way, and Roger had grown used to that. Every now and then he would have a girlfriend, but as sure as the sun rose in the East, eventually that would end also. He had been through that drill too many times to believe otherwise anymore.

Roger's life was not so much hard as it was anchorless. He was aware of that and tried hard to be of service, to have his life mean something, but he often felt that he was fooling himself. He was not completely convinced that he mattered to anyone for any reason at all. Life had made him a hardboiled observer of things in a way that would make a detective look like a meter maid. He believed nothing and he took nothing for granted. It was the only way that he could survive mentally and emotionally.

He thought about winning the lottery and the freedom that it gave him. It was not that he was ungrateful, he wasn't. It was just that now he had a whole lot of options because he was a rich man but his life had been so difficult in the past fifteen years that he had a difficult time enjoying his good luck, enjoying his wealth. He was always waiting for the other shoe to fall. His life experience had made him that way.

He had enough money available to travel where ever he wished but his IBS/Colitis and his physical limitations on travel made that very difficult. He was also very frugal from childhood. That was a New England trait. He found it very difficult to spend large sums of money, even when he had it available. It just was not the way he was put together. So he gave a lot of money away, invested the rest and lived quietly.

He kept his condo on the "harder side" of Alexandria, was learning to enjoy his home in the Del Ray section of the city and was slowly learning that life is what one makes it. There are no rules accept the ones you make and the ones you are expected by society to follow. If you keep a low profile and keep your mouth shut you can virtually do anything. Nobody will even notice that you are in the room. He learned that in the army. He liked living that way.

He thought about what he was learning from the reports that he had paid the two universities to provide him on American veterans. It was a good idea that Afet had given him. That idea was to pay two universities with a large minority student body to produce the report. Their vision of American veterans was different than it would be from a more mainstream group with strong ties to veteran issues and the defense industries.

Their assessment of things was much more realistic and frankly much more useful and their insights were compelling. It was a good choice to have them look at veterans' issues and then write a report.

And the third part of the report would be due him soon. He was eagerly awaiting it.

He pulled into the Del Ray section of Alexandria just as it was getting dark. He parked the car in the driveway, walked into the house and turned on the lights. He took off his clothes, took a shower and put on gym shorts and a t-shirt and decided to read quietly for an hour or so. He happened to walk into a back bedroom, one overlooking his side yard and Adriana's house and noticed a figure inside Adriana's bedroom. It was a man and he was naked. And there was Adriana and she was nude also. He looked away quickly but he could not help but see that they were embracing and they left the shades open in her bedroom window. Adriana had a lover other than Roger. That much was certain.

Roger chuckled to himself, "Well, welcome back Roger! It seems you arrived just in time to learn some things about life!" He turned out the light and went into his bedroom and went to sleep. Some things just never change in a man's life.

The next morning Roger awoke to a phone call. It was Adriana. She wanted to tell him that she had found someone "special" while he was gone and would not be seeing him again. Roger thanked her for her honesty and wished them both the best of luck. He hung up the phone and turned back to get more sleep. He was relieved. At least he did not have to confront her.

The truth was that the new lover had seen Roger through the window and Adriana did not want a scene, so she cut off any confrontation from happening by simply owning up to her new love. That was fine with Roger. The melodrama and her quirkiness was getting to be a bit much anyway. Roger thought to himself "Why is it that beautiful women are so quirky?"

Roger spent the day at St. Elmo's Coffee Pub watching the comings and goings in the neighborhood, reading the paper and just relaxing. He needed a down day. That afternoon the third part of the report arrived by UPS courier. Roger read the report that evening. It was always enjoyable to read.

Roger always felt able to understand veterans' issues better after he received these insights. It also gave him affirmation that he was not the only veterans' advocate who thought that something was amiss. He read the report with great relish.

The Third Section of the Report

This final section of the report dealt with the population that was to become service men and women and ultimately veterans after the Viet Nam War drawdown and into 2009. A large portion of the report was based on the work of two researchers named David Halbfinger and Steven Holmes. But it was much more than their work that was crucial here. Actually according the report he had received, Roger saw that most military scholars saw the Viet Nam war as the defining event in the birth and maintenance of the 21st century's blue-collar armed forces.

The opposition to the war had been so great and so all pervasive throughout American society that President Nixon abolished the draft in 1973 and the all volunteer armed forces was born in 1974. This was a watershed in the history of American veterans. When Roger read that he chuckled to himself. "No shit!" he muttered. "Viet Nam's ghost was all over the army when I got in."

Because the war was so unpopular and therefore service in that war would not lead to any significant advantage politically or in a business or educational sense for the children of the privileged class, they did not serve in any large numbers for the first time in American history. They used all sorts of subterfuge to get themselves excluded from the draft or from active service in a war zone. President George W. Bush and Vice President Richard Cheney were two such individuals in their youth. They would later become extreme hawks in American foreign policy. Their experiences were not isolated cases.

The hypocrisy of this line of thinking did not go unnoticed for huge slices of the American population during the Bush administration. In fact, it was a driving force in awakening the 21st century veteran to the surreal dimensions of pseudo-heroes running wars and ultimately dictating veterans' policies. There was no connection between "the deciders" and "the deceased." It was like a much more dangerous version of allowing ballet dancers to dictate to car mechanics exactly how to fix a transmission. It just made no logical sense.

But a lot of things made no sense relative to veterans' issues. Roger had certainly come to understand that.

It was certainly true that starting roughly with the Viet Nam war era that people of color could do very well relative to advancement in the armed forces. There were very high ranking officers in all the services who were not Caucasian. That was certainly a positive note. However, it was equally true that the demographics of the armed forces, and therefore of American veterans, was changing drastically from an evenly placed distribution throughout the national population to a very narrowly defined band of who chose to serve in uniform.

The report made it clear that the armed forces presently serving overseas in the summer of 2009 in the wars in western Asia was a far cry from that of the Viet Nam era and even more so from the eras preceding Viet Nam era veterans. The demographics of the service people involved show a marked departure from an equal share of the burden of service among the national population. Minorities are over represented and the wealthy and the underclass, those below the working class, are virtually absent. Self described political conservatives are over represented by a huge margin in the officer corps and North Easterners are very quickly fading from the ranks altogether.

In fact, according to the very well respected demographic researchers in the Department of Defense, the roughly one and a half million member armed forces of 2009 roughly resemble the demographic makeup of a community college or a trade school in rural America. Statistically, almost everybody serving in the early part of the 21st Century is coming from working class and lower middle class America, mostly from the West, Midwest and the South.

But that is not to say that today's soldier, sailor, coastguardsman, airman or marine is not educated. In fact, he or she is better educated than the population at large. For enlisted people the average reading grade is a full year higher than their civilian peer. Whites account for three out of every five soldiers. Black women outnumber white women in uniform. The armed forces are successfully integrated but there is also a sort of voluntary isolation from statistical reality at work here. In essence, the U.S. today has a working class military fighting and dying for the goals and aims of an affluent America. This is a recipe for eventual revolution. That is undeniable.

It is actually quite dangerous if this continues into the next decade the report writers observed. The U.S. armed forces are looking more and more like an economic version of the French Foreign Legion. Those who serve are serving largely because economically speaking there is no other place to go. The service is the last house on the block. There are no other options to keep a young person solvent. Roger said out loud after reading this paragraph in the report, "ain't that the truth!" he knew this from personal life experience.

From his work with veterans since he left the army in 1999 he knew that per data released in 2088, 12% of all homeless people were veterans. The report pointed this out. Once these people leave the service they are often so unconnected to society at large that they have no place to live.

At this point the writers of the article noted that Representative Charles Rangel of New York, a Korean War veteran himself, has publicly noted several times that the people who serve in uniform today do so because of economic realities, not a desire to be a professional soldier. He has called for the restoration of the draft several times since 2006. It is obvious that he sees the dangers here. What we have essentially is an imperial guard protecting the elite class and defending their agenda.

This cannot last for long when all the casualties are coming from the working class who are constantly fighting small wars, skirmishes, prolonged interdictions and police actions over the last thirty years ultimately to enhance the financial portfolios of non-combatants. At some point this will break down in bitter violence.

Roger liked Rangel's approach. He was smart, tough and tested. Roger tended to agree with Rangel. "He knows what he is talking about" Roger thought at this point in the report. "I think that I agree with him. This won't be able to continue much longer without violence."

Many military scholars have noted that since the abolishment of the draft in 1973 the U.S. has essentially developed a warrior class. It is perpetuated in many ways, often by promises of educational benefits and bonuses for enlisting and reenlisting. But it is also passed down through families that have had soldiers, sailors, airmen and marines serving in various past wars. Their attitudes are usually much more conservative than, and not nearly as diverse as, American society at large truly is.

This is believed by some sociologists to be an early foreshadowing of a huge social schism developing in American society between those who actually fight and die and those who believe that they have the right to do the asking that others do the fighting and dying. Wars are relatively easy to construct and carry out when someone else is doing the fighting and dying. They are harder to wage when the war's directors lose sons and daughters in combat.

The armed forces involved in the Viet Nam conflict were a universe away from the armed forces of 2009. The 2,954,000 troops who served in Viet Nam between 1965 and 1972 were much younger. They were much less likely to be married and almost entirely male according to data compiled by Richard Kolb the editor of VFW Magazine. The average combat soldier then was 19 or 20 years old and unmarried. Of the roughly 58,000 Americans killed there about 61% were 21 years old or younger. Of the enlisted men killed about 25% were married.

By contrast the average age of the service man or woman serving in the western Asian wars is about 26 and of those serving overseas roughly 35% are married. In the army of 1973 about 25 % of the enlisted people were married. Today that number is about 50% for the armed forces overall. About slightly less than 7,500 women served in Viet Nam and of that number 6,250 were nurses. Only eight died in Viet Nam and only one listed as killed in action. In 2009 relatively huge numbers of veterans are women and their needs often go unmet or they are underestimated relative to resources needed.

In the wars in western Asia today, 15% of the service people are women. In 1973 the average American serviceman or woman stayed two years in the armed forces. Today he or she stays seven years. Contrary to popular belief only about 25% of the American forces in Viet Nam were draftees. In World War II that number was 66%. In the early stages of the war, 1965 through 1966, black Americans bore the brunt of the casualties. By 1966 Army and Marine Corps commanders took aggressive steps to reassign black servicemen to other jobs in order to equalize deaths. By the end of that war 12.5% of the total deaths in Viet Nam were of black servicemen.

Servicemen from the South had the highest rate of battlefield deaths and soldiers from the Northeast had the lowest rate in the western Asian wars of the 21st Century. As of the Fall of 2000, 42% of all recruits came from the South.

Seventy-six percent of the soldiers in Viet Nam were from working class or lower income families while 23% had fathers in professional or technical/managerial positions. In 2009 about 60% of enlisted people are Caucasian. They tend to be married and upwardly mobile but they come from families that could not afford to send them to college.

Blacks currently make up about 22% of enlisted personnel. Half of all army enlisted women are black. The Hispanic population in the armed forces is slowly growing. They tend to be infantry grunts while blacks are heavily represented in the support functions.

The Air Force is substantially white in the 21st Century. It has always been that way.

The Triangle Institute for Security Studies in North Carolina did a study showing that between 1976 and 1996 the percentage of officers who saw themselves as non partisan or politically independent fell from 50% to 20%. Most of these identify themselves as Republicans. Many scholars saw this shift in political affiliation of the officer corps to be lopsided and unprecedented. It is also a strong indicator of a lopsided and skewed American paradigm relative to politics and the function of government.

The veterans that had served from 1975 until 2009 were a different bunch in many ways from those that had come before them. But for all the dissimilarities between the veterans of the two eras, the researchers in the report pointed out the work of a highly respected scholar, Andrew Krepinevich who worked at the Center for Strategic and Budgetary Assessments. He had made some very salient points in an article and a number of presentations showing the similarities between the Viet Nam era and its war and the present day war in Iraq. By extrapolation, the same set of circumstances would cause similar problems for war veterans.

He noted that "fighting another Viet Nam" was always a concern of both American strategists and the American people in the battles in El Salvador in the 1980s and in Somalia, Haiti and Bosnia in the 1990s. The American people demanded immediate knowledge of exit strategies. He noted that the conflicts in both Viet Nam and in Iraq had similar problems. His report noted these problems as follows:

§ In both cases the United States confronted an enemy intent in pursuing a protracted conflict with an eye toward seizing power after the American military's departure.

§ Early U.S. public support for the U.S. military involvement began to wane as they perceived that progress was not being made toward achieving the country's war objectives.

§ A number of America's closest allies were unwilling to support U.S.military intervention, and U.S. standing in the international community declined.

§ Although in both cases many close U.S. allies did not actively support the intervention, several states did provide significant military forces in support of the United States' efforts.

Overall however Krepinevich felt that the differences in the two conflicts outweighed the similarities. The troop levels in the wars in western Asia are drastically lower than in Viet Nam and theoretically this should keep veterans readjustment problems to a minimum. However, the suicides and murders of and by returning soldiers from the recent war do not support that theory.

Raw casualties prior to the Iraq War were down. The Gulf War had 2,225,000 servicemen and women serving. 467 were wounded and 147 were killed.

As of July 2009, there are 4,243 American dead in Iraq, 3 presumed dead and 46,132 wounded. As for Afghanistan there were 677 American dead and 2,379 wounded as of July 2009.

Traumatic brain injuries (TBI) are the signature wound of these wars on troops. Hidden explosive devices by the insurgents are the main cause. The effects of TBI last a lifetime and are usually quite serious. Roger knew that from personal experience and from his experience at Walter Reed Medical Center. Since TBI often literally changes a wounded veteran's personality and often requires lifetime medical assistance to help alleviate the symptoms, family is often torn apart as a result. It is the wound that never heals. Therefore the social consequences are staggering for everyone connected to the disabled veteran with this type of wound.

The casualty types from the Iraq and Afghanistan wars were different from other wars also. The report found that the primary causes of injury were explosive devices, gunshot wounds, aircraft crashes and terrorist attacks, in that order. Of these casualties 55% died in hostile action and 45% died in non hostile incidents. Chest or abdominal wounds or injuries were 40% of the casualties and brain injuries accounted for 35% of the total injuries and they were the main causes of death in this group.

The fatality rate in these wars was roughly half as high as in the Viet Nam war but the amputation rate in these wars was twice as high as in Viet Nam. According to military medicine experts, about 8% to 15% of the deaths appeared to be preventable.

The report pointed out another expert's opinion to be important. A military scholar of renown, Charles Dunlap Jr., made several salient points in his many writings on the wars in western Asia that were ongoing in 2009. He specifically points out that Americans do not want their armed forces to participate in another Iraq-style war. He is joined in this opinion by another solid military scholar James S. Corum. This is true, in their opinion, no matter how justified that war may be.

Dunlap states that 66% of all Americans oppose the war in Iraq as the researchers in Roger's report stated often. To state this simply, the army is fashioning itself to be used in politically motivated wars in precisely a manner that the American people strongly oppose. They simply find Iraq style wars out of the mainstream of American concerns.

The financial meltdown of the Fall of 2008 made it virtually unsustainable to continue to increase the $3 trillion dollar price tag of the Iraq War. Poll after poll suggested that Americans did not want to pay for it. Secretary of Defense Gates often tells his listeners that Americans must be willing to fight the "Long War" against insurgents around the world. The report states simply that Americans do not agree with him. Roger laughed and muttered, "Well, if that is the case, now what do we do?"

Generally speaking, the one who pays the bills wins the argument. And all the "heavy guns" in military thinking still conclude that America must be ready to fight a toe to toe war with a nation state if it is to survive. They generally say, these wars of insurgency can actually be lost and America will suffer little. But the price of modern warfare coupled with the price of taking care of each totally disabled veteran for perhaps five or six decades after he is disabled gravitates against such thinking. The most striking comment in the whole report came next. Roger was stunned to read it.

Toward the end of the quote from Dunlap in the report the authors quote him this way. It is a stunning admission from a top line defense strategist.

"This means we must explore how technology might serve to limit the numbers of young Americans who must be sent in harm's way. Certainly, we should unapologetically look for opportunities to replace people with machines. In that regard we need to acquire systems that can flexibly and economically be employed across the full spectrum of conflict."

The authors of the report made a compelling case. They stated the following:

"Extrapolating from this statement, we can now see the direction that America is going relative to producing veterans. The veterans of one hundred years from now will largely be machines. Essentially the cost of having to support shattered human veterans for six or seven decades is prohibitive, both financially and in social terms. America is moving inexorably toward fully mechanized armed forces in order to recoup or allay those lifetime veterans' support costs. The day of the human war veteran is, for the most part, quickly coming to a close."

The report essentially said that the human veteran is just too expensive to support over a seventy year life time if he is injured at age nineteen. Roger said quietly to himself "so it has come to this! I never would have thought!"

The report then basically when on to say that perhaps counter in-surgency troops supported by huge numbers of machines that were capable of semi independent thinking on the battlefield could bring the number of future veterans down to a reasonable level in the next fifty years. That is down from just under 23 million veterans in the summer of 2009. The authors of the report hastened to add that the sooner a fully mechanized fighting force was in place, the sooner huge financial and social savings could be reaped by American society at large.

Essentially, the report authors agreed with Dunlap. American veterans had now become too expensive over a lifetime to allow that population to grow. It had to shrink to keep the country solvent and that meant that future wars and battles had to be as mechanized as possible. No one pays a pension or provides medical treatment to a destroyed machine.

Simply speaking, the authors of the report said, "Mechanized war-riors do not leave grieving families when they are destroyed. They do not have to be supported for generations to come if they are incapaci-tated. They are simply discarded or rebuilt. They are not a constant drain on the national treasury. The Predator airframe of today with its "eye in the sky" capabilities and its ability to deal death precisely over the battlefield while being controlled from thousands of miles away is the prototype of the mainstay of the battlefield of 2050 and beyond. The veteran of the year 2050 will most likely be a machine.

The few humans still serving in uniform will be the ones that operate the machinery, control it in some manner or serve in counter insurgency and special operations units. The day of the Big Army, Air Force or Navy is fast drawing to a close for many reasons. Perhaps the most important reason is the high cost of providing for a totally disabled veteran over a seventy year period after his injuries incapacitate him."

The numbers were staggering and the authors gleaned these projections from the Department of Veterans Affairs. In the summer of 2009 approximately 22.9 million veterans were alive. That number of living veterans was projected to be 18.6 million by the year 2020, 15.5 million by 2030 and 14.1 million by 2036. The lion's share of all veterans' expenditures presently goes toward compensation and pension costs.

The total D.V.A. budgetary authority in 2009 was $47.2 billion dollars. Huge savings in national treasure could be realized by keeping the numbers of veterans low. And that meant either cut down on the number of wars or cut down on the number of humans fighting those wars. They were the only two feasible options to keep America solvent.

The report then closed with an executive summary outlining in very brief manner what had been found by the researchers in all three sections of the report. It asked that the government take care of today's veterans as best it could afford. It noted the discrepancies in how much money present day veterans needed to live a middle class life and how much that they were actually receiving.

It was a large gap by any standard and the authors noted that the present level of support was roughly 40% lower than it needed to be in order to keep a veteran living a substantially middle class lifestyle. The report ended by requesting that a fair pension and slate of benefits be paid to present day veterans and veterans of the future and that legislation always be ongoing to ensure that this happened.

Roger was more than satisfied with the report. It had been well worth the price.

He had paid an extra two thousand dollars to the researchers to have the report bound in leather, and have four official copies signed by the research teams sent to General Shinseki, President Obama and the Chairmen of the House and Senate Veterans Affairs Committees. His leather bound copy would be coming when the others were mailed out in a month.

Roger had felt that he had done his duty to inform his government as best he could regarding how the present day state of affairs among veterans could be contrasted with the life circumstances of veterans who had come before them. He felt that he had acted honestly and honorably as a citizen and a totally disabled veteran. He saw his duty and he did it.

VII.
No one saw this coming

The Veterans' War

AS IN SO many things in life, the most unpredictable things can happen in a flash with no real warning given to anyone. Such was the case concerning the Veterans War of the Spring of 2010.

For reasons still unclear to anyone involved in social issues, military planning, civic affairs, government projections, domestic intelligence activities or a hundred other government sponsored hard science and social science activities, no one foresaw the Veterans' War. It came completely out of the blue.

This was an odd fact considering that certainly there were precedents.

The Whiskey Rebellion of the 1790's was an early example of Americans resisting their government by force of arms. The Civil War is an obvious example of rebellion by the citizenry. The Bonus Army of 1932 was a precursor to what was happening with veterans in the early part of the 21st century. The civil rights riots in Detroit, Philadelphia and Los Angeles as well as a dozen other cities in the 1960s were a sort of template of what was now going to happen in just a few hours of Roger awakening that morning.

No one could have seen that 2010 would bring the upheaval that it did. But in February of 2010 veterans of all ages and from all backgrounds swelled up from virtually everywhere in the nation and took over the local post offices by force of arms throughout the entire country to stage a protest against ...against exactly what? Nobody seemed to know.

Simply put armed veterans aged eighteen to eighty walked into post offices around the country at 9:15 a.m. on Monday, 15 February 2010 and told everyone to leave. They went to the flagpole and lowered the flag, turned it upside down in a sign of distress and then ran it back up the pole. Within eight hours virtually every other small and medium sized post office in the country was occupied by armed and determined veterans. The takeover was spontaneous and seemed to have no purpose other than to call attention to the complete disillusionment of American veterans with American government. The immediate problem for local authorities was that the veterans were armed to the teeth.

Roger's phone rang repeatedly until he picked it up. It was 10:21 a.m. on the morning of Monday, 15 February 2010. Roger said "hello" and a man's excited voice loudly said "Roger! It is Wayne Coulter! Turn on the television set. Something is happening all over America. Veterans have apparently occupied dozens of post offices throughout the country. Something is going on; veterans seem to be staging a revolt!"

Wayne was a ninety-year-old World War II veteran, a Silver Star winner, who Roger knew from spending hours in conversation in St. Elmo's Coffee Shop on Mount Vernon Avenue many times. Wayne lived in an old age home across town but he kept in contact with Roger via email and phone.

Roger put the phone down and hurried over to the television remote laying on the sofa. He clicked the television on and put the channel indicator to CNN. Sure enough it was a live broadcast with a young reporter excitedly telling the story. No one seemed to know for sure what was happening. But this much was clear to CNN: veterans had occupied post offices all over the country by force of arms.

Apparently hundreds, if not thousands of veterans were involved. They had weapons. They made no demands. They sent everyone inside the post office buildings away from the sites. They were holding no hostages. Roger picked up the phone again. "You are right Wayne. Something is going on. I just cannot figure out what it is!"

Wayne, even at ninety, was always the rebel. A retired army major who had seen action as a young officer and had won the Silver Star at the Battle of the Bulge, he was an old Leftie. He had lost an ear in 1945 when his helmet sliced it off due to the close proximity of an incoming round smashing into the ground and knocking Wayne unconscious. He had been a forward artillery observer as a young lieutenant and had faced enemy fire many times. He was old in body but young in spirit.

"Do you think we should join them?" Wayne asked Roger. Roger replied quite seriously, "We don't even know what this is about Wayne. We better pay close attention to the news today!" Wayne agreed and the two men said goodbye. They both spent the day glued to the television set. At ninety years old, a highly decorated war veteran and almost incapacitated by age, Wayne was ready to stand with brother veterans at the local post office without even knowing what the beef was all about. He told Roger before he ended the conversation that his only regret was that he did not own a weapon. "The fire has never gone out in the breast of this old soldier" Roger thought.

By the end of the day and just before the evening news hour at about dinner time, the story was emerging. Somehow, veterans' groups on the left of the American political spectrum had used the internet in the preceding year to organize what was initially going to be a peaceful protest at post offices around the country. They were initially supposed to be protesting the wars in western Asia and the meaningless deaths and injuries from those wars.

And then others said that no, that was not the focus of their protest. They said that they were protesting the harsh treatment of recently injured American veterans by the Department of Veterans Affairs.

Still another group disagreed and said that they were protesting many decades of abuse, and frustration with the complete lack of interest that the D.V.A. had shown in their problems related to their service connected injuries, both mental and physical.

Yet another group said that they were protesting the million-case back log of disability cases at the D.V.A. that still needed to be adjudicated. Things were getting fuzzier and fuzzier. And they were getting more and more dangerous. Talk of imminent violence was growing.

Then there were veterans on the right who said that they were protesting the erratic and unsuccessful way that the wars in western Asia were being fought. They wanted a quick victory and were registering their dissatisfaction with the treatment of all the injured and maimed young veterans by this protest.

Other veterans on the right complained that the Obama Administration was not capable of running a war and that they needed to show everyone what real veterans thought about the latest administration.

There was even a small group of wheel chair bound veterans who were arriving at post offices throughout the country to openly proclaim that they were willing to die with their fellow veterans for whatever it was that they wanted. When asked specifically if they actually knew what their fellow veterans wanted, they said "no" but that it did not matter. They would stand or fall with fellow veterans. Blood is thicker than water and this philosophy had a dark side. That dark side was apparent now.

And everybody involved in this Chinese fire drill was now armed. The entire "peaceful protest" aspect of this group action which was originally intended to be civil disobedience had almost immediately turned into some sort of vague insurrection where everyone involved had a loaded weapon. This was now organized chaos.

By 8 p.m. that evening it was now clear to virtually everyone in the country that what was supposed to be a relatively small peaceful protest by scattered groups of veterans throughout the nation related to specific current events in the western Asian wars had somehow spontaneously spun out of control. Armed veterans in the hundreds of thousands had shown up at post offices throughout the country and told everyone to leave. Then they occupied the buildings.

When the first shots were fired it changed everything.

At 6:35 a.m. the following morning at the post office in Glenside, Pennsylvania someone fired a shot into the post office building that veterans had taken. No one but the armed veterans was inside. An old veteran using a walker, a Korean War veteran, was shot directly through the heart. He was dead before his body hit the ground and the thirty seven veterans that were with the dead veteran responded. They immediately knocked out the windows of the building with their rifle butts and returned fire.

Four Cheltenham Township police officers, including one woman officer, were killed outright. All were shot in the head. Seventeen bystanders who had gathered around the local news media mobile vans during the night were injured. Two teenagers were shot in the legs. Most of the others were hurt when the crowd panicked and trampled them down in the rush to get out of the way of the flying bullets.

By 7:45 a.m. the news was all over the country via the cable television news outlets and radio news. Shots had now been exchanged between veterans holding post office buildings and police agencies in Dana, Indiana as well as Gillette, Wyoming and Fargo North Dakota. Five veterans were killed outright and 23 police officers and federal agents were now dead. The police had attempted to storm the post office buildings in Millstadt, Illinois and West Deptford, New Jersey and three were shot and all attempts were driven back by the armed veterans inside.

In Petaluma, California a protracted gun battle was raging for over an hour now between police agencies and veterans who had taken over the post office building. Five veterans were killed outright and fifteen policemen and one police woman had been seriously injured or wounded. Three innocent children had now been killed when they were caught in the crossfire and one old Arab American grandmother caught in the crossfire in the Detroit, Michigan post office battle was now dead.

In downtown Manhattan, over one hundred veterans were occupying the General Post Office on Eighth Avenue and the New York City Police Department assisted by agents from several federal police agencies attempted to storm the building. One of the veterans had a machine gun. He opened fire and killed twenty two police officers outright. Fourteen federal agents were also killed or wounded.

By 9 a.m. that morning it was apparent that about half the post offices in the country were now occupied by armed veterans in a violent show of force over vague issues concerning the treatment of veterans over generations, unsuccessful western Asian wars, Second Amendment rights and about a dozen other vaguely defined grievances that the veterans registered with the media.

There seemed to be no clear leaders and there seemed to be no call for them among the veterans. These men simply wanted blood. They were out of patience, many of them were dying from service connected diseases and disabilities and they were more or less out of time.

Many of them apparently wanted to exact their vengeance on what they perceived to be an uncaring citizenry bolstered by a government that deliberately set up obstacles to their medical and pension needs in order to control costs. This now resembled a group vendetta. Reason and logic no longer seemed to matter to them. They apparently wanted people in authority to pay for what they perceived to be outright betrayal of their critical needs that was being inflicted by the government.

By this time federal police agencies had all divided up the various areas of the country to respond to the threat. They were working with local police to try and contain what looked to be some sort of low level insurrection from veterans for reasons not yet entirely clear. But one thing was clear, even to the Feds. There was no single spark that seemed to ignite this raging fire of veteran discontent. This cultural wild fire seemed to have been smoldering for decades at least. These men were armed and had already killed or wounded a growing and significant number of people.

Something was going to need to be done quickly to save the nation from a bloodbath where thousands of families were going to lose a brother, uncle, father or grandfather or great uncle to violence. Even some women were involved in the armed insurrection. This was completely unexpected and there was no precedent for handling it. The federal police agencies were deciding how to take the buildings back with the least amount of bloodshed. It was not going to be easy.

And there seemed to be no obvious mission overall. There was no real desired outcome on the part of the veterans. It just seemed to be group anger involving at least two hundred thousand young, middle aged and elderly veterans directed toward "the government", whatever that actually meant. This seemed to be an almost tribal thing, a rebellion of a group that saw itself as being treated badly by "the government" over a long period of time.

It all came down to basic rage vaguely aimed at the federal government and an uncaring citizenry for grievances, all of which could not be identified. These men and some women were simply acting much like minority groups had acted throughout American history. They were willing to sacrifice themselves to bring attention to their plight. There were many precedents.

The Native Americans staged several rebellions like this when pushed onto the reservation. American Blacks had often founded violent groups and supported them in order to gain attention to their plight. Even American Hispanics from time to time had been known to get violent based on their perceptions of how they were being treated by "the government."

The problem with this case was that at one time, each one of these armed insurgents had actually been the government. They made no demands. These veterans simply seized post office buildings throughout the country. This was basically an act of raw defiance for aims that were not clear or even stated. These were people bent on violence for the sake of violence. This was simple blood lust more common in the Middle East than in North America.

These people had felt raped by the "system" and now they were going to strike back. It did not matter who got hurt. And the government could not allow that. It would not allow that. This much was clear by the evening of the second day of the rebellion. Blood had to be spilled in great quantities to bring this madness to an end.

But it became clear on the third day that someone or some group clearly was in charge. If they had not been in charge initially, they were certainly in charge now.

The veterans had made arrangements in all cases to feed and water themselves. It turns out that they were stocking the basements of these buildings with canned food, rations and water for months. The provisions were hidden in basements and attics and back rooms of post office buildings for a period covering several months by participating veterans who worked for the postal service. Since there were so many veterans working at post offices throughout the country this was a relatively simple thing to accomplish. These people intended to stay in these buildings for a long period of time. Things had been previously organized, at least by some groups who had taken those buildings. That much was now clear. They would not move out.

The government simply would not let that happen. Plans were drawn up for massive retaliation by federal and local agencies and placed under the direct control and supervision of the Director of the Federal Bureau of Investigation.

By the end of the second week of the Veterans War the federal government had a plan in place. By this time all electricity and water had been shut off to the occupied buildings. But the insurgents had made plans for that, and they had makeshift latrines in the buildings and kerosene lamps ready to use. It was a month before all the buildings were back in the possession of the federal government.

The F.B.I. ordered a massive attack on all post office buildings being held by the insurgents at the exact same time. Within two hours of the coordinated attack all post office buildings were back in government control. Roughly fifty thousand veterans were killed in the standoff, most in the final assault by police forces to take back the buildings. Over twenty three thousand policemen and women and federal agents were killed by the insurgents, again mostly in the final assault by the federal government. The armed forces were never authorized to act and they did not. They stayed completely clear of this insurgency. That was by presidential order.

At this point over 50,000 veterans had been killed, about 50,000 wounded or outright captured by police agencies and it was estimated that about 80,000 insurgent veterans had escaped by orders of their high command. They melted back into the general population. About 10,000 veterans fled into the mountains, woods and deserts of the country in loosely organized armed bands. Their plans were not clear. After 31 days, the remaining 15,000 veterans surrendered en masse within twenty minutes of the order going out to hide their weapons and turn themselves in to authorities.

This was not complete chaos, as the government had initially thought. Many of the insurgents had a command structure. That much was clear now. Some of these insurrectionists had been in touch with some sort of ad hoc high command structure that they apparently finalized after the siege began. 55 of the veterans had died of natural causes during the post office takeover. Over 3,000 of the veterans were approximately eighty five to ninety ears old. All of those who had died of natural causes were from that group.

The insurrection was over.

Special courts had been set up to run for 24 hours a day for seven days a week to indict, arraign and assign to prison the captured insurgents. Special camps were set up all over the country, generally in or near the state capitals, to hold the insurgents for trial. The insurgents quickly elected their own officer corps and non commissioned officer corps to represent them and run things in the camp. There was a surprising discipline among the insurgents. They were not going to be quiet during their incarceration. They were going to use the media to air their grievances. They had certainly learned many lessons in public relations from the Wahabists waging war in western Asia and the Middle East. They would be tried for treason. Their basic defense would be that they were not the traitors, but rather the government was. This was going to be very interesting.

The Veterans Groups Take A Stand and the Pope Enters the Fray

The American Legion, the Disabled American Veterans, the Veterans of Foreign Wars, the Catholic War Veterans, the Jewish War Veterans and about twenty five other veterans groups strongly denounced the insurrection and called for public trials against the insurgents. Oddly enough, they never checked with their membership before the leadership of these groups banded together to do this.

They were roundly denounced as government patsies by a large minority of their memberships and there were mass defections and public denouncements from the members of these groups for many weeks. They did not necessarily agree with the insurgents but they would not take a stand against them. This was crucial and did not go unnoticed in congress or the White House. Although there was no real support for the insurrection, there was no willingness to denounce them among the population.

These people had simply been ignored for generations and they finally snapped. That was the general feeling among the American people. This was unprecedented in American history. An uprising had taken place. Thousands of people in positions of authority and among veterans had been killed and the American people just wanted it all to go away.

This was astounding. No one was crying for vengeance, justice or even trials. Obviously the federal government was moving forward on charges of treason.

Roger drove down to Richmond from Alexandria three times a week over the following months to interview incarcerated veterans in the Virginia Insurrectionist Detention Center and prepare them for trial along with volunteer attorneys from the ACLU, the Virginia Bar Association and several veterans' groups. He was astounded at the discipline these incarcerated insurgents were showing. They were not always young and were sometimes old, enfeebled and disabled men and women who had lost hope years before the insurrection.

The insurrection gave them pride and purpose. They were completely unrepentant. And what really touched Roger was the feeling among them that they had nothing to lose by being executed for treason. He was astonished at their inner strength.

Roger's job as a volunteer for the local American Legion was to get statements from whoever would provide them to him in order to present them to the judge during that veteran's trial as a sort of indication of the state of mind of the insurrectionist. The plan here was to try and convince the authorities that these men were in pain, had lost hope, had nowhere to turn and were not in their right minds. It was doubtful that this strategy would work, but it was worth a try.

Roger's first interview was with a young man who had served in Iraq named Dan Dawson. Dan had seen three combat tours in Iraq, had been wounded twice, treated for PTSD and returned to combat. He had been unemployed and drinking heavily when he joined the insurrection on impulse the morning it started. He was a highly decorated combat marine.

The third time Dan returned home from Iraq he found that his wife and young son had left him weeks before. She ran off with a day laborer to places unknown and took their four year old son with her. Dan didn't care if he was executed for treason or not. In fact he told Roger, "I am rather looking forward to it. At least it will put an end to all of this bullshit!" Roger was left speechless. This young man was deadly serious. He really didn't care if he lived or died.

The first trials started in a matter of weeks after the detention camps were set up all over the country. The government wanted to publicly try the leadership on television but it was not evident even six months later just who the leaders were. They were completely invisible.

The truth was that the leaders, whoever they were, had modeled the insurrection more or less on the Easter Monday Uprising in Ireland. It was a takeover of the General Post Office building in Dublin. That was Easter Monday, 1916. The entire veterans' insurrection had been based on that unsuccessful attempt to challenge British authority in Ireland. Eventually, that unsuccessful series of skirmishes in and around Dublin would lead to Irish independence from Britain just a few years later. And the stand that the Irish Volunteers took at the G.P.O. was the birth of it.

The veterans' insurrection had the feel of an Irish Republican Army operation and it was just as secretive and uninformative to the government in the national capitol. In fact the government knew full well that almost half of the rebels had escaped the post office buildings on orders of the Veterans' Army High Command. The government estimated that there were roughly 80,000 unrepentant insurrectionists among the general population. They had escaped under orders from the high command during the insurrection. The veterans insurrectionist high command made absolutely sure that the government knew that this had occurred. Everyone was going to be made to tread lightly here. That much was certain.

But the federal government was not completely blind. They had moles and informants in all of the camps, sometimes hundreds of them. This much was certain. Exactly like the early Irish Republican Army, the Veterans' Insurrectionist Army, now known as the VIA, had men and women of every conceivable political leaning, belief and religious persuasion in the country. Everything from left wing radical Democrat to active Socialist to extreme right wing neo-Nazi white supremacists were in the VIA.

Their common bond was their service in uniform, most of them having seen combat, and their absolute belief that the Department of Veterans Affairs had betrayed them at every opportunity. They felt no allegiance to any government that would hang them out to dry like the D.V.A. had done since its inception in the 1930's. Their common bond was their feeling of abject betrayal over many generations by the federal government. They had no common core belief but they did have a common enemy, the federal government.

This was not an army of true believers. This was an army staffed completely with non believers. It was really that simple. The basic ideology here was not so much a belief in anything cohesive for the group. It was more of a reaction to what was perceived as government betrayal and minimal intervention running to non intervention in the lives of millions of veterans which the government itself had broken by its defense policies over many generations.

To make matters worse, it was generally believed by the insurrectionists that they were sacrificed for the financial portfolios of the wealthy. The Veterans Insurrectionist Army leaders made sure that this got into the papers and that the European Union and all Asian allies were aware of this. The European labor unions gave the insurrectionists their unqualified support. And it got worse; the VIA had the Pope as an ally!

Early on in the summer of 2009 he released a long awaited encyclical entitled "Caritas in veritate" (Charity in Truth). It did not support the American government's secret hopes on many levels. As it turned out, when the insurrection occurred in early 2010 the Vatican Foreign Office referred to the encyclical written less than a year before and stated that it supported the rebels as morally correct in their desire to be treated fairly. This point of view was relative to their sacrifices for the interests of the wealthy in America over many generations. The government was apoplectic at the slam it had received from the Vatican. It had good reason to be.

The American population is made up of roughly 26 million active Catholics and another slightly more than 23 million people who claim to be former Catholics. That is roughly 50 million people or about one sixth of the American population of whom it could be said had their core value system formed by Catholicism. The Pope was a power to be reckoned with, even for a former Catholic in the U.S. in areas of life relative to moral questions. Since Pope Benedict XVI's encyclical clearly admonished the West for its many misuses of power and wealth at the expense of the poor, both in the Western countries and the rest of the world, the American government was largely silent when it was released. Now the U.S. government was being pummeled by it.

In part of the encyclical the Pope writes like a radical. The Pope disagrees with anyone or any government that believes that the economy should be free of government regulation. And that has traditionally been the way of the hard-right in American politics. He states: "The conviction that the economy must be autonomous, that it must be shielded from 'influences' of a moral character, has led man to abuse the economic process in a thoroughly destructive way," he writes. "In the long term, these convictions have led to economic, social and political systems that trample upon personal and social freedom, and are therefore unable to deliver the justice that they promise."

In the encyclical Pope Benedict even supports a sort of economic nirvana which would be hard to imagine let alone implement. He says that "a political, juridical and economic order which can increase and give direction to international cooperation for the development of all peoples in solidarity. To manage the global economy; to revive economies hit by the crisis; to avoid any deterioration of the present crisis and the greater imbalances that would result; to bring about integral and timely disarmament, food security and peace; to guarantee the protection of the environment and to regulate migration: for all this, there is urgent need of a true world political authority, as my predecessor Blessed John XXIII indicated some years ago."

And here was the part of his encyclical that was used by the VIA in its defense of its actions. The Pope states further: ."... the social doctrine of the Church has unceasingly highlighted the importance of distributive justice and social justice for the market economy."

The Pope unflinchingly supports the "redistribution of wealth" when he talks about the role of government. "Grave imbalances are produced," he writes, "when economic action, conceived merely as an engine for wealth creation, is detached from political action, conceived as a means for pursuing justice through redistribution."

What the VIA claimed in court was that since 1898 and the entrance into the Spanish American War the United States government had waged wars solely for the expansion of its markets overseas. It had seen as commonplace and acceptable the sacrificing almost exclusively of the sons and later daughters of the poor, working class, and marginally employable lower middle class of the American population. This was done for the sole purpose of protecting those markets for further expansion of the wealth and power of the minute portions of the population that were in the wealthy class of the country.

The VIA was essentially saying that the poor, disenfranchised and economically marginalized portions of the American population had spent the last 112 years fighting and dying and being maimed to make the American wealthy class even wealthier. They claimed that they had the moral support of Christian teachings as laid out by the Pontiff.

The Pope publicly agreed with them! This was making it very difficult for treason trials in a country that was one sixth Catholic or at least brought up as Catholic.

What made matters even more delicate is that the Pope sent a special envoy to the United States specifically to support the goals and aims of the VIA. Pope Benedict publicly declared just months after the insurrection that the rebels were right to protest their maiming and the deaths of their comrades as a result of the powerful elite in the United States placing them in harms way to make their group even more powerful and more elite.

The Vatican harshly criticized the American government for its medieval view of its right to force the economically lowly to routinely trudge off to war after war for the sake of the nobility and its hold over the use and accumulation of national economic wealth. The Pope was literally declaring war on the American view of its right to wage almost continual war in order to expand and secure markets.

The Pope publicly stated that the only reason he could find for wars in Afghanistan and Iraq was so that powerful elements of the American economy could gain a strong footing in the Middle East by any means possible. In short, the Pope declared that the insurrection was morally correct and that the veterans had a right to protest their historic abuse at the hands of American wealthy market manipulators. The Pope saw American veterans as serfs to the czars of American economic oppression worldwide. He pulled no punches. Leaders throughout American government were furious but publicly said nothing. What could they say? The evidence supporting the Pope's position was everywhere.

The Catholic Church in the United States immediately went into a strong defense mode for the insurrectionists. All of its resources and political power were now laid at the feet of the insurrection. But things got even worse for anyone expecting a hard line against the insurrection. The president, following the lead of President Lincoln, signed an executive order declaring that all insurrectionists were now cleared of any charges related to treason, although other criminal charges could be brought forward.

President Obama basically stated that if treason was being considered as a charge, these men were now granted amnesty on that charge. Although this was an executive order and federal judges were not required to submit themselves to this reading of the law by the president, all federal judicial districts eventually agreed to go along with the president's desires.

No charges of treason would be brought forward.

However, if any of these men or women were found to have participated in the deaths of the policemen, charges of murder or manslaughter could and would be brought forward.

The president had headed off a possible civil war. It was a smart thing to do. The hard part was now being handed over to the American federal court system. And this was not going to be something any judge would want to try. The country was deeply divided over the issue. That much was certain.

"What was this all about?"

Roger sat across from the old veteran with the cane and the crooked back. They were in a tent that the guards had provided for interviews. The old man was a Viet Nam war veteran and a retired Army colonel. He was about seventy five years old Roger figured. He sat upright. He was a West Point graduate, Class of 1960. He was ramrod straight and unrepentant. "Do you have anything to tell me to explain your actions?" Roger asked him. The man said nothing, he just started at Roger. "Who are you and what do you want with me?" the man said.

"My name is Rogier Magritte. I am a retired Army warrant officer, a helicopter pilot, and I got injured in the first Gulf War. I am totally disabled veteran. I am representing the Disabled American Veterans and we are trying to find a suitable defense for anyone going to trial from here. We assume that everyone here will eventually go to trial. I am interviewing you simply to find out what we can use to defend you."

The old colonel looked at Roger a long time. He had that professional officer stare that junior officers come to know so well. He stared at Roger for over a minute.

Then the old man said, "Where you a volunteer in the insurrection?" Roger said, "No." The colonel looked at him and said, "Why not?" Roger did not know what to say. Finally he uttered, "Well, things happened so fast and I could not sort out the issues, so I..." Before Roger could finish the colonel said, "So you sat at home and watched others take a bullet for your interests, is that right?"

Roger swallowed hard and put his head down. He looked at the colonel and said, "Do you want to be interviewed?" The colonel looked at him sadly and just said, "You and I have nothing more to say to each other." With that, the old man got up and walked out of the tent.

Roger waited for the next interviewee to step into the tent. More or less Roger was treated the same way by every man he tried to interview. He did not serve in the insurrection so they had nothing to say to him. Roger generally only got one or two interviewees a day to speak, and he would normally interview about twenty people in a day. They did not respect him, that much was obvious. Roger just drove home everyday in silence with the radio off. It was his duty to show up to do the interviews but it was not his duty to feel bad about being an outsider with the prisoners. It was just the way it was.

That night when Roger arrived home he turned on the television news to see that the European Union had formally supported the American insurrectionists in a document signed by all the members that day. The Dali Lama had also publicly supported the right of the American veterans to rebel. He gave a lecture at Oxford University and said that the rebels had a moral right to rebel against a central government that cynically used them over a number of generations to further the aims of an extreme minority that held a disproportionate amount of wealth and power.

The Dali Lama likened their plight to that of Tibetans attempting to right wrongs inflicted upon them by the Red Chinese. The White

House was secretly and quietly furious. There were no allies anywhere. The American government was essentially being seen as a shill for roughly two million extremely wealthy Americans who were using the apparatus of government, especially the armed forces, to further their own extreme agenda of wealth accumulation at all costs. That is to say, at all costs for virtually everyone but them.

The news broadcasts were now covering the full scope of the insurrection with comprehensive mini-documentaries every night. The Republican Party was furious at this turn of events. They were screaming for treason trials to take place immediately. They got limited public support from conservative Democrats in Congress. Fox News publicly ran several on-air rants demanding that these treasonous veterans "be dealt with seriously, immediately and with great prejudice."

The Quaker organizations in the U.S. supported the rebels and the American Buddhist Association joined them in that support. American Protestantism was about evenly divided in supporting treason trials and amnesty, as was American Judaism. Most American Muslims gave tacit support to the rebels. Both the Canadian government and the Mexican government stayed silent on the issue.

American families were divided on the issue of whether or not the rebels had a right to an insurrection based on the abuses they had suffered. America was swiftly descending into national social schizophrenia. The sooner that all of this was brought to some sort of conclusion, the better. Virtually everyone agreed.

The following weeks Roger travelled to Richmond as usual and found virtually no one willing to talk to him in the detention camp. At one point, a fellow interviewer, a woman named Elspeth MacDougle, asked him to have lunch with her. She was a Navy veteran and had served as a yeoman aboard a Navy fast frigate about fifteen years prior. She was cute, in her early forties and fit with a fine athletic build. She had a pretty face, strawberry blonde hair and had never married. She had no children.

"Where do you want to eat?" Roger asked her at lunchtime. "Any place but MacDonald's!" Elspeth said. Roger laughed, "how about a real restaurant? My treat, okay? What about Mexican food? Do you like Mexican food?" Elspeth said "Of course!" and off they went to find the nearest Mexican restaurant. There was one about three miles from the detention camp that was a nice place.

They took Roger's car since Elspeth had gotten a ride to the camp that day with another interviewer. They found the restaurant, parked the car, entered the place and sat down at a booth near the door. The waitress approached and handed them menus. They decided on chimichongas. "Always a good choice" Roger thought. They ordered cokes and waited for their lunch to be served. Roger sat quietly for a minute and looked across the table at his attractive lunch mate.

"So how did you get involved in all of this?" Roger asked the pretty woman across from him. She looked at him for a minute and then said softly, "I am a Navy veteran. I fell in love with a guy when I was aboard ship. We were going to get married. He got severely burned in an engine room fire one night when we were at sea. He spent about a year at the Bethesda Naval Hospital for his burns and then was retired medically. He then got his care from the Veterans' Hospital in Philadelphia. It was not the best of care. He killed himself in a fit of depression about a year after he left the Navy. He was severely disfigured. There was really nothing that anyone could do for him other than keep him alive. And that was simply not enough. We were both twenty five when he died. I kept in contact with him after his Navy days but he really did not want to have anything to do with me."

"Why not?" Roger asked her.

"Well, basically I think he thought that he was holding me back, that his burns were too severe for me to be happy being married to him. He was deeply scarred, and not just physically. As I look back on it now I am sure that he did not want that life for me. He wanted more for me."

"Was he too disfigured for you to love him?" Roger asked. The woman gasped a little and then looked Roger directly in the eye. Her eyes began to mist.

"I am not really sure. I loved him. That was certain. But after he was so badly burned, I must admit, my feelings changed. Now, whether that was right or wrong of me, I am not really in a position right now to say. I have questioned myself time and time again about it. I was twenty five. I was young and I wanted to live life. Would I have given my life to a man so severely disfigured? I am not sure, not even now."

"I would like to sit here and tell you that I was woman enough at twenty five years old to have embraced a life with him, but if I am going to be honest, I cannot really say that. I think he saw that in me and he did not want to break my heart by forcing me to slowly move away from him or to tell him that I was no longer attracted to him. He loved me and he knew me well enough to know that I was not strong enough for a life like that."

"So what are you telling me?" Roger asked her.

"I am telling you that he killed himself because he was twenty five years old, severely disfigured and in love with a woman who was not big enough, not strong enough, to love him back as his wife or his lover anymore. He killed himself I think to let us both off the hook. And frankly, that is why I work with disabled veterans. I owe him."

She looked down at the table. The waitress brought their lunch at that moment. She started to eat. So did Roger. But Roger had a lump in his throat. "Things are just never the way they seem!" Roger thought to himself as he ate his lunch quietly while sitting across the table from this petite and cute little Navy veteran. This had to be the most honest woman he ever met he thought.

After a bit Roger started up the conversation again. "So where do you work, what do you do?" Roger asked. "Well right now I am between jobs. I was an IT specialist for a financial company in D.C. but after the crash in the Fall of 2008 the company folded and about 300 of us lost our jobs. I get odd jobs every now and then working as a consultant for small businesses that are setting up computer systems for special needs within their company. It pays the bills."

Elspeth looked at Roger and said, "And you? What do you do?" Roger laughed and said, "Nothing. I do nothing." Elspeth looked at him with an odd expression. Roger continued. "I am retired from the army. I was a helicopter pilot. I got injured in the Gulf War and have full disability from the DVA. Between the two pensions and the fact that I came into some money two years ago, I don't need to work. So I don't work. So I have a lot of time and I use it working on veterans' issues." Elspeth simply said "Oh, that's nice" and continued to eat her lunch.

"So how are you getting home tonight?" Roger asked her. "I don't know. My ride left early so I guess I will take a taxi. I live in Arlington so maybe I will take a bus, its cheaper."

"No, I will take you home" Roger said. "I live in Alexandria. It is not that far from your place at all, I am sure. Anyway, I could use the company." Elspeth agreed. After lunch they returned to the camp for more interviews. That evening they had a pleasant ride home from Richmond. Roger took his time driving. What was the rush?

"This entire insurrection has set the entire country on its ear" Roger said to Elspeth. "Sure, that is what the entire purpose of an insurrection is!" Elspeth said. She continued. "It seems that the leader-ship had planned these actions years in advance and the government still apparently has no idea exactly who the ringleaders are. But I do know a few things about the movement from moving among them for months now. It is rather intriguing to say the least!"

"What do you know?" Roger asked.

"Well it seems that the insurrectionist leadership modeled them-selves and the entire movement on the Irish Republican Army. Every-one is arranged in a four person cell. No one in the movement knows the names of any more than eight other people. The most anyone can know is the identity of people in their own cell and one other cell and even that is for the mid- rank officers only." Roger listened intensely.

"Just as in the IRA, once a member is interned he or she loses all rank and holds the rank of volunteer within the insurrectionist army however as you know, they elect officers and non-commissioned officers to run things in the camps. These are temporary ranks and do not translate into rank or privilege in the insurrectionist army."

"They don't communicate electronically. Not ever. They have couriers who are almost exclusively homeless veterans who walk to the next courier and hand off the official communicade. Sometimes official communication can travel forty miles in an evening using these walkers. They have only four orders. Those orders are: Hold your position, Withdraw Immediately, Withdraw in increments, Attack. Those orders are given in the communicades which are nothing more than pieces of rope with one to four knots in the rope. The color of the rope denotes from what level the order is coming. Red is the high command, blue is the state level command and white is the local commandant."

"No one seems to know how many soldiers there are in the insurrectionist army. There are over a hundred thousand veterans interned right now as a result of rebel activities but apparently the government thinks that there are about this same amount of insurrectionists that have escaped internment and are awaiting further orders for action. It is a scary thought." Roger agreed.

"As far as delivering the more intricate and involved orders, they have worked out a simple system. One of the couriers will hold a portion of the newspaper under his arm and deliver it to the next courier in a mile or two. It gets passed on until it arrives at the intended destination. The meeting places and times have been worked out in advance. If it is the obituary section of the paper that is delivered, then the meeting is at a prearranged time in a cemetery. If it is the style section, the meeting takes place at a set time in a restaurant. If it is the sports section, the meeting is held at a designated sports arena or stadium or ball court. If it is the front page the meeting takes place in a designated public park or public area."

"Nothing is ever written down and all officers must be able to commit entire plans to memory. Everything is memorized. There are no notes. And here is what makes it so interesting. In order to help the officer memorize the plans, the orders are given in the format of a rhyming poem! They meet and are taught a poem. They memorize a poem. The poem is the battle plan. What an ingenious method of passing on the information!" Roger admitted to Elspeth that he was impressed.

"How do you know all this?" Roger asked.

Elspeth smiled and said, "I overheard a poem being recited and memorized by two men in the camp. It was fascinating!" Roger laughed. "You know what Elspeth? The CIA, Naval Intelligence, the FBI, all of them are completely out of their element here. They will never be able to defeat this because it is too simple!" They both laughed. Little did they know that the American intelligence community agreed with their assessment.

"I just could never figure out how all this came to a boiling point so quickly!" Roger said to Elspeth as they both looked out of the windshield at the greenery passing by them as they travelled north up Interstate 395. "I did not see this coming. Did anybody? There were no veterans that I know personally that were involved in the insurrection and I work with other disabled veterans every day. I have been doing it for years. How could I have missed this? It seemed to come out of nowhere and happened so quickly!"

Elspeth looked at Roger for a few seconds and decided to choose her words carefully. "That is just it. It did not happen quickly. The signs of discontent were everywhere for decades but no one wanted to look at them squarely and see the abuses. When the Bush administration took office and literally started a war on foggy grounds with the Vice President of the United States pushing business left and right on non competitive contracts toward his old company, even the most diehard jingoists had to look hard at what was happening. It was the beginning of the end of that peculiar American naïveté that resembles patriotism but is really cruel and unthinking manifest destiny. In short, we truly believe that the world is our onion; we can do whatever we want. That includes ignoring to a great extent the legitimate support needs of wounded, injured and dying veterans from old wars. We have now learned the price of that folly. And the price could ultimately be the violent overthrow of our government."

Elspeth waited to see how Roger would react to this and then continued speaking. Roger simply continued to drive and said nothing.

She continued her explanation. "The debacle in Iraq was basically about making the super wealthy base of the Republican Party and by extension, American war industrialists, even wealthier than they already are. The war was a partial fabrication based on incomplete and sloppy intelligence information to get American troops stationed semi-permanently in southwestern Asia to push our national business agenda forward. To state this simply, all key elements of the military industrial complex needed us squarely planted in the Middle East. Billions of dollars have been made by friends of the defense industries on weapons and defense related expenditures during our time there. This was no accident; this was carefully planned over many years."

Roger still said nothing but was listening intently. Elspeth continued talking.

"Then when the casualties started coming in the American psyche changed. That was when the IED explosions were giving brain injuries that ran from mild to severe to tens of thousands of troops, when over 5,000 Americans were killed in the wars, when troops were held against their will in the armed forces in a program called 'stop loss' and sent back into combat time and time again at that point the entire social contract between the government and the working class veteran and soldier changed. Now we had real oppression from a super privileged class of Americans dictating who would die from the lower classes so that they could grow even richer. The English speaking world had not seen anything like this bold and naked abuse of power by the nobles since the Middle Ages.'

Elspeth did not stop to even catch a breath. She was on a roll.

"The attack on the Word Trade Center and the Pentagon was engineered by the Al Qaeda who were protected by the Taliban, and hiding in Pakistan and based to some degree in Afghanistan. We boldly attacked Iraq. The war in Afghanistan has been a minor league effort since day one. The question now has to be, why is that? The only rational answer is that for whatever reason or group of reasons, Iraq was a greater prize to the military industrial complex than Afghanistan could ever be. So we attacked Iraq."

Elspeth stopped talking for a full ten seconds and looked out the window. She was getting emotional. Roger said nothing. She spoke again in a slightly louder voice.

"Hundreds of thousands of Iraqis, Afghanis and Americans have been killed and injured because the most powerful elements of American society decided that a military adventure into Iraq and Afghanistan would be profitable. In the end our government's actions comes down to money. And in the end, these insurrectionists decided to revolt. They had simply reached the saturation point once they saw through the government deceptions. They would not be abused by the powerful any longer nor would they allow brother and sister soldiers who would become veterans to be thrown into battles so that faceless and unknown rich men could become richer. It is now painfully obvious that there is no national security significance to our adventures in western Asia. So then there must be another agenda behind why we are there. The question is, what is that agenda? And who controls the agenda?"

Roger looked at Elspeth. She was tearing up. He said, "I don't know what the agenda is Elspeth. I am guessing that it is a war like other wars. It started slow and then got out of hand. Don't you think so?" Elspeth basically ignored his question and continued on with her explanation.

"The Obama Administration got into office largely because it promised to get us out of the wars in Iraq and Afghanistan as soon as humanly possible. We are still there. Veterans will no longer wait for either a Democratic or a Republican administration to come clean on the abuses and deceptions. They have had enough. When this phony series of wars is tied into the generations of abuses handed out to veterans by the lackluster performance of the Department of Veterans Affairs since its very birth as an organization, you have a recipe for massive violence. And that is what happened, we had violence."

Elspeth stopped talking, turned her head and looked out the passenger window in silence.

After a minute Roger said to her, "You seem to know an awful lot about this in great detail. Why is that exactly?"

Elspeth laughed and then said. "It is because of my cousin Ian MacGregor. He is an intelligence analyst for the State Department. He and I have been very close since childhood. There are no secrets between us. To make my case simply, Ian knows a whole lot more about this than most Americans and he tells me that the whole thing was a premeditated con on the American people from day one. I believe him. He has never lied to me. America's powerful stock speculating elite wanted a war to fatten their portfolios. They got one, in fact they got two. It is really no more complicated than that."

"Oh!" is all Roger could think to say at that moment.

They arrived at Elspeth's condominium within minutes of this conversation being finished. Roger called to Elspeth as she got out of the car, "call me sometime. Here is my card." With that he reached his hand out of the window of his car and handed a business card to her. She smiled and took the card, waved and turned and walked into the building where she lived. "Well one thing is for sure, she sure has spirit!" Roger muttered to himself. Roger never heard from her or saw her again. She never called.

The following months played out in the press, in the courts and in the camps. In the end, the veterans who were willing to sign an allegiance oath to the government and constitution were given a presidential pardon. There were about 500 who refused to sign the oaths. They were imprisoned on charges ranging from inciting a riot to involuntary manslaughter and everything in between. They were usually convicted and given long prison sentences. The insurrection was over but an insurrectionist army was extant in the country and organized.

All indications were that they would be more than willing to take up rebel activities at the request of their high command. And the nagging fact that the high command remained hidden, nameless and faceless and their agenda inscrutable bothered everybody, no matter what side of the issue one supported. Who were these people? Where did they get their power to plan, construct and execute an insurrection?

Chapter VII

Things in America had changed drastically. Things would never be the same between the government and the citizenry. That is what revolutions do; it was what they are meant to do. Insurrections change things in the mind of the citizenry. New rules come into play when revolutions happen. It is just the nature of the beast. Nations come off their foundations.

Slowly the country began to settle down but the nagging doubts that lingered in the minds of anyone who had the courage to think would always be there. The fact remained that an insurrectionist army of uncertain size and undiscovered leadership with a fairly vague agenda and populated by former servicemen and servicewomen who had served in the U.S. armed forces was unsettling at best and threatening at worst.

A large portion of the 22.9 million veterans alive in the summer of 2009 had decided to rebel from the central government in Washington D.C. based loosely on the history of how soldiers and veterans had been treated in the U.S. for generations. If these men and women had a broader agenda, the wonks in Washington D.C. could not find it. It all came down to group frustration at the way the group had historically been abused. It did not seem to be any more complicated than that. The beaten dog eventually bites. The lesson was there to be learned. But the real question was, had the government learned it? No one knew.

VIII.
And so
it goes

Movin' on!

DAYS TURNED INTO weeks, weeks into months and finally the year that the insurrection started and ended died a quiet death. All Americans were glad to see the year end. The New Year of 2011, held the promise of peace, if not prosperity. The Great Recession of the Fall of 2008 still had the country in its grip but unemployment was steadily falling below 7.5% and companies were beginning to hire mid range professionals and certified and trained workers again. America was getting back its self confidence.

A new manufacturing economy was beginning to develop in the U.S. The dollar had weakened considerably against Chinese and other currencies and this made exporting goods from the United States easier and more profitable to do. Foreigners were buying American goods again. Big money was being made at last and the U.S. was growing stronger every week.

Things were starting to look up in a big way and the Obama administration was working hard on veterans issues to ensure that the hidden insurrectionists had no reason to show their influence on national politics again. Happy days were here again. Veterans must not be allowed to ruin that fact. The president had spoken.

The country had come dangerously close to class warfare with over a quarter of a million veterans actively involved in armed insurrection. No one knew how many of these insurrectionists were hiding in an unrepentant mode, completely ready to take up arms again against what they perceived to be gross injustice. The FBI's best estimate was that there were about eighty thousand rebels among the citizenry who were ready and willing to strike if given the command to do so. That is a lot of people to be fifth columnists in a country that is not accustomed to dealing with violent subversion on a daily basis.

Americans are not Israelis. Americans do not have the proper psychology to deal appropriately with separatist groups, "freedom fighters" or underground armies of disenfranchised citizens. All the experts agreed. Americans have no experience with long term rebellions involving reactionary governments and radical groups who are not afraid to use violence on a large scale over many decades. Intelligence analysts agreed that the long term prospects for anarchy in the U.S. were frightening.

Everyone in the Obama administration was very aware that the nation had largely been spared massive damage by the president's unwillingness to use the armed forces to quell the rebellion. By using only federal and local police forces to stop the insurrection and by quickly pardoning the rebels who were willing to sign a loyalty oath, a full scale civil war had been averted. This young president was a lot savvier about handling large numbers of discontented veterans than most people gave him credit for being.

He had shown how shrewd he really was by bringing the insurrection to a close fairly quickly and by being able to characterize it as a criminal situation rather than a national security concern. Even the Russians were impressed with his ability to shut this thing off before it spilled over into general anarchy. He had every right to be proud of his understated leadership. It had won the day for peace in the nation. Virtually everyone in government agreed. The worst was behind us.

But that did not mean that it was all over. The danger was still there. The Department of Defense was organizing hundreds of focus groups containing veterans that were not involved in the insurrection. They needed to understand what had just happened in the country. The Disabled American Veterans organization gave Roger's name to the Defense Department as a possible member of a focus group and the department contacted him immediately. Roger agreed to take part. The group met every other Tuesday at the Pentagon. The first meeting was enlightening to say the least.

An admiral spoke to everyone and told them what the department wanted from them. Essentially he said they wanted to know "what the hell just happened?"

Chapter VIII

Over three hundred people were participating in the focus groups. The groups were comprised of ten people each. The Defense Department supplied the group facilitators. Each group would be given a different topic each week and they had two hours to reach conclusions to the problems presented to the group. Each group was given a name and a number. Roger's group was Tiger 14.

The first meeting of Tiger 14 was pleasant enough. Everyone got to know each other.

A young Navy lieutenant, a female named April Long, was assigned to the group as its facilitator. She explained the mission of the group and then asked the group to come up with rules of behavior for the meetings. The group did and then the meeting started.

"I just feel lost and overwhelmed by the whole thing!" a retired Marine colonel by the name of Mark Donohue told the group. "Me too" chimed in a guy name Ed Robinson who was a retired analyst with the CIA. "I never saw this coming and I used to research this stuff for a living" he said. "I wish I knew what to say. I don't. I am just as confused as everybody else." That was said by Arlene Pinto, a middle aged wife of a federal judge who was a mother of three teenage sons and who worked at the Library of Congress.

"Confused? I am downright flabbergasted! Since when do American veterans turn violent?" said Reynolds Parks, a thirty five year old Maryland National Guardsman, a Sergeant First Class on active duty.

"Are you kidding me? Veterans rioted in Washington D.C. over promised bonus money from World War I that they claimed was not going to be delivered. It was called the Bonus Army. They had to be routed out of D.C. by the Army at bayonet point. Several people were killed, including an infant, and their tent city burned down by troops. You never heard of that?" said Marian Williams, an Air Force veteran and an FBI psychologist. "And that was not the only time veterans were seen as a problem politically in the country."

Marian continued. "After the Civil War there was concern that Confederate veterans might stage a guerilla war that would last for decades and in effect they did, if you consider the Ku Klux Klan and other white supremacist groups in the South to be stand-ins for guerilla warfare. Lynching young black men was more than just racial hatred. On many levels it was terrorism directed at the central government which was imposing its will on the Southern population. It was a way for Southern sociopaths bent on subverting the national will for peace and reconciliation to show their strength."

Edwina Parsons, a black woman who was a GS-15 at the State Department concurred with Marian Williams. "I would have to agree. Lynching went on for decades after the Civil War all the way up until the 1960's and there was definitely an element of terrorism in the act. It was racial hatred for sure, but it was also the criminal element in Southern politics thumbing their noses at an inclusive political philosophy coming out of Washington D.C. It was a way to say, 'See? You do not control us' and I believe that deep down, this terrified the government here in the capitol. I think that now they are terrified of the veterans who have revolted in the same way that they were terrified of the KKK."

"Now wait a minute everybody!" Roger said. "Veterans have had long standing grievances for generations that the federal government either did not address or would not address adequately. To put them in the same category as KKK members is unfair. There was no hatred here. This was an insurrection based on perceived grievances of a group that had every right to demand attention and resources from the federal government. The government was not always willing to provide those resources in any effective quantity or appreciable quality. That much is clear."

Everybody looked at Roger incredulously. Everybody but Marian.

"You cannot be serious!" said Donna Flagle, a bio-chemist with the National Science Foundation. "They shot policemen and federal agents by the hundreds!" "You mean thousands" said Martin Bacher, a musician from the Kennedy Center. He played the cello. "Why are we meeting to find out anything about their motivations? Their motivations were criminal. They all needed to be placed into prisons, not pardoned!" he said loudly.

"Is it possible that their grievances were real and that they were not being adequately aided by the government over many generations? Is it possible that they participated in insurrection because their government betrayed them?" Roger said.

The entire room fell silent. Everyone looked at Roger. Several mouths fell open. Marian Williams watched Roger very closely after he said this. She was looking for something to register on his face, Roger felt that. He just did not know what it was.

"Their government betrayed them?" three people shouted at once with astonishment in their voices. "Whose side are you on?" said Donna Flagle.

Roger answered slowly. "I am not on anybody's side and I might add, neither are any of you! We are here to find out what happened. We cannot approach this thing with our minds made up relative to who was right and who was wrong. We just cannot get anywhere if we work that way. We must have an open mind. This country just suffered an insurrection that was cleverly portrayed by the present administration as a criminal act by a breakaway criminal group of veterans. They got away with that. Because it was portrayed that way does not in any way mean that this was actually the case. In my view, this may have been insurrection based on clear and just reasons for violence."

"What!" screamed virtually everyone in the focus group. That would be everyone but the FBI psychologist, Marian Williams. She held her tongue and looked straight at Roger with some admiration. She could not hide her emotions, showing agreement with what he said.

"Look" Roger said. "Even the Pope came out in support of the insurrection. That ought to tell us something. The Dali Lama supported the insurrection. He is no bomb throwing radical. The labor unions in Europe supported it. Now we have to realize that these people saw something of merit in what the insurrectionist veterans did. There was violence and people died. These were good people, on both sides of this issue."

People stirred in their seats but said nothing. Roger continued. "But we are being tasked with looking deeply at the causes of this thing. We are not being asked to support some government view of things so that we can whitewash the problems that are here that caused the insurrection in the first place. If we do that, we may very well have another insurrection in a few years. May I remind everyone that there is a guerilla army still among the population and completely hidden? Don't you see danger in that?"

Roger waited for their reaction. They all turned sullen and silent. He had a point. They could see that. No one would admit it however.

"So what are you saying, we should congratulate them?" said the retired Marine officer, Mark Donohue. "Yeah, what are you saying? We should look into the causes of why they damned near caused a civil war? They are criminals!" Ed Robinson, the CIA analyst shouted. "I have to agree with these guys" said Reynolds Parks the National Guardsman. "Me too" said Arlene Pinto the judges wife. Martin Bacher, Edwina Parsons and Donna Flagle simply looked at Roger like he was from another planet.

It was clear that not any of them were capable at the moment of looking at this thing from the point of view of the insurrectionists. This was going to be a problem and Roger knew that clearly now. He would have to wait until the group warmed up to his abilities to see things objectively before he pushed this any further.

Throughout the discussion the Navy Lieutenant, April Long who was assigned as the group facilitator said nothing. The meeting time was over. They were out of time. She called the meeting to an end and asked the group to consider their positions on the insurrection and be ready to discuss this fully at the next meeting. Everyone walked out of the Pentagon and to their cars in the parking lot.

Marian Williams, the psychologist, went walking toward the bus for the Metro line. "Need a ride someplace Marian? Roger asked. She said, "Sure. Can you drop me off at FBI headquarters in Northwest D.C.?" she asked. "Sure!" Roger said. The pretty woman of about 47 got into his car and the two headed out of the parking lot of the

Pentagon in Arlington and over the 14th Street Bridge into D.C. Roger noticed that she was not wearing a wedding ring. He filed that information into the back of his mind.

On the way into Washington from the Pentagon in Arlington Roger asked Marian for her views on the subject of the veterans' right to insurrection. "I notice that you did not say much in the meeting today. What's up?" Roger asked. "I did not say much because I do not have much to say—yet!" she said.

"I have to really think about all this and decide how to approach the insurrection and my view of its causes. On the one hand, it was a criminal act. It was an act of treason. On the other hand, some fine people with upstanding morals and moral authority in the world supported the rebels. I have to admit that. And I am duty bound as a member of this official focus group to take that into consideration when I try and make sense of this thing."

She stopped talking for a minute and then continued. "In the end, I have no problem seeing that the rebel veterans had very good reasons to demand action from the government to get their needs met. It just did not seem to be happening in any realistic way on a timeline that is reasonable. On the other hand, is that worth damned near starting a civil war? I just don't know how I feel about it yet. They were violent and took the law into their own hands. Thousands of people were killed. Does the fact that they had legitimate gripes against the government allow them to do that? At this point, I don't see that this was a reasonable response."

Roger pulled up to the side of the FBI Building and Marian got out. "I will see you in a couple of weeks" he said. "You can see me before that if you ask for my phone number" Marian said.

Roger laughed, "Well then, I am asking for your phone number!" Marian handed him her FBI Business Card with her cell phone number written on the back of it. She had written the number down in the meeting, hoping Roger would ask for it. She liked his moxie. And he was a good looking man. Roger drove off, heading back to Virginia and said out loud to himself, "this just might work!" He liked Marian.

And since he was unattached right now, this budding relationship had potential.

Over the next four months the group met at its appointed time and basically attempted time and time again to get to the root causes of the insurrection. However it was becoming obvious to everyone that almost everyone in the group had hardened their views on the rebellion and it was becoming virtually impossible for this group of people to see the veterans' side of things.

These people all worked for the government or had ties to the government in one way or another. Asking them to try and find the root causes of the insurrection was a lot like asking a northerner after the Civil War to find reasons why the Confederacy's existence was justified. Too much blood over too long a time was spilled for that kind of open mindedness to take place. The group was probably not going to be able to complete the objective. An independent view of the veterans' insurrection from any group of people controlled by the government in any way was simply going to be impossible. The group agreed that this much was true. The facilitator reported this to the Defense Department command structure sponsoring the focus groups.

It turns out that all of the groups were more or less saying the same thing. They could not see the veterans' point of view and they reported that. After four months of attempting to find the root causes of the insurrection, the project was stopped. It had failed. For whatever reason or group of reasons, the people involved in the study simply could not find a way to justify and explain the insurrectionist's behavior. The Defense Department was now no closer to an answer as to the root cause of the rebellion than it was months before. The project was quietly disbanded.

But it was not a total loss for Roger and Marian. They had grown close and started dating. Roger of course had to explain one more time that his genitals were a bit different and that his sex life was therefore affected. Marian of course was willing to work with the situation and eventually got comfortable with the physical parameters of Roger's sexuality. Affection has a way of overcoming all sorts of oddities in a personal relationship. That much Roger knew from experience.

When the time for intimacy came, Marian was shown how Roger's genitals worked and was open to the situation at all levels. Things were moving ahead nicely for both of them. It was nice to just slow down and smell the roses. They both needed that in their lives and it was just working out that way.

The VIA and Long Term Plans

Jim Baslow had been a Master Gunnery Sergeant in the Marine Corps when he retired on thirty years in 2007. An eighty percent disabled veteran when he left the Service, he found it hard getting a job or keeping one once he did. He suffered from combat PTSD and had lost part of his foot from an IED explosion while serving in Iraq. He had suffered a very bad experience with the Department of Veterans Affairs relative to his disabilities and when he retired from the Marines, he felt as if his service to his country had been taken for granted. It just seemed like another routine day in the Corps the day he left. No one really said much to him and his retirement ceremony was perfunctory at best. It was an impression that many military retirees have on departure day. It does not leave a person quickly, especially if he leaves the service disabled.

No one really gave a damn whether or not Jim Baslow was retiring, or had ever served. It was not just all that important to anyone he knew. Two combat tours in Iraq meant very little to most of the people that knew him outside the Corps. Reality is harsh some of the time and to a professional soldier it is harsh most of the time. Family from back home tends to treat a professional soldier like a visiting cousin and spouses are often estranged. Kids are often simply angry because dad is gone a lot. And generally speaking the citizen in the street tends to take all the sacrifice and pain and chaos in the life of a professional soldier for granted.

When its all over, there is precious little appreciation in any substantial way for a hard life in the service of one's nation. Retirement usually comes hard. It is not a pretty picture for most military retirees. Jim would sometimes laugh sarcastically underneath his breath when he would think of how he was treated and mutter to himself, "thanks a lot Jim for your service to the country. Now, take your meager pension and get the hell out of here!" That is pretty much how he felt about himself.

As for Jim's personal life, his wife left him soon after he retired. She found a married man that owned two delicatessens and bought her a new car. She would rather be the lover to a married man than a wife to Jim Baslow, retired marine, disabled veteran and unemployed day laborer. At this point in his life he did some major league introspection about his life path and struggles. This all led to him being involved with the Veterans Insurrectionist Army.

He was recruited by one of his old executive officers who held the position of a state commander of the rebel forces and the growing insurrectionist army. Jim received a captain's rank in the army and commanded two different units. These units took and held two post offices for three days. When the army was ordered to have some men escape rather than be captured, Jim was ordered by the state commander make sure that he was not taken prisoner. He was to escape from the post office building and be available to rebuild a more effective, leaner and meaner fighting force. He did as he was ordered.

Of the forty men and women Jim commanded in the two post office buildings that he was assigned to take and hold, only five escaped of the eight that were ordered to do so by the state commandant. The others were either killed or captured and interned. They all signed the loyalty oath. That was fine with the VIA. The rebels still had plenty of volunteers and officers to stage a healthy response to any government foot dragging on veterans' issues. The men and women that were killed or captured had served their purpose and those that were now pardoned were off the hook and out of the VIA as far as the high command was concerned. Whatever plans the rebels had now could be carried out successfully by the smaller and leaner VIA that was still intact after the insurrection.

And the rebel high command had plans.

Now that they had a battle hardened army that was insurrectionist in spirit, secretive in nature and guerilla war-fighting in technique, it was determined by the high command that another statement had to be made on behalf of forgotten veterans. Right or wrong, fair or unfair, the high command determined that it was time to strike again in a largely symbolic but compelling series of acts that would avenge what the VIA believed to be ongoing government abuse and neglect of veterans.

This time the hope was that the public relations value of the strikes would make up for the fact that the VIA had not been able to ignite an insurrection among the population at large. That was the ultimate goal. It was proving almost impossible to orchestrate. The American people simply did not identify with the veterans or their needs to the point of joining the insurrection.

Major General Jason Nesbith of the Air Force Special Operations office in the Pentagon had been concerned that some Special Ops people had taken part in the insurrection and were still at large. Almost none of the interned had any special ops background in the past twenty years and that concerned him. The operation went too smoothly and was much too organized for special ops people not to have been involved. But who were they and where were they now? He had made his concern known to the Air Force chief of staff who told the joint chiefs of the problem. No one else seemed too concerned. He wondered why that was the case.

The truth was obvious to anyone who wished to open their eyes and see it. Large portions of the Pentagon staff and of the armed forces in general had been involved on some level in the insurrection. There were rebels among the general staff of the armed forces because the insurrection went off too smoothly for the situation to be otherwise. This made a bad situation worse. Betraying the needs of working class and lower middle class veterans in order to protect the nation's elite was going to be a bitter pill for the nation to swallow for many generations to come. The price would be ongoing, low level, never ending civil unrest. And it would be violent.

Nesbith tried over and over to get to the bottom of things. Who was in command of the rebels? How did they communicate their plans to the rank and file? Why was the Pentagon seemingly taking the recent insurrection so lightly? He just could not get proper answers to those questions. And that bothered him. He had even spoken to the Director of the FBI, Robert Mueller, who seemed just as befuddled regarding the Pentagon's disinterest in the insurrection. What was going on?

The only appropriate answer seemed to be that of collusion of one high command with another. It was hard to escape the perception that professional soldiers, sailors, airmen and marines were in league with the rebels. And it was not necessarily the generals and admirals. It seemed to be coming from the mid rank officers and high ranking enlisted people. The working class was protecting its own.

And since the mid ranking officers were the ones largely involved with the insurrectionists, it had to be noted that they were the actual field commanders. They were the ones who commanded the troops. They were the dangerous ones, the part of the chain of command that actually held the weapons and gave the orders, or in turn, refused to give the orders. The mid rank officers were the doers; and if the "doers" refuse to "do" an army or navy grinds to a screeching halt. Things had certainly changed in the U.S. armed forces since 1945.

No one could have foreseen this problem at the end of the Second World War. With the nation flush with patriotism and relieved to be ending a world war, it only seemed natural to the captains of American war industries that Americans would be happy to serve in the armed forces out of a sense of national pride. And for a period of time, this was a correct assumption. But eventually too few were getting very wealthy over the broken lives of too many who were not even being adequately cared for in their pain and brokenness and by the 21st century the number of broken veterans was staggering.

Most soldiers and sailors were aware that by 2009 even the basic cost of living adjustments for disabled veterans was far below inflation when measured against a disabled veteran's pension as calculated on the actual value of the dollar in the base year when the DVA pensions started. Young people were being severely disabled in combat and action and by the hard realities of service life and their pensions were grossly inadequate to keep them more than barely surviving.

Hard and faithful service to the nation was being rewarded with a lifetime of government supported poverty and a disability system that virtually everyone agreed was broken. This was an open sore on the soul of the American veteran and a cancer that was eating away at the social contract between the government and the individual service man and woman.

There were fewer than 3 million disabled veterans in the U.S. in 2009. There was some evidence that a majority of these disabled veterans lived in substandard conditions without any real quality of life. And worst of all, they were becoming politically savvy and very aware of what had happened to them on behalf of America's "business interests." Wars, skirmishes, police actions and all sorts of violent raids and actions had been fought since the end of World War II to ensure American supremacy in world affairs.

But now, these veterans were much too aware of how they had been used to be taken in by parades and patriotic talk and the occasional bone thrown to them by politicians. They were bitter and they had good reason to be bitter. They were broken and then thrown aside. They endured almost endless waits for disability claims to be fully adjudicated. And then substandard medical care was routinely considered the norm for their needs. A class war had been brewing for generations. Now it had spilled over onto the national scene. This dissatisfaction would not be easy for the government to quell, quash or misdirect. There was too much pain over too many years for too many people for a band-aid approach to fixing the problems noted to work.

For the FBI, the situation could not possibly be more volatile. An awakening bear was hungry for justice, maybe even revenge, after a long hibernation from politics and activism. The politically active and even violent veteran of the 1930s was being reborn in a new time, in a new incarnation over more or less the same issues of neglect and deception. A national nightmare was on the cusp of becoming a reality; veterans were organizing and executing carefully laid plans in great numbers. But plans to do what? General Nesbith wanted to know.

An informal verbal agreement between Major General Nesbith and the Director of Federal Bureau of Investigation came into being. They would share information relative to whatever they would learn about the Pentagon's involvement with the insurrectionists. "Thank you director for your time" the general said as he walked out of the director's office. "Please stay in touch general, we need to work together. The situation is dangerous" Director Mueller said in parting.

The two men would find out just how dangerous the situation was in less than a week. The insurrection was entering its second phase.

The Rebellion Never Died

Jim Balsow received his orders from the state commandant the same day that the commandant had received them from the national high command. There would be an attempt by the VIA to start another insurrection among the population by using violence, and this time it would be against the heart of the problem, as they saw it.

Selected gas stations around the country would be blown up while at the same time the front doors of local banks would be blown off. The actions would be symbolic but powerful reminders to the government that the insurrection was still very much alive. The oil and gas and financial entities that were behind so much of the pain and misery of the veterans would be getting a direct message from the people who were harmed for their supremacy. It was time to pay the bill that they had run up in the lives of American veterans.

Roger and Marian were returning from a late night date when they literally found themselves in the middle of the chaos. At 1:00 AM Eastern Standard Time one hundred gas stations on the East Coast were blown sky high. Plastic explosives had been secretly mounted late that evening on the bottom of the gas pumps in each service station selected and detonated by remote control from rebels in passing cars.

Just as Roger and Marian passed the Chevron gas station at Seven Corners at the Falls Church section of Northern Virginia it was ignited by Jim Balsow. He was following them in a car.

Jim was too close to the explosion when he drove by and ignited the explosion electronically by radio signal. His car immediately caught fire and the car drove off the road and into a telephone pole. The force of the explosion had already killed Jim. He did not have much experience with this type of plastic explosive and the blast was much more powerful than he had expected. His career as an insurrectionist commander was quite short. He was essentially killed by the blast he incorrectly set up himself.

Roger's rear window shattered and the force of the secondary explosion knocked his car off Route 7. The car careened into a traffic barrier and he and Marian quickly got out of the car, slightly hurt, and limped away. The explosions continued for an hour. The Vegetarian Restaurant next to the Chevron Station at Seven Corners was completely engulfed in flames. Flames were shooting a quarter of a mile into the sky from the burning fuel. Secondary explosions went off every minute or so. The scene was pure pandemonium.

At the same time, the front doors of three banks in Falls Church were blown off. Jim Baslow had made arrangements for a rebel cell to attack each bank. There was chaos everywhere. Fire engines and police cars were running all over the community trying to help however they could. Luckily, almost no traffic was on the roads at that time.

There were five deaths in Falls Church, all to people who had been at or around the gas station at 1:00 AM. Throughout the east coast states of the U.S. the tally was about the same. All in all about 700 people were killed in the blasts and subsequent fires. The VIA was declaring war on the government. The government was stunned.

Roger and Marian were taken to the municipal building that housed the police department in Falls Church and from there they were taken to the hospital in Alexandria, nearer their homes. All over the states on the East coast the story was the same. Gas stations were blown up near major intersections of highways and banks had their front doors simultaneously blown off.

The command center at the Pentagon went into war mode and General Nesbith immediately rushed to his office at the Pentagon from his home in Arlington. His adjutant, Colonel Mike Nance, U.S. Army Special Forces was already on scene at the Pentagon and wearing a side arm when the general arrived.

"What have you got to report?" the general demanded of the younger man. "I am working on that now sir" the colonel replied. "I should have some solid information to you in the next hour." Nance left the general in his office and returned to the crisis operations center.

Nance had just reported into the job the month before. He had served two tours in Iraq and one tour in Afghanistan with special ops teams. He had an older son serving there now as a young captain with an armored brigade and a younger son who was seriously hurt in an IED explosion in Iraq just six months after he graduated from West Point. He was presently at Walter Reed Army Hospital recuperating from brain damage from the explosion. The young man was not responding to treatment very well and in fact was pretty much a vegetable. Nance was heartbroken. He no longer believed. He had been involved in too many special ops to believe in "America the Beautiful" any longer.

Nance now believed that America was run by a cabal of wealthy manipulators who would sell their mother into slavery for more power, more control and more overseas influence. He knew that now. He should be the one to know, he had commanded many special ops mission in his days in the field and the majority of the time it did not involve something he would be proud to tell his family. It was usually simple assassination.

And it usually involved some sort of drug lord or warlord or mainstream politician somewhere on the planet who would not do America's bidding. It was all about the raw use of naked and primitive violence to get done what the American super-wealthy class had wanted done in any situation. American soldiers and sailors had been dying for that reason for centuries. Nance thought that it was time to stop. He had a belly full of this hypocrisy. He was done now.

He reported back to General Nesbith within the hour, just as he said he would. He was still wearing his sidearm as senior officer of the day on watch in the crisis operations center. He knocked on the door, entered the office and quietly locked the door behind him without the general noticing.

"What do you have to report colonel?" the general asked.

"We have mayhem essentially all over the East coast. Gas stations have been blown up and banks have been damaged. We are not exactly sure what the message is here but the messenger is definitely the VIA. They are back in full force." Nance did not mince words.

"Damn!" Nesbith screamed. "The bastards were given a chance by the president against the good judgment of the Joint Chiefs of Staff and they abused their pardon. They have gone on the warpath again and for no reason. They were treated more than fairly after the insurrection. They were pardoned for the most part for Christ's sake! Now they will pay."

"I will notify the chairman who will notify the president and we will get the Army National Guard involved and this time we will crush the bastards. I will call the Chairman of the Joint Chiefs now. He should call the president."

Nesbith reached for the phone. Nance said quietly "Put the goddamned phone down and put it down now." Nesbith looked over to see a pistol pointed right at him. "What the hell are you doing Nance? Have you lost your mind?" the general asked the colonel with great astonishment and more than a little personal fear.

"No. I think I just found my mind" Nance said in a low voice filled with white hot rage.

Nance continued. "You see I would have been on the team five years ago. I would have done whatever you fuckers wanted. Whatever you told me to do tonight, I simply would have done out of some goofy sense of duty or honor or some other bullshit word you hang on a wall for the rest of us to follow and then refuse to follow yourselves."

"You and all the rest of the self-appointed big deals who sit over at the Army Navy Club on weekends and talk about your days at the academy and how fucked up this or that secretary of defense or president was or is at the present time. You have all deluded yourselves, you admirals and generals. You all think you stand aside from the system. You don't. You are the fucking system. You are the fucking enforcers. You are the "capos", the head men in charge of breaking arms and collecting protection money for the criminal gang that runs this country. You perpetuate this insanity with your blind allegiance to the powerful and their endless greed. And you support them. Why? Because you have bought into the need for this use of force to keep the rest of us down. Fuck you general!"

The general could see that Nance was furious. He continued with his tirade. "I was wounded three times in special operations that turned out to be more like a drug drop off or a mafia hit than a military operation. I made sure that America's darkest business could go on unimpeded by killing local leaders in over ten different countries that wanted our illegal and immoral shit to stop. They just wanted their people to be left alone to direct their own destinies without our endless meddling."

Nesbith could see tears of rage in Nance's eyes. This did not bode well for the general. Fear gripped him deep in his throat. It was getting hard for Nesbith to breathe. He was close to panic.

"My sons are involved in it now too. One is a previously wounded captain facing combat every day for reasons that are unclear even to me. The other is a vegetable lying in a bed right now at Walter Reed with no hope of ever becoming a human again." Nance swallowed hard and continued his raging.

Nesbith was now very much afraid. He had been in special operations long enough to know that this type of man is a doer, not a talker. Nance narrowed his eyes and spoke in a lowered voice filled with spite and anger.

"The veterans that are in open rebellion are right. They have been fucked a hundred times over by people like you. You and people like you have allowed them to be broken and fucked-over for generations; and for what? What was in the national interest here? What was the need? You supported sending them into combat for reasons that absolutely no one with a rational mind could support. This was all about money for the powerful few to be gained by pain and death and injury by the powerless many. And I paid for it and my sons have paid for it. My life is over. And now, so is yours."

With that Nance leveled his weapon at Nesbith's face and then placed two rounds into the general's forehead. The general slumped to the floor, deader than a bag of hammers.

Nance walked over to the door to the general's office, opened it, locked and closed it. He left the Pentagon, got into his car and drove home. He drove into the driveway of his large home in the Mount Vernon section of Alexandria, Virginia. He sat in his car for fifteen minutes and wrote a note to no one in particular on the back of a large brown manila envelope that had been lying on the back seat and then shot himself in the head.

The police found his body the next morning. The Pentagon was notified within an hour of the police finding him. The duty team had found the general's body by that time.

Colonel Nance's note read as follows:

I shot and killed General Nesbith early this morning for no other reason than he needed to be dead and I needed to kill him.

He was not an important man and neither am I. He was a player in this game of constant warfare for the sake of money and this morning I decided not to play anymore. He was a believer. He actually believed that what is good for America's wealthy class of business tyrants is good for the country. It is not.

And now maybe the Pentagon will listen when some long haired peace activist or some broken disabled veteran with his legs blown off asks to be heard by the powers that be. Maybe now somebody in power will attempt to rein in this madness. Maybe now people will begin to understand that all this killing to make a buck for the very few is costing our nation its very soul.

Killing people all over the world to ensure our economic superiority is not valor, it is not fighting for freedom. It is murder. I don't want to play anymore. I have killed too many people in the name of "freedom" to believe it is the way to conduct foreign policy.

I am not killing any more people for the sake of economic superiority or to preserve the "American way of life." It is all bullshit. I am done now.

I hope my sons understand. I had to do this. I had no choice.

Colonel Mike Nance
U.S. Army Special Forces
Deceased

It was now ten hours since the explosions began and people started dying and the Pentagon had still not adequately responded per the operations plan. The veterans' army allies in that building were making sure that there was no cohesive response from the federal government. They frustrated all attempts at a cohesive government response to the violence.

It was more of a gut reaction to allow the fire of rage to burn itself out than it was a cohesive plan of support by active duty people at the Pentagon. They simply refused to do their duty. They more or less looked the other way while preselected parts of the country burned. Each man and woman had his own reasons. They carried on for the most part as if they had no part to play in the drama unfolding before them.

It seemed that soldiers and sailors, airmen and marines had no stomach to go to war with older relatives who had worn a uniform at one time. They were not going to kill fathers or mothers, uncles and aunts and older brothers or sisters because someone told them it was their duty.

A night of anarchy had now set in across the nation. Gas station explosions and bank security breaches by plastic explosive were now taking place in the Midwest and on the west coast. Mayhem and death was the calling card to low level and long lasting insurrection in the U.S. starting that night. It would last for decades until the Republic was reformed.

America had now entered a time of constant low level rebellion. It would never end now, not until the very republic that had been known prior to the insurrection had died. And veterans were now committed members of an insurrection that would live as long as the Irish rebels' insurrection that they had modeled themselves upon.

The Irish resistance to British rule lasted almost 800 years prior to Irish independence. That was a sobering thought to Americans who held power. The wealthy, the privileged, those who do not serve in uniform or bear the fight know that they cannot long prevail without the cooperation of those who do the fighting and dying for them. Those days were quickly drawing to an end.

The day of the American robber baron influencing government in sending Americans overseas to fight and die for oil revenue and market share and economic leverage that benefitted the relative few was coming to a violent close. The serfs were refusing to die for the nobles.

A new America was being born.

Roger and Marian sat in the Alexandria Hospital emergency room where the Falls Church Police Department had taken them and waited, bruised and battered, to see a doctor. Citizens all over the country watched television and followed the news closely for many weeks. In the end, the entire thing went largely unexplained. The rebel high command was never identified. About 300 rebels were killed in the explosions due to lack of experience with plastic explosives or due to police gunfire during arrests. Not one was taken prisoner. The armed forces did not involve itself in the conflict.

Orders went out from the White House, from the Pentagon and from all the major military commands within the continental U.S.

Somehow or other these orders got confused, misdirected, or simply did not arrive at their destination. The armed forces refused to involve itself in killing veterans. The message was clear to anyone who wished to acknowledge it. The Army and Navy would sit this one out. The Marine Corps and Air Force simply went off line for a day or two.

The Coast Guard, as always, was a day late and a dime short. Coasties walked around in a perpetual state of feigned confusion for a week. It was not all that hard for them to behave this way since this is usually their normal state.

All in all the armed forces of the nation sent a very clear message. They were not interested in quelling an insurrection that was being waged by former service men and women who had been raped by government for generations. They simply walked off the playing field. The president, the congress and the American people got the message. This insurrection was well deserved.

Happily ever after?

As the months went by Roger and Marian grew close. Their brush with death brought them closer. Roger felt that he knew Marian well and liked what he knew about her. After a year Roger asked Marian to marry him and much to his surprise she said "Yes."

They honeymooned in Jamaica. Marian picked the place where they vacationed. Roger liked Jamaica. Marian agreed that Roger should write a book. He had plenty of time on his hands, and as a lottery winner, he certainly had the financial wherewithal to do it.

"What should I write about?" Roger asked his bride as they sat on a lovely Jamaican beach and looking out into the surf. "Oh, I don't know" his bride purred, "how about writing about the realities of being a disabled veteran in 21st century America? Why don't you write about your experiences in the insurrection?" Roger laughed and looked at her with mild surprise on his face.

"And if I wrote the book, would you read it?" Roger asked her. She laughed and looked at her husband and said "Probably not. But that is only because I have lived it with you. It would not have any suspense for me." They both laughed. And she was probably correct. When a storyline becomes crystal clear and the suspense is wrung out of it like water wrung out of a wet towel, people just don't seem interested in the story anymore.

Roger thought about that for a minute and then looked at his wife and said "I sure hope that what you say is not the case. This would be a very dangerous storyline to ignore."

With that said the two of them continued to look at the surf for twenty minutes when two men walked directly in front of them. They were both surprisingly fit. One man about forty years old had his shirt off and a long scar ran from his right shoulder down to his abdomen. The younger man who was about twenty eight had slashes on his upper right arm and walked with a very slight limp. They both had short haircuts and they had the look of military men.

They walked straight and in step, even on the sand. Roger thought that it was probably his imagination but the older man seemed to look at Marian and smile at her the way a colleague or co-worker would smile at someone in the workplace. He just found it odd but put it out of his mind.

Roger looked at Marian in great surprise when they overheard the conversation that the two men were having.

The older man spoke in a voice that seemed to indicate that he did not realize that he could be overheard above the crashing surf. "Now let's try it again. I will recite the poem and then you recite it after me. You must memorize every line. We cannot write anything down. Let's do it again. We have to do this until you get the whole poem down correctly. You must be able to recite this over and over to yourself under pressure so that you know your standing orders for this mission. Let's try it again. Now listen carefully." With that the older man recited a short poem.

> "Crinkle, crinkle with the cars
> Drive them fast, you'll go quite far.
> Slam them hard on 5 July

Into buildings we'll identify.
Crinkle, crinkle with the cars
Lots of chaos or no cigars!
When the blazing fire is gone
When there's nothing to blaze upon
Then you show your fearful might.
Crinkle, crinkle through the night.
Crinkle with the remote cars
Cause many explosions from afar.
In the dark black night so deep
When the people are asleep
You shall not ever close your eyes
Until the morning sun does rise.
Crinkle, crinkle with remote cars
Blow the federal doors ajar.
Crinkle, crinkle with the cars
Your targets will have painted stars.
In shining red on walls you'll spy
These targets you must nullify.
Crinkle, crinkle with the car
Blow them up at the midnight hour.
Crinkle, crinkle with the cars
They'll be packed with gas filled jars.
Pick them up the night before
Set the timers in the front door.
The car explodes as the timing bar
Slides across the contact spar.
High Command will get the cars.
State Command will place the bars.
My job is the contact spar.
I must make it blow the jars.
It's held in place with wire and tar.
I make sure it ignites the car.
The cars are parked on 4 July
At local coordinates X and Y.
I will be told those points that day.

I send one cell to each car and say
"Do not forget to stand far away
when the bomb is sent on its way."
And when the job is surely done
And the havoc has begun.
When explosions rock the night
Each cell shall then go into flight.
I then await with ready ears
To hear further orders for many years."

The younger man had listened intensely to the poem and started to recite it again.

The men continued to walk down the beach. Both Roger and Marian heard the entire poem recited by the older man. Roger turned to Marian with shock on his face. The men did not seem overly concerned that they were overheard, Roger was sure of that. He said to his wife, "What do we do?" Marian looked at her new husband and said "I don't know Roger, what do we do?" Marian did not seem interested in interfering and seemed oddly detached from the whole situation. Roger found her response strange. He looked off into the surf and watched the two men walk away slowly from him and his new wife.

Suddenly, Roger did not feel that he knew his new wife very well at all. She put on her sunglasses and picked up a paperback novel and started to read. After about twenty minutes Marian, the FBI psychologist and Air Force veteran, looked at Roger and said "What do you want to eat for lunch?" Somehow or other Marian's detachment from what had just happened frightened Roger. Roger was more frightened than he let himself realize. Something was very odd here.

After about ten seconds Roger said, "All of a sudden I am not very hungry. Maybe I will skip lunch today." Marian laughed and said, "Okay honey, whatever you want. I am going back to the room. I have had enough sun for today."

Marian got up and left for their hotel room which was located just off the beach. Roger sat on the beach in a beach chair looking up and down the beach and out into the surf. He was very confused. And now he was also very afraid. Roger looked out into the ocean. A slow and simmering panic overtook his mind.

Marian walked into their hotel room and undressed. She walked into the bathroom, turned on the water and stepped into the shower stall. She soaped herself up and started to recite a poem slowly and quietly to herself that she had recently learned.

She knew the poem quite well having memorized it the week before her vacation started. She kept her voice low and recited the poem and over and over to herself as she showered. She listened intently to every word that she spoke, just as she was instructed to do when she memorized the poem weeks before.

"Crinkle, crinkle, with the cars..."

About the Author

Tom Barnes is a retired Coast Guard warrant officer, a retired employee development specialist from the Smithsonian Institution (GS-13) and he spent a little time teaching public high school business courses in Northern Virginia after he retired from the service. He is a totally disabled veteran.

This book has been written as an attempt to get inside the mind of disabled veterans in the 21st Century using a fictional set of characters to tell one disabled veteran's story. Although many of the characters in the novel are real people, there must be no presumption that the author has any unique insight into their thoughts or intentions. They are used simply to move the story forward.

Tom's education is extensive.

B.A. in Liberal Arts from Mount Saint Mary's RC College, Emmitsburg, MD 1975

B.S. in General Business from University of the State of New York, Regents, in 1995

M.Ed. (Secondary Education) Beaver College, Glenside, PA in 1995

M.A. (Human Resources Management) from Marymount University, Arlington, VA in 2000

M.A. (Human Performance Systems) from Marymount University, Arlington, VA in 2003

Tom studied for a short while toward his Ph.D. in Adult Basic Education at George Mason University in Fairfax, VA earning 26 credits toward that degree. He took classes at both GMU and Virginia

Tech. When he was declared totally disabled by the Department of Veterans Affairs, Tom saw that study was no longer possible.

Tom would welcome the opportunity to hear from you and gain your insights into this novel .

Tom can be reached at:
6300 Stevenson Avenue, 614
Alexandria, VA 22304-3572

Other websites for Tom Barnes books:
TheMcGurk.vpweb.com
FinneganTales.vpweb.com
ADACV.vpweb.com

3990226

Made in the USA